Furr

Axel Howerton

FURR

Axel Howerton

TYCHE BOOKS LTD.

Furr
Published by Tyche Books Ltd.
www.TycheBooks.com

First Tyche Books Ltd Edition 2016

Print ISBN: 978-1-928025-59-7
Ebook ISBN: 978-1-928025-60-3

Cover Art by Sean Yang
Cover Layout by Lucia Starkey
Interior Layout by Ryah Deines
Editorial by M.L.D. Curelas

Author photograph: Liz Howerton Photography

This book was funded in part by a grant from the Alberta Media Fund.

To family,
In all its myriad forms.

1

I CAN SMELL the smoke coming down from the mountains. It's still a long way off, days even, but I can smell it all the same. Or I'm due for what my mother called a spell. Because I can't possibly smell the trees burning four or five hundred kilometres away, but it's there, coating the inside of my nose the same as if it was a campfire two feet in front of me.

"You smell that?"

Devil looks at me from under one doubtful eyebrow.

"Do I smell *what*?" he grumbles, paying little attention to me and serious attention to the hundred bucks I just put in his hand. "You just want the usual, right?"

"Of course."

Devil and I were friends. Had been friends. A very long time ago. Now he was just my weed dealer, and I was just one more awkward desk jockey nerd scoring off him in a back alley.

Devil DeVille, master of every possible way to be cool. Leaning against his gleaming black Charger, in his black leather jacket, his black leather boots. Fonzie boots with the little buckles. I can smell the oil on those boots. Fresh oil. They gleam even in the sickly orange streetlight glow.

Devil reaches into his pocket and tosses me a little plastic-bag coated bundle. The ripe stink of it brings water to my eyes and I pull back, while my fingers miraculously wrap around the bundle and pick it from the air.

"Nice catch, Jimmy."

"Thanks." I want to tell him how I've been oddly coordinated lately. How every wastebasket three-pointer has sunk, how every jagged sidewalk block that has tripped me up for the better part of three years has suddenly smoothed out in front of me. How I hear like a bat and pounce like a cat. I want to talk to him about the woman across the road, how I can smell her perfume when the balcony door is open. I want to share it with somebody, but I know what he'll say. He'll think I'm losing my shit again. Once upon a time, Adam DeVille was the only person I could talk to. We'd hide out in his basement, listen to AC/DC records and talk about girls like Amanda Sorensen, and her step-sister Megan who had double-D breasts in grade nine. We'd eat mac and cheese and bitch about our crazy mothers and their stupid boyfriends.

I want to talk to Devil, but I know what he'll say. *You're imagining things, Jimmy. Maybe you should go talk to that shrink of yours, Jim.* Or worse, he won't give me the time of day without a fistful of twenties for a bag of indica.

"That's a lot of green, Jim. You're gonna bleed me dry, man, you keep buying this much this often."

I want to tell him how I have to smoke three times what I used to, just to get calm. I want to tell him how I have a bottle of whiskey sitting on my kitchen table, staring at me.

"I'm meeting some friends at Flames Central."

Devil chuckles.

"You? At a sports bar?"

"Yeah. So?"

"Since when are you into sports, let alone *hockey*? Or bars? You're not drinking again, are you?"

I feel the pause. One of those pauses that I know is different for me than for everyone else. It's a breath for Devil, and an excruciating ten minutes of panic for me before I finally mumble my reply. "I just need to be around people. It's just some guys . . . from work . . ."

Devil stands and throws his hands up in surrender.

"None of my fucking business anyways, Jimbo. Drop me a line when you run out."

He fishes keys out of his jacket, gives me a strange sideways glance before he opens the door.

"Stay out of trouble, kid."

I offer a gawky salute and step to one side as the black beast rumbles to life and the headlights slice through the alleyway. A strange tang of sulfur cuts the smell of woodsmoke, as I watch his tail lights curve around the corner, leaving red lightning behind my eyelids.

2

I AM BROKEN.

That's what they've been telling me for most of my life, anyways.

When you're little—six, seven years old—fresh out of an abusive home, cute, terrified, easily manageable . . . that's when they get the hooks in. Doctors sitting around, deciding how your brain went sideways from everybody else's.

Oh no, Jimmy. You can't feel that way. You can't possibly understand. You're not old enough to really get what's going on with you. You're just broken.

Broken. Wrong. And no damn good.

And Ma, in her abject terror and endless lazy guilt, she takes me to church. A bunch of churches.

She takes me to more doctors.

She reads all the books on how to fix a broken boy.

And then she leaves all that on the windowsill and goes out to find a new man to fix her own broken life.

New men.

And I sit, wondering.

What was the thing that knocked my brain astray?

How did I get this broken?

What is it about me that's wrong?

"SO HOW ARE we feeling this week, James?" Doctor Rhodes sits in his same spot, legs crossed exactly the same, in the same grey trousers, with his same bald head, and the same long beard, only slightly whiter every year. Every week it's the same thing. *How are you feeling, James? Have you talked to your mother, James? Have you been taking your medication, James?* And always, without fail, *Have you been sleeping, James? Have you been dreaming?*

He sits there in his grey trousers, stroking his beard and wondering if it's time to send me away again. Am I feeling violent? Am I acting out and opposing authority? Am I using alcohol and illicit drugs to cope with my mental health issues?

Three times thus far. Three times good ol' Doc Rhodes has had me committed *for my own well-being*. The first time I was all of fourteen years old.

Broken. Dangerous. No damn good.

How did I get this way? That's what Doc Rhodes pretends he's asking questions for. Really I think he just takes my money and waits for me to lose my shit again.

All I have for an answer is the dream. This dream and these bunches of words, almost a poem, but never all together. Half a poem and one faded dream. Like some half-torn picture of somebody else's life.

"COME ON, FINN! Run with me!"

I'm standing in a room with no walls. White flows from the edges of this place, fluid, shifting. No walls, just movement. Like I'm standing behind the waterfall, looking out into a vast white nothing.

The little girl laughs. It echoes from the walls of this place. There are no walls. It echoes from nowhere.

"Emma!" I hear my mother calling from the end of a long hallway. Echoes with no walls. Echoes from nowhere.

I'm six years old. Running. Jumping. Spinning. Long white-blond hair flowing behind me as I spin. Me. That's me. Jimmy Finn. I remember that boy. I remember him as if he was a cousin I met one sunny afternoon full of people I was supposed to remember, but never really knew. *Ran athwart the gloom.*

The little girl—little Emma with the dark hair and the green eyes—she spins too. Nothing else in this place but the feeling of the earth moving beneath us, the earth spinning, wild and out-of-control, and her green eyes. Dark, olive eyes. I remember all that. It's the only thing I remember. The olive green eyes and the world spinning. *The maidens of the moon.*

Then comes the blood. *Dressed of fur.*

The teeth. The anger. *Fierce of tooth.*

Tearing, ripping, screaming.

The teeth, howling as the echoes close in.

The world turns backwards, white becomes black becomes red.

Blood red.

The waterfall has turned to blood.

And the echoes have turned to screams.

I remember all that. I know it. I breathe it. It's at the very middle of my bones.

Little Jimmy. Little Emma.

The screaming teeth inside me.

Tearing, ripping.

Devouring me from the inside out.

Hunger, and blood.

So much blood. An ocean of blood. Rising and crashing. Pink foam cresting dark waves.

It's just outside of where we hide.

Little Jimmy. Little Emma.

Inching ever closer with the tide.

And always my mother's voice calling from a place without time. And never calling for me.

"Emma! Run! Run home and hide!"

And then comes the blood.

"HAVE YOU SPOKEN to your mother since our last session, James? We had discussed you being more open with her."

"No."

I want to explain how miserable that makes me. How guilty. That the one person I'm supposed to be able to count on is the last person I want to talk to. I can't tell her anything. She judges, sermonizes, cries, and beats her hands against the phone like she's at the Wailing Wall. She begs forgiveness of God, Jesus, Doctor Rhodes, her latest gentleman friend, the ghost of my father . . . anyone and everyone but me. That's on a good day, when I don't have much to say.

"How have you been handling your depression? We discussed you trying to be more social, now that we're out of those winter doldrums, as it were."

Rhodes thinks my issues are tied to a multitude of things. I think he just likes the technical, officious-sounding labels—*Seasonal Affective Disorder*, because I get miserable and tired in the winter, and crazy, horny, and violent in the spring; *Oppositional Defiance Disorder*, because I don't handle demanding people very well. *Attention Deficit Hyperactivity Disorder*, despite the fact that I am almost never hyper, and can't focus because I'm in a constant state of sensory overload. Which brings us to *Sensory Processing Disorder*, on account of my supposedly delusional, though somehow real-enough-to-label overactive senses and the confusion they wreak with my mental state. My file is literally a foot thick. Any slight issue I've had since seven years old, diagnosed, pigeonholed, labelled, stamped, and recorded in triplicate, then added to the List of Me. Rhodes is organized, I'll say that for him. And after twenty-some years, he's about the only person I ever really talk to, whether I trust him or not.

I want to tell Rhodes about Devil. I want to talk about that bottle of whiskey that's waiting for me. I want somebody to tell me I can say no, that I have something inside of me that is strong enough to persevere. I want someone to tell me I'm okay, or at least tell me that other people are as fucked up as I am. I want to tell him that I could smell the coffee and day-old doughnuts in his waiting room before I got off the elevator.

He'd just smile knowingly under that beard, fingers working the scent of pastrami and pickles into the white tuft under his chin. Then he'd write some notes on his clipboard, tap the pen against his temple, and ask me, "What do you think about all of this, James?" Round and round and round we go, until he can pick out the right label and slap it on the file, then tuck it away in the archives of Jimmy Finn.

Instead, I swallow a lump of skin inside my throat, grin like an idiot, and bow slightly as I fumble for the doorknob on my way out.

3

"GOOD GAME THE other night, hey Jim?"

"What?" My head cracks the inside edge of the photocopier door and the birds scream out and claw at my eyes, instead of the cute tweets and stars you always see in cartoons. "Fuck!"

Benoit slowly comes into focus as I pull my head out of the copier's ass, ears still ringing.

"Shit. Sorry, dude."

"No. My fault." I smell blood and feel something hot and sticky on my fingertips as I reach back and touch my thundering head.

"Jesus. You're bleeding!"

I smile and wave off his attempt to poke the wound, or lead me to help, or whatever he's trying to do.

"I'm fine. Thanks. It's okay. Really."

I'm hunched over and creeping down the hallway toward the bathrooms, hoping not to run into anyone else. Benoit's smoked meat poutine and three-beer lunch breath follows me all the way down. My stomach starts to growl at the thought of shredded beef, despite the pain in my head and the cacophony of all of my senses going off at once.

"Jimmy? Jimmy, what happened?"

Chanel No. 5, and the sweet cocoa scent of mochaccino.

"Jimmy?" Margaret hustles down the carpeted hallway on her heels, wrapping a silk-covered arm around my waist. The taste of blood and meat are replaced by something else. I can feel her pulse through three layers of clothing. I feel the heat of her skin and I can smell her panic. It fills my nostrils and crowds out the cocoa and perfume. I breathe deep and feel a surge of energy well up from my chest.

We hit the door to the men's room just in time for me to fall through the door and onto my knees, panting and vibrating.

The door swings shut behind me and dulls the smell of her as she repeats my name and raps lightly on the door.

I retch and unleash my own meagre lunch of crackers and V-8, a lousy red slop that tastes more or less the same coming up as it did going down.

Twenty minutes later the crowd outside the men's room has dispersed, and I'm mostly recovered. I leave with a sheepish nod to the janitor who's come in to mop up my remains.

Margaret is waiting at my desk.

"Are you okay? I think you should go down to three and see one of the doctors in the clinic. Do you feel well enough to get home?"

The look of concern on her face is like some weird hieroglyphic that I can't decipher. It's beautiful, and it makes my heart ache. I suddenly want to talk to my mother, to apologize for everything I may have ever done wrong. I want Margaret to hold me, to run her fingers through my hair and tell me that I'm going to be just fine.

"I'm fine. I'm sorry. I . . ."

"Sorry? Don't be silly, Jimmy. You had us all worried sick. Ben said you cracked your head on the copier. Must have done a real number too."

She reaches out towards the bandage on the back of my head. I want to turn and meet her, guide her hand to that place, feel her pulse against my skin again, and let it heal me.

"Really. I'm fine. Maybe I should go home though."

I'm already clawing my stuff into my bag as the words tumble out of my open mouth.

"Okay. Take the rest of the day. And get that looked at. You may need stitches." She touches my shoulder lightly as she passes, and I feel a crackle of electricity pass from her fingers.

I'm in the elevator and down two floors before her scent has faded enough for me to breathe.

I STOP AT the convenience store in the lobby of my building for some aspirin and a bottle of club soda.

Outside I get that whiff of sulfur again as something black and enormous swirls into and out of my periphery. It's gone before my eyes can find it, some lousy concussion symptom. Unlike the wave of hobo musk that suddenly fills my entire sinus cavity. It almost knocks me to my knees. I look for the homeless man I'm sure must be standing right behind me. There's no one on my side of the street. The other side of the road is filled with trees and concrete. Oddly quiet until a sudden gust of wind blows the stench past me and brings the campfire smoke back down from the mountains, and something else. Perfume. Not Margaret's, something light and French. I look up and see her across the street, at the end of the block. The redhead from the 30th floor. Long gazelle legs stretching and curving on top of six-inch heels, her scarlet summer dress flowing behind her, and her long auburn hair blazing in the sun. She was a slow-motion vision, the smell of smoke driving her forward like a phoenix rising out of the ashes and across the city sidewalks.

The swooping tail of her dress disappears behind the glass of her own front door, and the spell is broken. I realize that I'm staring like a goon, and hard as a marble pillar.

I SIT AT my kitchen table, the bottle an arm's length away, the phone slightly further, and stare out across the empty space between us. I can still smell her, all the way across the street. I can see her when she passes in front of the window, a gauzy daydream of thin linen blowing in the wind the only thing keeping her safe. What the hell is wrong with me?

My hands stretch out across the table, in the slowest race in human history. Who loses? Sobriety or sanity?

Every night. Same story. I sit here and brood and wait to go over the edge. Then I smoke a lot of weed.

A lot of weed.

And then I stare at the bottle some more.

Tonight I let my hand creep to the right. The look of worry on Margaret's face still haunting me.

"Hello?"

As soon as I hear her voice, I regret the decision.

"Hello? Who is this?" The vague brogue and forty years of cigarettes and whiskey painted over with a fresh coat of schoolgirl giggle. "Marvin? Is that you?"

"It's me, Ma."

"James?" Here it comes. "Ohhhh, Jimmy! I've been sooo worried about you, son." So much sickly-sweet syrup hiding the arsenic in the words.

"I'm fine, Ma. How are you?"

"Oh, I'm just fine, Jimmy. Your Uncle Marvin is taking me out dancing, so I can't talk long." Like I'm still seven years old and believe every skeezy married car salesman who bends her bedsprings is some mysterious "uncle".

"I don't have an Uncle Marvin, Ma."

Pause. Disappointed glare telegraphed straight across the continent via the utmost in telecom technology. Wearied sigh.

"Fine. My *friend*, Marvin. Did you call me just to spread your misery, James? I don't have time for your attitude."

"Nice to hear your voice, Ma."

Click. Thanks, Ma.

I can hear through the walls, everything around me like I'm inside some glass bowl with everything reverberating. The couple fighting next door; the people on the opposite side having a quickie in the bedroom closet, while their friends are watching *Friends* in the living room. The old man at the end of the hall with his ugly, groaning, slapping, and screaming pornos constantly playing. Every few hours he grunts something in German, opens a new bottle of vodka.

At least it's Friday. I get to spend two more days and nights sitting here with my swollen brain and my slow right hand.

4

Dressed of fur

"Run!"

Fierce of tooth

"Run home and hide!"

I'm awake.

Awake, and I still hear the screaming.

A shroud of whiskey sleep and black morning clog my eyes, and I'm still hearing the screaming.

Black shapes bouncing and hopping in front of me. Screeching. Screaming.

"Get out of here! Get! Goddammit!"

I blink the confusion away and am unsurprised to find my face in the grass.

The birds are running, bouncing, hopping away. Jumping into the air as shiny black boots stomp around in the dirt.

I roll onto my back and look up into the accusatory glare of Officer Friendly's flashlight. I don't know what his name is, but he knows mine. We must be pals.

"Hey! You! Get up. What did I tell you about sleeping it off in the park?"

"What? Lemme just . . ." I feel a squirt of bile hit the back of my throat as I twist and contort to put my arms underneath me.

I roll back over to help the process, steadying myself for the first push-up of the day.

"Get the fuck up!" Friendly's boot under my ribs doesn't help me.

Instinctively, my hands go up, and my face comes down, back into the grass, which is much less comfortable from a one-foot drop.

"Fuck!"

"Come on, pal. What's it gonna be?"

I'm up. Half-sitting, legs still splayed out into the wet grass. Or maybe it's just my pants that are wet. At this point my senses are all shades of messed up, and I can't tell if the urine tang is coming from me or from the alley forty-feet away. The birds are still winging around my periphery. Always with the goddamn birds.

"I warned you before," Friendly says, struggling to get a grip under my armpits and haul me to my feet, "you can't keep passing out in the park."

Before? *Keep* passing out?

My knees are wobbling. They just keep hitting snooze and rolling over. None of me wants to cooperate.

"What's it going to be? You only get one warning and you used that up last night. So . . . Drunk and disorderly? Or were you on your way ho—"

He half tosses me up off the ground, spinning me to face him. The sudden change of direction leaves my stomach a half-step behind, and I retch, bile-flavoured whiskey and tepid soup bursting out of me like a swollen rain pipe, straight into the air like a goddamn fountain.

Friendly's face is dripping. His hat is raining slop onto his belly. He is no longer friendly.

"You asshole!"

Two thick hands hit my chest, full force, releasing another geyser of gruel straight into the officer's face. I'm tripping over my own feet, stumbling back, one foot coming down on top of the empty whiskey bottle and rolling underneath me. I feel my feet and my arms running in different directions, the momentum flinging me back onto the concrete where I land on already bruised ribs and wail like a kicked dog. The birds come swarming down around the bastard, and he swats them away with his puke-laden hat. It would be comical if he wasn't so pissed off.

"Drunk tank it is, shithead," Officer Used-to-be-Friendly says, laying another boot into my side before he grabs my collar and drags me, like a bag of garbage, toward the cruiser.

5

Officer Friendly's name turns out to be Whitfield. That's what it says on my paperwork, anyways.

I'd call him an asshole, except I would have done the same. I would have done worse. I would have wanted to kick the stupid drunk's head into the curb. He would have been doing me a favour. I'm the asshole.

The papers I sign have lot of complimentary terms like intoxicated, belligerent, and *resistant.* Repeated issues. *Recommend psych eval.* That means they'll forward a copy to good ol' Doctor Rhodes. Which means my mother will hear all about it by lunch. Why the fuck did I tell them about the doctor? Why did I tell them about the smells, the noises? Why can't I just keep my goddamn mouth shut? Maybe I do need to be locked up. Taken care of. Kept safe under lock and key. That's the curse though, isn't it? They can't save me from myself, and they'd only lock us up together.

This is how it always starts. Even when I was fourteen. The first time I woke up, face down in the grass, covered with somebody else's blood. Even then, it would have been a favour to stave my head in, teach me a lesson. Then I was twenty, maybe twenty-one, floundering in University, drinking, fucking anything that moved. Then it happened again, six or seven years ago. Wild, drunken bar fights, blackouts. Those days, those mornings, waking up confused and drenched in red. No Officer Friendly that day. I panicked and ran to the only people I trusted.

Like an idiot.

My mother treated me like I was some kind of sideshow freak. She refused to talk to me until I *got help*.

My doctor, good ol' Doctor Rhodes, the man I'd talked to every week since I was seven years old, he'd put me in the hospital. Again. Only it wasn't really a hospital, was it? It sure didn't seem like they were out to really help anybody, just lock up the nut bags and the troubled teens. I was dumped off like a bag of trash, piled in with cutters, and drug fiends, and people that were so strung out on crack, or so out-of-touch with reality that they were little more than toddlers in overgrown bodies. Defective pod people. There was a guy that fucked holes in the dirt. There was a skeleton with skin, a woman who cut off her own labia because she thought it made her look fat. There was a man who had eaten his own fucking foot. And me, confused and angry. A sad, alcoholic kid with abandonment issues, turned sad, alcoholic, should-have-learned-his-lesson-by-now man. Broken. Wrong. No damn good.

IT'S SIX IN the morning. *Monday* morning.

I have to be at work in an hour and a half, and I smell like Officer Friendly's hat.

The rest of the world smells like campfire, and the city has fallen into the clouds. I knew it was coming. I've been smelling it for a week, while everybody I mention it to looks at me like I'm having a stroke.

One thing about living in the shade of the Rocky Mountains. Mid-August to early September, without fail, the smoke comes down from the mountains like a death shroud for the end of summer. And it came fast. The last glimpse I'd had of the moon—while being shoved sour-head-first into the back of Friendly's cruiser—the sky was clear, and black, and full of stars.

Four hours later and the city is a ghost.

Athwart the gloom

Where the hell did that even come from? Some snippet out of my deep dark memory? Some morbid fairy tale when I was a kid? Something my mother used to say?

How much forest was burning out there? I wonder. How much

forest can there be?

The mist is somehow calming to me. It dilutes the evidence of my own self-abuse and hides me as I stumble through the street, dodging in and out between the spotlight arcs of the streetlights cutting through the thickening smoke. Everything's turned black and white. Sepia tone, like some old Orson Welles movie with weird angles and crazy shadows. Shadows that move as if they're following me. Swooping from corner to corner like liquid crows. That sledgehammer stench of sulfur comes with it. Maybe I *am* having a stroke. Maybe I am crazy.

At least the acrid smoke cuts the stench I'm carrying all over me. There's precious few people out here with the dawn, to stare at what's left of a blood red moon, and wonder at the blanket of grey. I'm inside my building, up and out of the elevator before anyone passes close enough to turn up an offended nose.

"Jesus!" the old man from 3312 croaks as he elbows past me.

I might say the same for him. The stories my sensitive ears could tell. The nasty words and ancient German salutations he grunts into his pillow as his television rumbles with turned-down screams of agony and lust. Some of those voices too high and too terrified. Too young. I can smell the lube still dripping in his jockeys. I've seen the red flag waving from his wall as I pass his open door, heard him moaning "Sieg Heil" in his sleep. None of these people keep their secrets from me. Or maybe I've just imagined it all. I don't even know anymore.

I'm locking my door before the elevator closes. I hear him whisper.

"*Schweinhund.*"

THE SHOWER IS hot and fast, scraping the foul taste of a cell full of drunks and hobos off of me. The foul taste of me. I'm scrubbing. Brushing. Clawing away the night. The skin itches and burns, but I keep scrubbing. The clean, fresh smell of Irish Spring. Ridiculous, and cliché, right? *Jimmy Finn uses Irish Spring, for that ol' wholesome smell of home on the Emerald Isle! Faith and Begorrah!* Somehow, it's the only thing I've found that smells clean and doesn't give me a headache after five minutes. The only soap or shampoo or cleaner that doesn't overpower me to tears. Fucking ridiculous. That's me.

I let the heat and the water pound into the back of my head, like a torrential downpour, masochistically trying to hit that wound from the photocopier, maybe bust it open and bleed a little restitution. The water can't find it. Neither can I. My fingers fumble and claw and stab at the spot, but there's nothing there. Not a scab, not a scrape, not even a bruise.

I rest my forehead on the cool, hard tiles. This is how it always begins. I'm going to lose my mind again. I try to focus on the water, on the sound of the artificial rain. I try to turn it real in my mind, falling hard on the ground, through the trees, turning that solid earth into something soft, thick, and free. My feet sink in, and my toes shorten, pulling in to the pads. My spine straightens, my shoulders rotate forward. I'm breathing deep the smell of pine and cedar and wet earth. I open my eyes to see it, the green. What I see is claws. Hair. *Fur*. My feet turned to something alien and wrong. Wet fur and black claws. I fall back screaming and land hard against the edge of the tub, cracking my ribs so hard I see stars. My eyes go straight, and my feet are where they should be, pale and long and full of toes. I close my eyes and weep. What the fuck is wrong with me?

Dressed of fur

NOW I'M LATE again. Pulling myself together. Fingering the back of my head, still looking for the gouge I was missing. I stand for twenty minutes staring out across the divide at the woman in the opposite building. I can smell her from across the street. I watch her move graceful and quiet through her morning routine. Transfixed. Mesmerized.

Then a drink. Four drinks.

The bottle is clanging around in my bag as I jog to the train, each bouncing step pounding in the back of my head like too much bass, then reverberating through my sore ribs like a knife twisting in my side. This is how it always begins.

The smoke clings to me, swallowing me up. There's something comforting in it, something familiar. I want to run. Instead, I climb into a packed train, shoved and muscled and pressed by the mass of humanity into a corner by the door. There's some oblivious haircut in a suit, drenched in body spray, absently sticking his elbow in my face so that he can get his phone to his ear. I'm trapped. Cornered. I feel the panic growing. The wide-eyed demon of proximity is bulging at my seams, ready to explode. This was a bad idea. A very bad idea. Babies are screaming. Who the fuck brings babies on the train at 7:30 in the morning? There are a hundred clashing conversations—phones, friends, strangers making small talk, bums harassing teens with blaring headphones. The wheels are screaming, and the joints between cars are creaking with the weight of all this madness. The late-summer heat, already stifling, is a good ten degrees higher now that the smoke has pressed its way in. The inside of the train car has to be in the high thirties, with no air circulating, other than the hot, stale breath of every person in there. I can taste eighteen different types of perfume, cologne, somebody has a tuna sandwich. Somebody smells like they've shit their pants. The baby spews. The bum is pissing down his leg. All these people, all this madness. Concentrated city. I'm choking. I'm dying. I'm going to explode. Or I'm going to crumple, like an old tin-can under foot. My eyes are clenched shut against the spattering lights, the strobing images out the window, the snarling faces and nervous eyes. I feel weak and overwhelmed, but that demon is there, so close, springing his heels, ready to pounce.

I'm two stops away from work, when I'm rocketed back into the Plexiglas barrier. My eyes open, and there's a face, inches away. Some hipster kid with a shave-side barber cut and a twirly-fucking moustache. I feel something press against me. I look down at the tightest pair of baby blue chinos that have ever been. Pointy leather shoes. The train bounces again, and his balls are in my hand.

"Dude."

I snap.

I shove this creep back the few inches of free space that are left in the car. The domino effect takes three people with him. The hipster loses his footing and topples over into the lap of some woman with a face full of paint and the smell of lavender all over her. She screams. The car comes to a shuddering stop at the station.

I shove past the screaming faces, past the nineteen or twenty people trying to force their way into the six square inches of free space left in the train. I fall past them, doubling over the railing a few feet away, and gasp for air, sucking in the smoke and thanking whatever-gods-may-be for it.

6

THE PHONE HASN'T stopped ringing all goddamn morning.

The split in the middle of my cranium is throbbing, teaming up with the stabbing pain in my side, humming with the overhead lights, buzzing down the middle of my brain like a circular saw, sitting in one place, carving an endless spray of torn grey matter.

The first four times, it was that nimrod Kari—Kari with an *i*—wanting "an updated ETA on that TPS report".

The fourth time, I bark at her, "It's not going to be any fucking sooner than the last three times you fucking asked me!"

The next two calls are from H.R., followed by a call from Margaret.

She warns me, *for the last time*, for the first time today, "Get your shit together, Jimmy!"

The next two calls are from Kar*i*. Asking again about the TPS.

By ten-thirty, the mickey is out from the bag and I'm flavouring my coffee.

Irish. Just like me.

When the phone rings again, I'm ready to throw it out the window and into the street, and I'm ready to throw myself out after it. I'll chase it straight to hell. At the very least, it might kill the headache.

"Jimmy dear?"

"Fuck."

Now I'm wishing it was Kari with an *i*.

"What's that, Jimmy?"

I reach back down under the desk for the bottle.

"Nothing, Ma. What do you want?"

"I just wanted to make sure you were all right, honey. We didn't really get a chance to speak the other night. Dr. Rhodes said . . ."

"No. You were too busy with *Uncle* whatever-the-fuck-his-name-is. And why are you talking to Rhodes? Isn't that against the shrink code or something? Why the hell is he still talking to you?"

"I'm your mother!"

"And I'm thirty-five years old."

"I'm still your mother."

Today she's my mother. Three days ago she couldn't give me two minutes. I splash liquid into liquid in the white porcelain mug in front of me. It's more whiskey than coffee at this point. Fuck it. I pour it straight into my mouth before replacing the cap and clumsily dropping it between my legs. It clatters against the side of the desk. I swing around too fast, trying to make sure nobody is watching, but only making my head swim.

"What was all that noise?"

"Nothing," I sputter, coughing up a hot mouthful of whiskey into my lap. "Shit!"

"What are you doing, Jimmy? Are you drinking?"

"I'm at work, Ma."

"Jimmy!"

I tug the sweatshirt away from the back of my chair and stuff it down between my legs to mop at the puddle of liquor there. The smell of it, always overpowering, makes me woozy.

"Fuck! I'm not drinking, Ma!" I whisper. "Why are you calling me at work?"

"Doctor Rhodes said that you were arrested."

"Detained. Not arrested. And that was three hours ago! Do you two have some fucking Batphone emergency line or something?"

Goddammit. What if somebody overhears? They listen in to everything. A bunch of little field mice, swarming and digging and nipping at every little scrap they can sniff out with their little rat faces.

"Oh, Jimmy. Why won't you just come home and let me take

care of you? You're all alone there."

"Home? To your new house in the buttfuck-middle-of-nowhere? With your uncle-of-the-month? That's not home."

I can see her face in my mind, contorting at my *nasty* language. So deeply offended by her own terrible, broken son.

"Why do you insist on talking to me like that? I didn't raise you to . . ."

"You barely raised me at all, Ma. You and your boyfriends."

I know it's harsh, but my head hurts. My day has sucked. This is what she does. Cut me off, make me wait to get attention on her terms. Her schedule. She's in control. I'm at fucking work. How many times have I told her not to call me at work?

"James!"

Here come the hollow tears, the improvised hysterics. Next would be the guilt trip. The poor-single-mother, making-ends-meet-any-way-I-could speech.

"Ma. I'm sorry, Ma," I offer, caving in to my ingrained Catholic/Baptist/Mormon/Whatever-the-fuck guilt. I've been brainwashed by the best. "I haven't been sleeping. I've been having those dreams again."

Silence on the other end of the phone.

"Ma?"

"You've been dreaming about *her* again?" she asks, quiet and pointed. Always to the obvious. How dare I dream about some *girl* when poor mother has sacrificed her whole life for me?

How could I not wonder? I don't even know who she is. All I have is this nightmare. This nightmare, and her. My mother won't tell me why she's in my dreams, calling out some other kid's name, won't tell me who the girl is, why we're running. What we're running from.

"The little girl, Ma. *Emma*." Even saying the name feels strange, like it's lighting some magic lantern deep in my belly, some tiny warm light way down deep inside. All the more motivation to rub it in my mother's face. "Tell me about Emma."

"I'm sure I don't know what you mean, son," she declares. Hard and fast. Shutting me down with that slight Irish brogue slipping into her voice the way it does on those rare occasions when her meagre instincts for mothering pop up, like some long forgotten quote. Like how to be a mother is something she remembers, but can't place. Something she has no context, or use for, but sticks in there anyways. For a broken boy with no past, it sure adds a salty aftertaste of neglect.

“Ma, don’t lie to me. I know that was her name. I know she was real. I feel it. I just can’t quite remember.” I’m forgetting I’m at work. I don’t even care anymore. I need to know something, anything. *Athwart the gloom.*

“I really don’t know . . .” Rolling the r’s, dragging the o’s.

“Ma!” I shout into the phone.

“If there was a girl you knew in Bensonhall, I truly don’t remember it! Now stop this nonsense!”

Bensonhall? What the hell is *Bensonhall?*

I’d never heard that name. Had I?

“Was that the town? Bensonhall? Is that where we’re from, Ma? Is that where we left him?”

“I have to go, James.”

“Ma? Tell me the truth. One fucking time!” I’m out of my chair, gripping the phone so tight that my hand aches. “MA?”

“Goodbye, Jimmy.”

“MA? What the fuck! MA!”

She’s gone. The click followed by the subtle static of the line resetting. I slam the phone down into its cradle. Over and over, willing it to knock against my mother’s head with all the intent of my impotent fury.

“FUCK!”

Faces are lining the tops of the cubicles, peeking around the corners. All the little rat faces, looking for their crumbs. Benoit is standing frozen with one hand on the copy machine. All eyes on Jimmy Finn’s crazy ass. Jimmy’s having a nervous breakdown. *Did you hear about Jimmy Finn in records?*

I can smell Chanel No.5 and mocha latte, and hear the soft steps of Margaret’s flats, plodding quickly down the hallway carpet.

“Jimmy Finn! What in the hell is going on here?”

Margaret, red-faced and eyes bulging. There’s a tiny vein popping at the corner of her forehead, just under a wisp of curly brown hair. It’s too bad. I kind of like Margaret. She was always decent. Never gave me a hard time, unless I wasn’t doing the job. I never heard Margaret gossiping around corners or fucking around in the supply closet. I never smelled secrets on Margaret. Now I was disappointing her. Just like Officer Friendly. I was the asshole here. Best to just walk away. I'm done.

I know I'm done. She knows I'm done.

I fumble around for the bottle from underneath the desk, gather up my sopping wet sweatshirt and my bag.

"What are you all looking at?" she shouts at the rat-faces. "Get back to work!"

When she opens her mouth, the rich chocolate-coffee smell overtakes the sweetness of her perfume.

I step past her into the hallway, holding my breath against both.

"Where do you think you're going?" she asks. Then her face twists as the strong peat-moss whiff of scotch finally wafts up to her nose. "Jesus, Jimmy!" She waves a hand in front of her face.

"I'm sorry, Margaret. I am sorry. I'm sorry." Guilt overtaking fury.

I walk off down the hall, not even waiting for her to finish the thought. She doesn't move. She takes a deep breath and sighs, her smells following me all the way down the hall, until I shut her behind me with the stairwell door.

7

"I RECEIVED A call from you mother, James. She's quite concerned about you. After this latest incident, I can't say as I blame her."

I'm sitting in my usual spot, tucked into an overstuffed armchair, facing good ol' Doctor Rhodes. Rhodes with his bald head and his white beard. I just want my drugs. I have to sit through the bullshit and beg like a leper for alms, but I need him to up my prescription and do it in a hurry, before I get any worse. I've already been arrested, lost my job, started drinking again. This is how it always begins.

I shuffle in my seat, adjusting, picking at a seam along the arm. How long have I been sitting here? An hour a week, at least? For, what? Twenty-eight years? Do that fucking math. That's like four *years*' worth of days. 1500 hours, give or take. That's like me sitting here in this goddamn chair for two full months, night and day, staring at this asshole, listening to all the ways that I'm fucked up.

"Do you just have a warehouse full of these fucking chairs?"

"Excuse me?"

I savour the shock in his voice. Just like Ma. *Watch your language, James!*

"These chairs. I swear it's the same damn chair I've sat in every week for my entire life. But it can't possibly be the same chair, can it? It's like brand new. So I'm thinking that you have a warehouse full of this shitty, uncomfortable chair, bought *on clearance* sometime around 1980."

"What are we avoiding, James?" Rhodes with his pandering tone, staring down over the shiny rim of his glasses. Always toying with them, shifting them. I could smell the nervous on him whenever I walked in the room . . . but of course that was all in my mind. Another delusion in my broken, sideways mind.

"I'm avoiding your bullshit, Doc. You telling me all the ways I'm failing to be a proper human. Isn't it supposed to be the other way around, Doc? Aren't you supposed to listen to me? About my problems?"

Rhodes adjusts his glasses again. I can smell the salt in his sweat. I can taste it, mixing with his Old Spice.

"As you say. Tell me about these problems, then. Tell me about the incident last night."

I sit. Quiet. Just for a minute, and stare at him. Fixing him with my eyes. He can never look me in the eyes.

"What's to tell? I got drunk. I fell asleep. I puked on a poor, brave officer of the law, and he ran me into the drunk tank. What was he supposed to do?"

"When did you start drinking again, James?"

I can feel the snarl forming on my face. "You really haven't listened to me once, have you? Do you have any idea what it's like?" The anger is welling up in my chest, swelling like a balloon. I know it shows in my face. I can see it, reflected on *his* face. His fear, it's like a pulsating light, leaking out of every hole in his head.

"Do you know? What it's like? Hearing things? *Every* thing? Smelling things so loud that it knocks me on my goddamn knees? I have to pinch my fucking nose shut when I fill up at the gas station. Do you know what that's like? The looks I get, standing at the pump ready to puke, hand clamped over my face?"

He's twitching. A tiny involuntary muscle on the side of his forehead, in his temple. "If you're drinking again, with your medication . . ."

"Well, the pills don't do anything for me! I can't walk down the street without being assaulted by chaos! So yeah, Doc! I drink. I smoke weed." Mocking him now, shrugging demurely, tenting fingers over my face. "I smoke . . . *marijuana*!"

"We've talked about this, James. Without *proper* medication, your symptoms will take over and you will lose touch with reality."

"Jimmy. How hard is it to just call me Jimmy?"

"These delusions of yours require medication. You don't want to be institutionalized again."

He uses that word like a scalpel. Like a real doctor, for once. Slicing right through my skin and poking at my bones. Cold and sharp and purposeful. Regaining his control. Better doctoring through intimidation.

I feel the muscles knotting in my neck, between my shoulders. The knife is still there, wedged between bones, ready for him to twist and separate. I crack knuckles and push back against it, wondering if I'll actually hear something clatter to the floor. The scent of strawberries and Brazilian dark roast distracts me. The nurse back from her break, strawberry tart wrapped in cellophane, next to her little cup of coffee—double sweet, double cream. I breathe deep and play my hand.

"You want to hear about my delusions, Doc? Is that the idea? You naughty boy." I know what to tell him. He wants to hear the juicy stuff. In my experience there's two types of shrinks. The ones fascinated by human behaviour, who might actually want to help somebody . . . and sick fucks like Rhodes, who just want a contact crazy high.

"The other day, I was outside on my balcony, just sitting there, having coffee. About the only place I'm not totally overwhelmed by noise and lights and chaos . . ."

"James, we need to discuss the medication, especially if your drinking problem has . . ."

I let the smile come, wide and devilish. I'm staring through him with my eyes, owning him like an x-ray. He's no more human than a coat rack.

"I'm sitting up there, minding my own business. Looking out across the city. This woman—a girl, really—maybe nineteen or twenty . . . she comes into view in her kitchen, *across the street,* and I can smell her. Two-hundred feet away. Thirty stories up. Her window is open, but she's inside. I'm sniffing her out. I'm opening my nostrils at the scent of her, breathing her in. Because she's *bleeding*. Between her legs, Doc. I can smell it. I can taste it in the back of my throat, sweet and salty. I'm swallowing it, drinking it up. I get hot all over, sweating, even though it's cold outside. The rest of my senses peak with it. It's rising in my chest, in my stomach, in my balls. I'm hard as a rock, and I'm watching now. I'm seeing her like I'm looking through binoculars. Every little movement, every twitch of her muscles. Her long legs are folded at the knee, her t-shirt barely covering her to mid-thigh. I realize I'm fucking growling. Growling. Like an animal. And all of a sudden I'm starving, my stomach is cramping, I'm so hungry. I have this urge to jump off of the balcony, like I could just bounce, and bound, and run across the nothingness between us in a few powerful leaps, like I could fly through the air and catch her and tear those legs right off of the bones and swallow them whole . . ."

I'm keeping my voice low, feeling the tension build in Rhodes' joints, feeling him squirm and twitch. More than that, I'm back on the balcony, tasting her again on the back of my tongue. Licking my lips, feeling my eyes roll back in my head. Knowing that Rhodes is dying inside. Wanting to chain me, to diagnose me, to stick me with some Latinate medical name—slap it on the label on my jar and watch me bang and clatter against the glass—but he can't. He doesn't know if it's real, or if I'm fucking with him. He doesn't know if I'm going to laugh, or bite his fucking face off.

Rhodes tugs at his collar and clears his throat.

"Well. Yes." He stammers, "About the drinking though."

I've got him now. I know it. He knows it. I can smell the lust overtaking the fear.

"You want to know what I did then, Doc?"

Rhodes sits rigid, holding his breath. He's a deer in the headlights.

I let a wide grin peel the lips from my teeth, let Rhodes see those long dog-teeth and wonder what I'm going to do. What I'm going to say. Let him shudder at his own deviance for once.

"What I did then, Doc? I went inside, and I opened the fridge, Doc. I pulled out a fresh new rib-eye I was planning on grilling up that night. I tore open the plastic and I jammed that fucking meat into my mouth, and I tore it apart. I tore *her* apart. I ripped and bit and gnawed at that slab of raw meat until I had devoured every last bit of it, blood and fat and gristle, and then I licked that package clean, man."

I flick my tongue at him, let him want the feel of it, bursting in his mouth, blood running down his throat. He smiles. A terrible, tooth-filled smile. I had him.

"Next time I'll warm it up first. Leave it out in the sun while I look at her there, across the street, out on her balcony, safe and unaware on the thirtieth floor."

Rhodes finally takes a breath, shuddering slightly as he draws a lungful through his nose.

"How's that, Doc?" I ask him. "Is that what you're looking for? You old pervert."

"James!"

"Just give me the script so I can go home." I sink back into that chair. That goddamn overstuffed, miserable chair.

Rhodes is still twisting and shuffling in his chair, trying to cover up his erection with the clipboard.

"We've, uh, covered this many, many times, James."

He's back into his spiel. Shifty, shifty Doctor Rhodes.

"You create these neuroses for yourself, and project these deviant desires onto others . . . *onto me* . . . in order to absolve yourself of your true feelings. Your feelings of abandonment, of loneliness. To escape the memories of your childhood abuse."

"You want to know how I feel?" I hold up one finger of each hand. "That's how I feel."

"You have to harness your anger and face these issues, James."

My fingers are digging into the arms of the chair. I want to tear that thing to fucking shreds. I want to tear *him* to fucking shreds.

"What issues? That I'm fucking crazy? That you and my mother have twisted me up into some kind of human pretzel for your own amusement?"

I've got a thread loose. One little thread from the arm of that goddamn chair.

"About your mother, James."

"What about her? The only thing she's ever given me is grief. And this fucking poem I can't get out of my head."

"What poem, James? Can you tell me the poem? Surely, that shows a connection with your mother. She is very worried about your well-being."

"Fuck her," I say, still picking at the thread. "Fuck you."

The thread pops. Unravelling, spinning out of control, springing out in an endless loop under my fingers.

"There's no need for that language. As you have pointed out yourself, James. We have been friends for a very long time, have we not?"

I'm spinning it around my finger, pulling the life out of that chair, stealing the thing that holds it together, twisting it into my hand.

"Certainly *not*, Doctor Rhodes. Not friends. I don't have friends. As you have pointed out yourself."

He's staring at my finger, twisting and twisting, pulling that thread. What does he care, anyways? He has a warehouse full of these fucking chairs.

"I'm broken and wrong, and at your mercy. Unless I want to have you send me to the nuthouse. Right? Isn't that how this works? I kiss your ass and tell you these little delusions of mine, and you give me pills to keep me safe for public consumption?"

The string is tight. Turning my finger purple, but I can't stop. Not now. He's finally coming apart. Fucker.

"That's very hurtful, James. I believe we have a very important relationship. I'm only here to help you."

"Well, you're a lousy fucking doctor if you haven't figured out how to do that after nearly thirty years."

Rhodes stands up, steps in toward me, and plucks the end of the thread, snapping it from the seam just as the stuffing begins to burst. He extends a stiff hand, hesitant and awkward. Making the gesture without having the balls to back it up. Letting me know that my time is up. Another week, another hundred bucks. There's the door.

"You really are a lousy fucking shrink." I slap the hand away. Then, it all caves in. I hesitate. He fucking beats me again. I give in to decades of conditioning.

"Script?"

Rhodes, tall and proud once again, pulls a scrap of paper from his pocket—always well-prepared—and holds it out toward me, just out of reach. Twisting my leash like so much thread from an armchair.

"You should really try to be more open with your mother, James. She is quite worried about you."

I'm heeled, and broken.

"I bet she is."

I slam the door behind me, but we both know it means nothing now. A futile expression of over-baked angst.

I throw a glare at the fat receptionist. She has strawberry on her face.

I think about jumping across the desk and licking it off.

But it's too late. I just want to go home.

8

I'VE SPENT FOUR hours walking in circles in my apartment. Turning and turning. Pacing like a dog in stir.

Every so often, I sit in front of my laptop screen for an uncomfortable minute or two, trying to focus on Facebook, or YouTube, or some other forced facsimile of modern normalcy. I have no friends in either reality. My Facebook page is a depository for pat motivational bullshit, old *Bloom County* comics, and movie trailers for movies that I'm never going to actually watch. All of it feels so false and manufactured and pointless. I type the poem out. It doesn't make any goddamn sense either.

From the South, three sisters fair . . .

The maidens of the moon

I stand on my balcony and stare at the sinking red glow behind the edges of the haze. The smoke is so thick now that the sun is no more than the glow of a cigarette, a dying ember in a snowstorm.

I try to sniff out the woman across the way. All I get is a nose full of cremated nature.

I'm trying to maintain. I'm trying to contain. I walk in circles and tell myself that I'm just imagining all of this.

Maybe it's all a dream. Maybe I'm still sleeping.

Then the nightmare starts tearing through into my conscious

mind. Snippets of dreamland. Her voice echoing off the walls of my apartment. The smoke outside solidifies and flaps in the wind, man-sized bat wings slapping against the coming night. I close my eyes and it becomes billowing white curtains filling my mind. I hear the screams far off in some dark corner of my head. I see the blood, seeping from the walls, pooling on the kitchen floor.

Fuck Rhodes.

I need something else. I need something to keep me awake and not dreaming.

I need something to take the edge off and let me relax and let me stop seeing and hearing and feeling everything.

I need to see Devil.

IT TAKES ME an hour to find my keys. I haven't driven my car in weeks. I find them buried under the couch cushions. The car starts easy enough. Which always shocks me. I always expect my neglect to result in it just fading into a quiet death. I love to drive, when it's late and quiet and the city is empty and I can open the windows to breathe in the night, and it feels like I'm running, flying through the darkness.

Tonight the air is full of smoke, and for some unfathomable reason, I'm terrified of what's out there in the shadows, in the mist. Those man-sized wings. *Athwart the gloom.* So I keep the windows up tight and suffer through the claustrophobia and the stale car stink.

I prowl through Coach Hill, past the mini-mansions, the McMansions, and the ornate palaces beyond. Houses with stone walls surrounding them like castles. Homes with gates and trees and more grass than I step foot on in a week downtown.

I'm looking for the car. His car. That unmistakable car.

I know he lives around here. I just don't know exactly where. I'm looking for that car. I'm praying that he doesn't park in a garage. I'm praying that he's home. Which is lunacy. What kind of drug kingpin is sitting around at home on a Wednesday night at midnight? What would he be doing? Watching *The Daily Show* and smoking a bowl? This is Devil, we're talking about. Adam DeVille. The Devil himself.

Then I see it. Curled up in a long white drive, deep-space black, gleaming like the cosmos, nose poking out into the smog and the smoke, that little chrome gargoyle on the hood. Nobody else has a car like that.

I park on the street and hunch my shoulders against some invisible predator. I can smell something on my tail, following, lurking. I've been smelling it for days. Or maybe I haven't. It was there in the park. Leaving work. Even on the train. Maybe I'm remembering wrong. Imagining things. Maybe paranoia is the next step in the Total Mental Self Destruct chain. I still smell it. Sulfur stench, black ink shadows, followed by something ripe and meaty and dark. Like the monkeys at the zoo. Like the wild dogs out behind Lee Ho Fook's Chinese restaurant, waiting for a half-eaten Styrofoam cup of beef chow mein. It was there all right. Some strange thing, some wild animal in my periphery. Always in the corner of my mind.

I shuffle fast to the door, wary of tripwires and land mines and god-knows-what. This is Devil, after all. He might have a sniper on the roof for all I know.

I rap lightly on the big oak door. Then a little harder. Hushed whisper.

"Devil?"

Harder still. Knuckles to wood. Feeling something weird under my skin. Outside of my skin. I'm not sure. Something soft between my knuckles and the door.

"Devil!"

I hear clomping steps. Devil in his boots. Those goddamn Fonzie boots.

"Who in the hell?" he's mumbling. Maybe I've woken him up and he'll put a bullet in my face. Serves me right. I'm the asshole here.

I feel him press his face to the peephole in the door. I smell his aftershave seeping through the door by osmosis.

The door swings wide. He's in his boxer shorts. And his boots. He's covered with strange markings. Beautiful, ornate tattoos, but interspersed with ancient-looking letters and symbols. Viking runes and tribal swirls in hard blacks, odd Arabic-looking symbols in seven different colours, lines and circles and triangles topped with more triangles and crescents and letters I don't recognize. I haven't seen him without a shirt since High School gym class. He has a hard, rectangular piece of black metal in his hand. It's a gun. A handgun. The kind of gun you see in cop movies, the kind with a clip and a hundred bullets.

"Jimmy? What the fuck, man?" He's rubbing sleep out of his eyes.

"I'm sorry. Can I come in, please? Please, Adam."

Devil bugs his eyes wide open and clears his throat. He looks at me closer, makes up his mind.

"Yeah. Yeah, man. Get in here."

It's a nice house. A big house. Open and clean and tasteful. Everything smells like wood and leather. Real leather. It smells like heaven. A soft, natural heaven. The whole place is a monument to the good taste of understated sensibility. No noxious perfumes and ammonia smells. No bright lights, and loud TVs, and blaring music. Just shelves full of books, paintings on the walls, and tastefully matched pieces of art. He has swords on the wall, and some sort of Zulu death mask. I don't have to ask to know that they're authentic, or that he knows how to use the swords. I always thought that, had he not become the city's biggest drug dealer, Adam DeVille would have travelled the world writing books. Probably more Henry Miller than Hemingway, but he would have been huge, and he'd be the same man, the same Devil. Or maybe he could have been a professor—Archaeology, maybe—like Indiana Jones.

"Sit down, Jimmy," Devil says. He's pouring himself a drink. He looks back at me, eyeballing me, pondering something. He pulls out another glass and splashes some scotch into it, but barely half of what's in his own tumbler.

He sits down across from me, motioning me to follow suit. The chair swallows me up like a Venus flytrap, wrapping me in soft, brown leather.

"You look like shit, Jim," he says, passing me the drink. Slouching back in his chair. He's still just in his boxers and those big black boots.

"Do you ever take those off, Devil?"

He's in a good mood now. Comfortable. He shuffles forward and leans down to stare at his feet.

"Only when I'm fucking your sister."

I don't have a sister, but he always says it anyways. He sits back again, working his way into the seat, pushing his muscles into the flesh of the chair. The hundred arcane symbols twisting and writhing with his skin. Once he's there, held in good and tight, he takes a swallow and sets the glass on the thick roll of leather and wood beside him.

"You look like shit," he says again.

What he's really saying is *why are you here, Jimmy Finn?*

I feel the aggression in the way his shoulders are tensed, in the way his fingers are locked around the glass, the way he looks at me without blinking.

"We've been friends for a long time, Adam. I was in the neighbourhood. I thought I'd drop by."

All of the bullshit. All of it. But he knows. He keeps watching me with his devil eyes.

"We *were* friends, Jim. A long time ago. Now I'm the guy who sells you weed." He shakes his head and mutters under his breath. "Do I look like a guy who does fucking favours?"

"I'm sorry I came here. I get it. Not cool." I'm up and backing my way out of the room.

Devil stops me with a look. "What do you want, Jimmy? And don't say meth, or crank, or any of that shit, or I'll beat you to death and leave you in the trunk of that shitbox car you parked out in front of my house."

"I . . . I don't do that stuff, man. Look, you've always been into this weird, supernatural kind of shit, Adam."

"Don't call me Adam." He takes another swig from his glass. Losing patience, but holding himself back. "I don't call you *James*, do I?" Not wanting to take care of business in his living room. In his sanctum sanctorum. "You sure look like you've been tweaking out to me, Jim."

"No. I . . . I don't know what's wrong with me, man. I'm . . . I'm broken. I've been seeing shit . . ."

"Then the last thing you need is more fucking drugs, Jimmy."

He's right. I know he's right. He was always right. In High School, he was the one with all the answers, coasted through class after class. Already making more money selling pot than most of the teachers made in salary. Always with a plan, never getting caught. He has rules, and plans, and calculated business models. He has a Zulu death mask on his wall.

"Devil. I just need something to stay awake. OK? Something to take the edge off, sure. But something to stay awake. No more nightmares. No more blood, no more screaming."

Adam DeVille looks at me with pity on his face. A look he used to give me when we were sixteen and comparing shitty mothers and sharing cigarettes outside the gymnasium doors.

"You still having those dreams?"

I'm weeping. Bawling. Sobbing like a baby in the dark. I'm falling apart in Devil's living room.

"I don't know what the fuck is happening to me."

Devil gets up and clomps across the room, sits on the arm of my chair and holds me in his arms. I cry harder at the first human touch I've felt in months, outside of somebody's crotch in my hands on the C-train.

"WHEN'S THE LAST time you ate, man?"

Devil's piling my third plate full of eggs and bacon.

I'm feeling raw and nervous, but lighter than I have in weeks, months maybe. Almost . . . comfortable. My head feeling clear for the first time in as long as I can remember.

Devil has a half-dozen books piled next to us. He's flipping back and forth looking for something. Index to contents to page numbers, book to book to book. It's an odd sight—this hard-ass, muscled and tattooed drug dealer, glasses balanced on the end of his nose, buried in textbooks and thick reference books. When he finds what he's looking for, he taps his finger on the page, nailing it down, the other hand stroking his chin. Like Rhodes, but Rhodes played by somebody with a six-pack and a handgun.

"Clinical Lycanthropy."

The eggs sink from my stomach into my pelvis, and I feel like I'm going to soil Devil's kitchen stool. I know that word. Of all the words he's been muttering and mumbling for the last half-hour, I know that one—*Lycanthropy*.

I choke on a pebble of scrambled egg as the standard equivalent for that word creeps past my lips.

"Werewolf. You think I'm a werewolf?"

Devil sighs. It must be annoying always being the smartest guy in the room.

"No, dummy. *You* think you're a werewolf."

He sits down next to me, wrapping a thick arm around my shoulder, pulling me closer as he reassures me.

"It doesn't even mean that you think you're a werewolf. Maybe you just believe you're reverting to some kind of animalistic state

. . . wolf, cheetah, an albino fucking alligator. The point is that you're having some kind of breakdown, and this is how your brain is dealing with it."

He slaps me on the back and hops off of his stool, walking around the counter and rummaging around in a cupboard, coming up with a messenger bag of some sort, pulled out of who-knows-where.

He pulls out pill container after pill container, examining the labels, looking down his nose through his glasses to read. He finally finds the two he wants and slides them across the countertop at me.

"Here," he says, almost proudly. Maybe he should have been a psychiatrist. He'd already been of more help to me in an hour than my own doctor had in a quarter century.

"These will keep you awake—if that's what you really want . . ."

He picks up the second plastic tube.

"These will help you sleep, which is what I think you really need. No dreams, no nightmares, just rest."

He comes back around and hops onto his seat.

"The human brain is a delicate piece of machinery, Jimbo. You can't fuck around with it so much."

"Says the drug dealer," I mumble behind a mouthful of bacon.

"I'm not the one losing my shit, Jimmy." Cold, but accurate. Definitely should have been a doctor. Then his lips curl up and eyebrows arch. "Unless you *are* turning into a werewolf," he grins.

"Don't tease me. Please."

"Who's teasing? You have no idea what kind of shit is out there, man. You see this?" He points to a patch of ink on his chest. A cross with *fleur de lis*, smaller crosses and snowflakes surrounding it, a star at both ends. There's a crescent moon on a stick crossing the central image, Victorian flourishes on every terminus, except the moon-stick.

"What is it? A weathervane or something?"

"That is a *Veves*. The symbol of Papa Legba, gatekeeper to the spirit world. *Voudou*."

"Voodoo. Seriously?"

"*Voudou*. Yes. Seriously. This dude from New Orleans cursed me. He killed my dog and sent all kinds of nasty ghost-shit after me. His poltergeists trashed this place, crashed my car . . . almost killed me . . . I don't know how many times. A *Voudou* priestess gave me this symbol, and it all stopped."

"What the fuck did you do to the guy?"

"I killed him. Obviously." Devil winks.

"I mean what did you do to make him curse you?"

"I slept with his mother."

"Obviously." I laugh, a little more nervously than I intend. "But you don't really believe that shit, do you? That I'm actually some kind of mythical man-beast?"

"I've seen shit that would turn you white, Jimmy-boy."

"Isn't that from *Ghostbusters*?"

"And *Voudou* was some silly shit from an old Bela Lugosi movie, until I met Dominique Dufresne."

I LEAVE A half hour later with the two pill bottles and a big bag of pot. Devil hands me a little box. It's a phone. The kind you buy at the 7-11. The kind drug dealers use and throw away.

"My number is the only one in there. Don't use it for anything else. Call me if you get in any trouble you can't get yourself out of, all right?"

"*From the south, three sisters fair*
Ran athwart the gloom
Dressed of fur and fierce of tooth
The maidens of the moon."

I don't know why I say it. It just comes to me altogether for once.

"Poetry, Jim? Not really your style."

"Have you ever heard that before? You're into poetry, right?"

Devil smiles softly, pats me on the shoulder.

"Well, it ain't Whitman, if that's what you mean."

Devil DeVille. Gangster. Drug dealer. Scholar. *Voudou* expert. Poetry lover. Hugging me as I step back out into the night.

"Be good, man. Be *careful*," he says.

I PICK UP that same dangerous scent again, as soon as I turn away from the door. Sulfur, followed by a rush of air, then replaced with some kind of monkey-stink. It's coming from the trees in the yard next door. I run to my car and clamber inside in a panic, every ounce of hope and normalcy and compassion I'd scraped together in Adam DeVille's living room, gone. I try to pull myself together. I'm imagining things. This is all in my head. I pull out the two pill bottles. Blue for sleep. Red to keep running.

Clinical Lycanthropy. Werewolf. Fucking maniac. *Dressed of fur and fierce of tooth.*

I'm losing my mind.

I have to keep running.

9

I'M BACK WALKING in circles.

Maybe Devil was right. Maybe I took the wrong pill.

Blue for sleep. Red to keep running.

Too late now. Too very late. Three A.M. and I'm still running.

I can't stay locked up inside anymore. I need freedom, and space, and air . . . even if it's filled with smoke and death. I'm wide-awake and my brain continues to bubble and spatter, frying itself into nothingness inside my skull. I can feel it shrivelling up and drying out, my last connections to reality sizzling off like so much fat. Very soon there won't be anything left in there to argue, nothing left to hold me back from . . . whatever it is I'm becoming.

Clinical Lycanthrope. Beast-man. Werewolf. Crazy person.

They're going to lock me away again. This time for good.

The bottle is clinking in my pocket. None of it seems to make a difference anymore. Not the booze, not the weed. I smoke half of what Devil gave me. Enough to paralyze an elephant with mellow thoughts of cool water and plentiful fields of bamboo. Me? The noises and smells get fuzzier, the inside of my head becomes a vast echo chamber. Just a bigger pot to fry in.

I pop the top and guzzle it back. The icy fingers of whiskey snake out from my stomach, into my chest and my arms, and turn from ice to fire, but never reach my head. I'm whispering to the bottle. Whispering to myself. I'm crying again. Anger, frustration, misery.

This place is keeping me crazy. These walls, always talking. All of these TVs blaring, endless noise, and disembodied voices floating through the walls. All these smells and vibrations. Trapped inside, alone, yet surrounded. A hundred strangers forcing their way into my head.

I don't even realize I'm doing it until I'm dressed and my keys and my bottle are tucked into the pockets of my jeans. I'm already fifteen floors down, my legs carrying me down the stairs in a daydream. I pass the other human refuse on the way—a Russian I've seen in the alley, drifting in a corner, strap still loose around his arm, sour pus on a half-dozen sores that smell like death; in the fourth floor stairwell there's this girl—a hooker, I guess—she's maybe seventeen, all wrapped up in a purple, fake fur jacket, and I'm walking through a cloud of tangerines and wine cooler. Her arms and legs are twisted around some skeezy bastard with his pants around his ankles, his legs all pimples and wiry hair underneath her.

I'm not any better than these other cast-offs, am I?

Lost. Alone. Broken.

But even these scraps of humanity don't notice me.

Even to them, I'm a freak.

IT'S LIKE SOME kind of apocalypse out here. Streets cold and empty. Filled with smoke and devoid of movement, except for the dense charcoal cloud that seeps off of the pitch black sky. The smoke is so thick now that the streetlights stand muted and impotent, teardrops of grey in perpetual shadow.

Goose-pimples rise on my arms.

I shouldn't be out here.

I know it. I feel it. *Athwart the gloom.*

Thick as that fog is, as crushing to my senses, I still imagine a faint odour of unwashed primate.

I hunch my shoulders against the formless night and the strange quiet, and I jam my hands into my pockets, wrapping my fingers around the comfort of that hard glass bottle. I want to steel my reserve. I want to comfort myself. Delude myself. I want to swallow that bottle down right now. Part of me wants that, wants so badly to just curl up in the gutter and swallow that bottle down and feel warm and forgetful and justified.

But the other part of me knows that's a lie, and it keeps me moving. My feet shuffling, faster and faster, until I'm running through the darkness, rubber soles pounding against the cement, until the concrete gives way to soft earth and grass, and I collapse, heaving for breath, but warm and filled with something other than misery. I roll and spread myself out on my back in the grass and look up into the black-smoke sky. It's moving, swirling with black shapes, turning in slow circles, coming closer and closer.

As much as the smoke suffocates the smells, it seems to amplify the sounds of the night, or maybe it's just that there's nothing left alive out here. But that would be a lie too. I can hear them moving. I hear whimpers, tears. Soft and low. Begging for mercy in some ancient tongue. Then I hear the reply.

"Fucking bitch! Hold her down!"

"Shut her up!"

I'm creeping through the trees, weaving through the shadows like a ghost.

There's three of them. *Bros* with flat-brimmed ball caps and belts around the middle of their asses—except one—his belt is around his knees, and he's fighting his way between the legs of a young Asian girl. She's thrashing away, clawing, kicking. She doesn't want to be there. The other two *Bros* are holding her down. They don't think I can see them. They think they're all alone in the dark. They think this is a secret. Officer Friendly, so territorial when I'm sleeping peaceful under the stars, he's nowhere to be found tonight.

I can smell her. Lilacs and lemons. The lilacs aren't real. Perfume, false tones of springtime, cloying and sweet. The lemon is real. It's covering a hundred other things. Spicy, fragrant things, but the lemon cuts through it like a knife. I smell her fear. Stronger than the lemons.

Her fear is sharp and exciting, but it's soon over-powered by a testosterone stink, mixed with cheap body spray and stale beer.

Then comes the blood. Not much, but I can smell it. I can taste it.

My heart is pumping faster, my limbs are flushed and tight, muscles knotting and twisting. Some strange new energy is pulsing through me. There are drums pounding in my head, blocking out the misery and the doubt and the fear. Taking away everything that used to be me.

My hands are curled around the tree, clawing the bark. I feel the wood snap under my fingertips.

I'm watching them like they're three little piglets and I'm the big bad wolf.

Dressed of fur and fierce of tooth.

The birds are screaming in the trees.

"Fuck is with those birds, yo?"

"Shut the fuck up and hold her down!"

The one that's trying to wedge himself inside of her—he's first.

I bound in from the treeline—fast—faster than I've ever been.

I grab his neck and pull. Rip. Tear. I hurl him on the ground and pounce.

I smell lemon fading with footsteps in the dark. Smart girl.

My fists are hammers, heavy and thick, swinging from high above me, as if they were thrown down through the black clouds by Thor himself. Left and right, back and forth, one after the other, swinging wide and high and coming down with all the weight of every terrible misery that has ever darkened my mind or my heart. Nothing is wrong here. No questions, no judgments. Just blood.

His face is coming apart beneath me. His eyes are lost in folds of swollen meat and awash with red. He's shoving fingers in my face, clawing for my eyes, finding my jagged teeth. More blood, more screams. The joints pop as they separate, the sinews snapping against my tongue.

The other bros are pulling at me, pummelling me with their fists and their feet. They are screaming, but their voices swirl and combine with the cheers of the crows in the trees. There's a legion of them, calling to me, urging me on, daring me to make their supper an easy one.

I hear them. I understand. I'm hungry too. So hungry.

His swollen ear bursts in my mouth. The lights behind his eyes have gone out, candles snuffed with a hurricane. He doesn't even twitch when it pulls free. The cartilage is chewy, rubbery, but the hot rush of fresh blood quenches me.

I feel something cold slide into my leg, a sharp pain, then the rush of warmth and a glorious, fresh ocean of blood. It overwhelms the rest of my senses. I lift my head and breathe deep. I scream out into the night—not of pain, but of joy.

The second one freezes when he sees my face. The knife is still in his hand, coated with red. My red. My blood. He staggers away from me, like some stupid kid in a bad slasher flick. He's holding the knife between us, but so shaky that I could blow it away with a breath. He's trembling, crying. I feel the heat of the stream of piss before I even smell it. His pants go two shades darker down the front. I smile and spit, launching what's left of his pal's ear into his screaming face. Number three is long gone. I hear his manic steps fading into the distance a block away. Number two is mine. I curl my fists in front of me, lick at the blood between the knuckles. There's something else there, in the spaces where my own skin has faltered and split. Tufts of pink-stained hair stand out where there was none before. Fur.

I've finally lost my mind. Finally.

It fills me with a tremendous sense of well-being.

And I smile.

He doesn't like that smile. A fresh stream of piss and he shudders and shits himself.

He throws the knife at me, crawling way on all fours. The birds are all around us, black messengers from the darkness, sent down through the black cloud to announce me. The new me. The better me.

He screams when I sink my teeth into his cheek. Thrashing away, clawing and kicking.

He doesn't want to be here.

Alone. In the dark. With me.

10

I WAKE TO sunlight.

My eyes open to the light and stare up into the pale blue expanse of the sky. There's still smoke in the air, but it's faint, a thin veneer of sepia on the few scattered clouds.

I move to sit up, expecting the usual creaking and knotting, the initial misery of my day—sore muscles, twisted up in a lack of sleep and reminding me what abuse I have in store for it again. Pleading with me to leave them alone, to rest, to die peacefully and be left to rot.

Not today.

I'm on hard ground. In the middle of a broken landscape of carved-out earth. Gravel and grey dirt. I'm surrounded by lagoons of milky white water and towering piles of darker soil. Ant-hill pyramids twenty-feet high.

I look around, clear-eyed and oddly calm.

I'm in a construction lot—the scraped earth where nature gives way to man—there's a tall wire fence on one side of the lot, but the rest is bordered by trees and hills of grass. I'm somewhere near the river. I can smell it, forcing its way through the concrete, metal, and glass. I'm miles away from home.

I stand and brush the sand and dust from me, feeling taller, stronger, and calmer.

I realize that the one thing I don't smell is the monkey stench that had been following me for weeks.

My hands are black with dirt and something sticky. Red.

Blood dried into hard shell gloves, cracking and pebbled with grime.

I breathe deep and long, enjoying the cool morning air free of downtown smells and the press of a thousand other people in my periphery. I kneel at one of the huge pools of rainwater, and I don't recognize the face that stares back.

My face is a mask of red, two day stubble turning to a spiky beard, run through with the same sticky black as my hands. There's a stranger's eyes staring back at me. Still emerald green, but brilliant and gleaming. Clear and confident. No longer filled with fear and doubt and misery. This face is rugged—handsome even. I splash the water onto my face and scrub, washing my hands, my face, cupping the surprisingly cool and fresh water to my lips.

I shove my head under and come up laughing.

I feel . . . good.

I WALK UNTIL I recognize my surroundings, feeling new strength and surety in my legs. Every muscle in my body feels new and strong. People stare as I pass, ragged and terrible with my shirt and my pants filthy with old blood. It's not my blood. I checked. Whatever happened to me in the night, it left its mark. Just not enough for me to remember, or care. I scratch at the scrub on my neck and feel the urge to run swell up in my new legs.

It starts as a jog across the beltline into Seventeenth Avenue, bouncing across in front of traffic, pouncing through cars locked in stasis, humming at stoplights, rumbling at the curbs. I bound into the crowd and break free, legs pumping harder, body moving quicker. My lungs are open, every part of me working as if I was made to run. The faster I run, the less I notice the world around me. The smells merge and disappear, the voices fade, the faces melt into a blur, and I'm sensing my way forward, dodging bodies and cars and turning corners by feel until I come roaring across First Avenue and that smell hits me like a wailing siren. The hot monkey stink. I trip once coming to the curb and barrel—shoulder first—into the endless brick tower of my own building, crumpling against the wall and slumping to my ass on the sidewalk.

It's filling my nose now, so close. Closer than it's ever been. I turn a wide nostril toward the alley, following it, seeking it out.

And there he is, down the alley, staring right at me. The monkey man. An unwashed animal wrapped up in dirty jeans and a leather vest. He's smiling.

"Are you ok? That was a pretty hard landing. I think you're bleeding."

Another smell I knew all too well. I turn my head to stare up into her curious eyes. The redhead from the thirtieth floor. I flick my eyes back down the alley too late, and my stalker is gone.

"Hey. Are you ok?"

She's wearing a purple sundress, and she has an armful of books and a leather purse clutched to her chest. Those long legs are bare to the thigh.

The scent of her blood is faint, stemmed with cotton, her time almost passed, but it still overpowers everything else around me. My eyes roll back as I breathe it in. Taste it. The taste of it is in my mouth, but stronger than before. There are terrible things flashing through my mind. Screaming and fear, and geysers of blood. The taste of flesh on my tongue. My stomach cramps at the thought of it. Hunger. Deep and terrible hunger.

She backs away as I get up from the ground, creeping forward, matching every step she takes.

The fear comes into her pretty blue eyes. Wide and pleading. She's backing out into the sidewalk, people are passing us by, turning to look, but no one stops, no one utters a word. They all start backing away. I'm clearing a path between us. The blood is feeding me, drifting through my lungs, into my heart, pushing it harder, faster, the power of it pounding in my ears, rushing through my bones like lightning.

She turns to run. I can see it now, like a red trail behind her, flowing out like a line on a map.

She breaks for the intersection, ten steps ahead of me. She's in the street, screaming now, the red is flowing like a river, forging a path between us. My eyes are locked on her legs. Those legs I want to tear apart, swallow whole, juicy and firm and full of life. I see it in my mind, gnawing on the bones beneath, feeling the soft sponge of the marrow in my teeth.

I pounce, launched like a rocket by new legs, through the air and flying. Powerful. Free.

Yellow fills my eyes. There is the sound of thunder. The force of the entire world screeching to a stop. A thousand screams. I am swatted into darkness. Her smell and her screams are fading. There is blood. New blood. My blood. I recognize that smell, but it's fading too. Everything is fading. Everything is black.

11

"COME ON, FINN. Run with me."

The echoes. The white walls that move. Her voice. Young and high and calling me.

"Finn. Come on, Finn."

The room is shifting, the echoes longer, farther away. I'm losing her to the darkness, the white walls shifting quickly to shadow. My mother's voice gone. Little Emma calling me.

"Run, Finn."

I'm staring down at my own hands, bloody and torn. Something sticky there. Something mixed with the blood.

Cloth?

Hair.

I scratch at my own hands with long nails—not nails—*claws*. Pulling at bits of stuff. Stuffing. Fluff. I'm bursting at the seams like Dr. Rhodes' fucking chair. I claw deeper, skin splitting and tearing away like paper. There is no more blood. No blood, just thick white hair.

Fur.

Dressed of fur and fierce of tooth.

The scream comes from deep inside my throat and bursts from my nose, my mouth, my eyes.

My hands are in front of my face, out toward the distance. I'm staring down the long hallway, between the white fur of my hands, ribbons and scraps of paper-skin left dangling like streamers from my clenched fists.

The screaming. The blood. They begin like another echo, down that long hallway.

I blink, and my eyes open wide in new light. I'm under the bed now, watching, as they change.

Two people. Naked. A man and a woman. She is beautiful. Like the little girl, dark hair and olive eyes. He is tall and thick with muscle, covered with thick hair.

She claws at his face as he grips her arms, both drawing crimson trails beneath their fingertips. Their faces are twisting, breaking, falling apart in front of me, faces falling away to reveal gnashing fangs beneath. Nothing but teeth. So many teeth.

I hear screaming. Loud and piercing. Like a thousand crows calling in unison, screeching with all their might. It's coming from inside me. I feel a touch against my hand. I don't recoil. I don't start. It's warm, comforting. Tiny fingers wrapping around mine. She is beside me. I turn and look into those olive eyes, so deep and calm. There are vast forests inside the green of those eyes.

"Run, Finn," she says. "Run away home."

I WAKE TO white hot fluorescent light.

My eyes open and stare at the water-stained, pockmarked tile ceiling of a room that scares me. Deep in my bones, I feel that this place is wrong. Dangerous. False.

Machines clicking. Beeping. A cavalcade of noise beyond the walls. Crying. Pleading. Groaning. Shouting voices.

And the smells. So many smells. Cleaners. Harsh and poisonous. Shit and piss. Vomit and blood. I'm in a hospital. Whether it's a hospital, or a *hospital,* remains to be seen. Whichever kind of place this is, there is death here, I can smell it.

I can smell *him*. The ape-man. The unwashed man, sweaty and dirty, no chemicals and perfumes on this one.

I try to move, twisting at my wrists, heaving against thick leather straps at my wrists, ankles, thighs, and chest. My head is free, with enough give in the straps to strain a few inches to turn and look at the man standing against the wall, his stink sheathed in light blue hospital scrubs. His face is tan and leathery, his cheeks and neck textured with a scrub of thick stubble. His long dark hair is tangled behind him with some sort of leather strap. Not the sort of man who works in a hospital, or wears light blue.

"Where the fuck am I?" I croak, in someone else's broken voice, "Tied down."

"Yes, mate," the man warbles back. Kiwi? Aussie? "The doctors think you might pose a spot of trouble, I reckon."

"Please?" I groan, tugging weakly at the straps.

"Oh I couldn't do that, Jim. Not yet." He grins a mouth of yellow teeth, blank spaces here and there, like a broken fence. He's flipping through pages on a clipboard. "Says here you puked up some bloody fingers, mate! Fingers! That must have been a bitch to bring up."

"I didn't . . . what am I?"

"What are you in for?" The man chuckles, "All I know, son, is that they've been out there in the hall talking about your Doctor Rhodes. Something about *second time this week*, and *mandatory psych evaluation*. Whatever it is you did, they think you're bonkers!" He sits down next to me on the bed, reaches out, and playfully pats my head. When he raises his arm, the smell of him punches me right in the face. I try to twist away from it, feeling a mad terror spread through my body like wildfire, welling up in my chest and bleeding out into my limbs, twitching at each spot that was locked down against me.

"Now!" this fake orderly continues, "I have been tasked with making sure that your paperwork is correct, Jimmy-boy!"

Australian. Definitely Australian, and badly in need of a bath, or a firehose.

I know his smell. The smell that has followed me for weeks. Who the fuck is this guy? Where the hell am I?

"*Finn Bar MacTyre*, aged thirty-five . . ." he grins again, showing me all the spaces in his face, "Now ain't that a bloody handle?"

"Finn. *Jimmy* Finn. James." I cough, "You've got the wrong fucking guy!"

"Not what it says here, boy-o. Age thirty-five. Next of kin, one *Barry* MacTyre—father—Bensonhall, British Columbia."

Bensonhall. I twist at the word, hard, and feel something crack in my side. I choke back a sharp breath.

"What did you say?" I bark at him, "Bensonhall? What does that say? Where did you get that? Why are you following me?" I'm straining with everything I have against the straps. All the strength I had this morning, sucked away with whatever put me here.

"Tut-tut-tut, Jimmy!" The orderly pats my head again, absently, without even turning from the clipboard in his hand. "You're going to attract attention, Jim. You don't want those doctors getting the wrong idea about your mental state, now do you?"

I tighten up again, yelping as the crack in my side becomes a red-hot knife between the ribs, forcing the air out of me, laying me flat and stiff, breathing slow and shallow.

"That's a boy. Now," the orderly leans over me, putting his dark face in close and taking a long sniff running up the length of my face, "Yeah. You're the one all right. I can smell it in you. It's right there, under the skin, just dying to get out, ain't it, Jimmy-boy?" He smiles wide and terrible, a foul stench of stale beer and something fishy wafting out between those broken teeth.

I wince and feel the stab of the blade in my ribs again.

"I guess it won't hurt none to loosen these straps a little. You're not going to do something foolish, like try to escape, now are you, Jimmy? Wouldn't want you to run off on us, now would we? No."

The orderly stands, slowly and methodically moving from strap to strap, unbuckling me, starting with my chest, then each leg, and finally the arms. He steps carefully away and lets me fumble loose the last wrist strap myself. I sit up slowly, struggling through the cramping pain in my side. I drop my feet to the floor and notice the jagged scar across the outside of my thigh. It looks like an old scar, white and faded, still thick. I know I didn't have that scar before. I run my hand across it to feel the ridge, make sure it's real.

"Nothin' a change and a good hunt won't fix I reckon, eh?"

He's already backing toward the door.

"Injury report says you've got some broken ribs. They'll heal up fast too, but they're gonna slow you down some for now. Jimmy be nimble. Jimmy be quick."

He winks at me then takes one quick glance over his shoulder, out the tiny window in the dirty white door.

"I'll just be going now, Jim. You'd be best to do the same. Heard tell of shock therapy. I didn't think they were allowed to do that anymore in a place like this." He grins his gap-tooth grin again and tips an invisible hat as he slips into the hallway.

"Get a move on, Jimmy-boy. Go see your ol' dad. That's my advice."

The door flaps in his wake, sending waves of his musk back to haunt me.

THERE'S A PILE of clothes at the foot of the bed. New, and clean, still ripe with the chemical smell of the factory. All my size. Jeans, boxer shorts with the tags still on them, wool socks rolled together, a black t-shirt, a canvas field jacket, a hooded sweatshirt. There's a wallet in the pocket of the jacket. My wallet. The wallet that I know damn well is sitting on my kitchen counter. I flip through it, looking for somebody else's cards, somebody else's ID. Everything is there, everything that proves that I'm Jimmy Finn, thirty-five, five-foot-nine and one-hundred eighty pounds. Everything where it belongs, plus five hundred dollars cash that sure as hell didn't come from my chronically overdrawn bank account.

The work boots on the bottom of the pile are a size too big, but they'll do to get me out the door.

I chance a look through the tiny window, only to see the orderly loitering at the end of the hall. He gives me a wave and a bounce of the eyebrows before he reaches behind him and tugs at something on the wall. The quiet is shattered with the wail of a fire alarm. Spigots across the ceiling of the hallway begin to sputter and spray. He waves me after him as he disappears around the corner.

I make one painful step in the clunky boots before remembering the clipboard, roughly tearing the sheets from it and shoving them beneath the new jacket before zipping it up tight and limping out the door.

I'm sure as hell not waiting around for Rhodes, or any other doctors. No cops. No judges. No court-assistance lawyers.

No electrodes bolted to my head. No walking coma for weeks on end while they poke and prod and explain why I need to be locked away. Why they need to break me more—break me again, and again—so that I can be remade. No thank you. Not Again. Not Ever.

Time to run.

And now I finally have somewhere to run to.

Bensonhall.

12

THE PHONE IS in my apartment. The apartment I have no keys to. The apartment directly above where I had apparently tried to kill someone. The police are probably already looking for me here. The white coats from the hospital too.

I'd made my escape from the hospital easily enough in the panic and confusion of the fire alarm. In new clothes and walking on my own, nobody would have mistaken me for the broken maniac chained up and crippled in that room.

I shuffled out and down the hall, past the policemen hovering nearby, trying to calm down old ladies in hospital gowns, dragging their IV stands toward the exits. I ducked into an alcove and pretended to be drinking from the fountain as Doctor Rhodes hustled by, his bald head flushing red down into his face. He had two orderlies and the two police with him, hustling toward the room I'd just vacated. I limped past the nurse's station and down the long hall to Emergency, stepping out into a night as clear and fine as I had ever seen.

There was a bum with a cart full of cans passing in the street. I gave him a twenty for the three bucks change to take the bus.

Once I was safely packed into the back corner of the bus, I pulled out the crumpled sheets of paper and, for the very first time in my life, looked at my own past.

Which is why I'm back here, at the scene of my crime. A crime

I don't remember. The reports on the clipboard say I attacked a girl, right here on my own doorstep, chased her into traffic like a rabid dog. Got hit by Checker Cab #336. Driven by a man named Manji. There was a second report attached, about two young men being attacked in the park, mauled by some kind of maniac. One of them *facially disfigured.* The other one now short a few fingers. *Attacked without provocation.* That's what the report said. Just two guys walking in the park at three A.M. I don't remember any of it. I've become some kind of monster.

I need to see Devil.

Clinical Lycanthropy.

Dressed of fur and fierce of tooth.

He's the only one who might understand. The only one who might help me. Might.

So I need that goddamn phone.

I creep around the back of the building. The cops are there, but they're busy. There's two of them, raining down fists on the poor homeless bastard that sleeps in the corner next to the kitchen of the pizza place next door.

I hop the cement wall into the parking lot and wind my way through the cars, finding a spot right next to the door, tucked in front of a blue minivan. I wait.

The cops finish with the bum on the other side of the wall. I hear them laughing and talking in their cruiser. Football. Which of the sixteen-year-old hookers on third they wanted to nail most. Which Disney princess would be hottest in real life? A couple of times, one of them walks past the outer wall and waves a flashlight past in a lazy arc.

Finally the lock clicks, I hear the bar clack against the metal of the door, and somebody steps out, framed by the light from inside. I pop up behind them and dart inside before they even register me. If they thought they saw something, they might have turned back to an empty doorway and momentarily cursed their own paranoia.

In the few hours since my breakout, my ribs have hewn back together. The cramping pain is gone, the throbbing weakness in my leg is gone. I'm stronger, faster, more focused than I feel I've ever been. I bound up the stairs without losing a breath. Thirty floors running. Not even running. Skipping.

I land at the thirty-third floor and sense them immediately. I can smell them. I realize that cops have a smell. Their own scent. Maybe it's the oil on their holsters, the plastic in their radios, or the cleaner in their uniforms. I can sniff them out as easily as a black banana, or a tuna sandwich that's been left out that little bit too long.

There's two of them. Same as downstairs. They're hovering at my door. These two are quieter than the bozos in the street and likely better at their job, but I need that phone.

I open the door slowly, carefully, eyeballing them through the gap, trying to calculate how close I can get before they recognize me, or want me to explain myself.

It comes to me in a flash. I walk calmly down the hall, trying not to tense too much, but ready to move if they recognize me. Maybe they have pictures, or a description from Rhodes or the girl they say I attacked.

I walk right past the officers and knock on 3312. It's around the corner and out of their sight line. I hear the old man fumbling and straightening things, putting himself in order. I hear the TV click and the electronic moaning stop.

"*Vas ist das*?" he yells. "*Vas ist* you want?"

He's plodding to the door, sock feet on carpet, old steps, soft and unsure.

"*Vas*?" he hollers through the peephole. I back away from the door, against the adjacent wall, away from the peephole.

I hear him patter away, and I knock again, sliding up against the wall once more.

"Who ze fuck *ist das*?" He's screaming now. I hear the cops mumbling to themselves behind me, wondering what the problem is.

I wait, then knock one more time. This time I duck out of his eyeline and across the hall, behind the giant fake palm by the elevator. 3312 explodes into the hallway, screaming in German.

"*Scheisskopf*! *Vas ist Das*? I vill cream your asses!"

The cops come running. 3312 sees them coming and screeches like a Great Owl, slamming the door in their faces. I reach behind me and hit the button for the elevator, as the cops are banging on 3312's door, demanding he let them in. Contempt of Cop. Works every time. The more he refuses them, the more furious they get. The elevator hits, dings, and I pop out of my hiding spot as if nothing could possibly be amiss. I smile cordially as I pass, dropping my head as any of us would do, avoiding the maelstrom—*letting the officers do their job*. They've already forgotten me from the hallway, and I walk past completely unremarked.

I'm hoping, and I'm right, that they've already been in my apartment and didn't bother locking up. The hallway cops have doubtless used my bathroom, been through my medicine cabinet, raided my fridge. I'm likely missing change from the big jar by the bed. The car keys are sitting in the middle of the table, instead of lost between couch cushions or placed haphazard on a shelf full of paperback novels.

I only need the phone.

It's still packed up, under the bed, cast aside like an empty box, and they've assumed exactly that.

I take one look around, cataloguing a lifetime of possessions, realizing that none of this shit is mine.

Some other guy. A broken guy. That strange, crazy asshole with the miserable life.

That's who lived here. That asshole, Jimmy Finn.

Not me. Not the monster who tears people apart and eats little girls in the street.

I'M BACK OUT and down the stairs, listening with some small amount of contentment as the officers say, "What do we have here, Fritz?" and "I suppose these videos don't belong to you, huh?"

"Sieg Heil, Schweinhund," I whisper as I bounce down the stairs, tearing the box open with my teeth.

I walk right past the two cops in the alley. I flip up my hood and hustle down the alley as if I'm late for work. They're busy arguing about the best sauce for an Arby's roast beef sandwich.

The little pigs don't notice the Big Bad Wolf.

13

DEVIL IS ALREADY waiting outside Lee Ho Fook's when I jog up a half hour later. The sleek black car is sitting silently in the side parking lot, the little chrome demon on the hood reflecting the streetlight like a beacon. Devil is lit from inside the black depths of that cosmic Challenger by the blue glow of his cell phone. I knock on the window. He doesn't look at me, just holds up his first finger, *I'll be right with you*, and finishes his call.

Devil rolls down the window and inspects me with a cool eye. "Christ!"

I smile, and it comes shooting up through my body, fed by that warm lantern light, deep inside. I feel it there, growing. Except I'm not dreaming anymore. I'm actually feeling happy to see him.

"It looks worse than it is."

"You still look like shit, Jim. Like ten pounds busting out of a five pound bag."

"Let's eat. I'm fucking starving."

I'm already seated and sipping at water by the time Devil saunters through the door, casting a subtly cautious eye to all four corners of the room before joining me in the booth at the back.

We used to come here when we were kids—teenagers—hiding out from the world behind these red silk tapestries and chintzy zodiac statues, all the worst clichés of oriental culture, and the best damn ginger beef in town—something that wasn't even Chinese.

Devil motions for me to get up and switch sides with him. He wants his back to the wall and his eyes on the door. He's that kind of smart.

"You don't want anyone walking in here and recognizing your face anyways."

I quietly acquiesce, happy to just be out of whatever dark force had been holding me down.

"I've been looking into all this shit you're dealing with. Werewolf lore? There's some interesting shit out there. Every culture has werewolf legends, from the ancient Greeks to the Chinese."

I'm uncomfortable at the mention of the word. *Werewolf*. Is that what I think I am? Is that what kind of beast is inside of me?

Devil continues as if I'm not even in the room. That motormouth know-it-all thing he's been doing since we were kids. He's just going to keep talking, telling me everything. He's a walking live-performance PBS documentary on every single damn topic you can imagine.

"You'd be Irish, right? Finn? Whatever parts of you aren't wolf parts." Devil laughs at his own jokes when he's in this zone of his.

"Are you asking if I've got wolfman nards? Like that fucking movie you loved in grade seven?"

"*Monster Squad*. No. I'm trying to explain your fucking cultural history to you, if you'll listen for two seconds instead of being all hairy about your situation."

"Jesus."

"No, Saint Patrick." Devil smiles. "The legend is that Saint Patrick, when converting the Gaelic and Viking hordes in Ireland around fifteen hundred years ago . . ."

"Did they have green beer and get fucked up every March?" I'm being sarcastic, trying to piss him off. A big part of me doesn't want to hear it. I don't need a history lesson right now. I need an answer to what's happening to me.

"No, idiot." He reaches across and slaps my head. "Pay attention."

If it was anyone but Devil Deville, I'd be tempted to swing back.

"Saint Patrick . . ." He pauses to make sure he has my

attention. "Saint Patrick was there to convert heathens to Christianity. When the tribes of Ireland refused to listen, booed him off the stage, as it were, he cursed them to turn into baying wolves. Cursed to actually physically transform into animals. Crazy, right?"

I'm still not getting it.

"And your poem," he continues. "There's another ancient Irish legend about King Airitech, who had three daughters who turned into wolves at Samhain . . ."

"Sa-who?"

"Halloween. They turned into wolves on Halloween, does it matter? They were fucking werewolves. These two warriors lured them out with their harp-playing, then speared all three to keep them from eating the sheep."

I feel myself pale. The blood falls out of me like a waterfall.

The maidens of the moon.

Monsters murdered by heroes.

The conversation stalls as the old man that runs the place comes over to take our orders. Once we've pointed at a half-dozen numbers on the list, he takes his leave, and Devil launches right back into his lesson.

"You remember Bowmont Livingston? Big native kid from high school?"

There was only one big native kid that I remembered, and he'd been a miserable bully. I remember Devil knocking his lights out by ramming his head into the goalposts in the field behind the junior high.

"You mean Larry? Big, fat, sloppy Larry? Didn't he call your mother a cunt?"

"Yeah. A long time ago. He's changed since then." Devil gives me a look. "People change, Jimmy. You've changed . . . since yesterday. Try to respect that." He keeps those sharp eyes on me, wary, careful.

He's not wrong. I nod my acceptance.

Devil chews on a straw. "Livingston is an Anthropology professor at U of A now. Specializes in Ktunaxa folklore."

I chuckle at the name. Devil shoots a warning straight through me. I guess if Devil could turn out to be the Pablo Escobar of Southern Alberta, and I could turn out to be an escaped lunatic, anything was possible. It's just that the other two weren't as surprising as Fat Larry becoming a papered scholar. A papered scholar named *Doctor Livingston.* I keep my surprise to myself, and my mouth shut.

"I asked Bowmont—*Larry*—about this Bensonhall place. He says the Ktunaxa . . ."

"What the fuck is a Ktunaxa?"

Devil sighs. Still lonely as the smartest dude in the room.

"Ktunaxa. *Kootenay* tribe. From the Kootenay area of the Rocky Mountains?"

My face must be a shiny blank slate. Devil shakes his head and continues.

"The Kootenay Indians lived in the low areas of the Rocky Mountains, right? Just over the border in British Columbia, when there weren't any borders, and it wasn't British anything."

He's tapping his fingers into the plastic menu to make sure I'm paying attention.

"The Ktunaxa have tales about wandering white men. White men with what the Ktunaxa called 'the power of the wolf'. They came and traded with the Ktunaxa, and built themselves a secret town up in the mountain, called *Binn Connall.*"

Blank slate.

"Jesus, Jimmy. Binn Connall . . . Bensonhall . . . It's classic misappropriation."

I'm trying to keep up. Slowly connecting threads. Bensonhall is in the mountains. Larry is a doctor. Some white men built a wolf town on Indian land.

"*Binn Connall* is Gaelic . . . *Irish* . . . means 'Mountain of the Strong Wolf'. Over a hundred-and-some years, to non-Gaelic ears, it becomes Bin-kon-all, Bin-son-all, *Bensonhall.* Get it? It's not on any maps that I could find, but *Professor* Livingston says he knows exactly where it is."

I'm still lost, but my ears perk up at the last bit. I'm waiting. He's dragging it out. It's a game to him. A puzzle to challenge himself with. Now he's pausing for dramatic effect. Or maybe it's on account of the waitress coming with our food. I smell her as she breaks through the swinging doors, an ocean of strange and powerful scents pouring past her like the tide coming in. But there's something else. A so-subtle trace of lilacs and lemon.

The hairs on my neck prick up as the girl sweeps around beside us with an armful and clatters them all to the table, dropping one on the floor as she stumbles back, a horrified mask of recognition frozen to her face. She lands on her ass on the floor and crawls away, muttering in Chinese as I jump to help her.

The manager, or host, or owner—whatever he is—old man scoops her up, firing off an explosion of Chinese words in a rising tone of displeasure, and carts her off to the back again. A magical ninja busboy appears from the shadows and gathers up the remnants of the chow mein from the floor. The room is silent and still mere seconds later.

I'm at a loss. Lost. I sit down and turn to find Devil staring a hole through me. Again.

"You know that girl?" he asks, coldly.

"I have no idea what the fuck that was about. Maybe they've shown my picture on TV or something. It wouldn't be in the paper yet, would it?"

Devil leaned forward. "She called you *láng rén*."

"I don't know her." She smells like lilacs and lemons.

"*Láng rén* means werewolf, Jimmy. They wouldn't have said *that* on the TV. We need to go. Now."

Devil pulls a wad of bills from his pocket and drops a few on the table, shoving me in front of him toward the door. The old man jumps in front of us, bowing and muttering.

The old man is holding something out to me. He's unleashing another volley of strange words at us. Devil nods his head like he understands, but he doesn't say anything, just shoves me toward the door again. The old man thrusts this rock into my hands. It's some kind of tiny statue. It looks like a hippo strangling a bird.

"Thanks, I don't . . ."

"Just take it and go." Devil says, "Take it, bow, say thank you."

I follow the instructions to the letter.

"*M goi! M goi!*" the old man is repeating.

He follows us into the parking lot, still bowing, still shouting, "*M goi! M goi!*"

DEVIL THROWS IT into drive and peels out from Centre Street onto Sixteenth Avenue. We're two blocks away before either of us says a word. The little statue is still wrapped up in my fist.

"What the fuck was that? And how do you speak Chinese?"

"There are five times more people in China than on this whole side of the planet. How do you *not* speak Chinese?"

We drive in silence for what seems like an hour, even though it's only ten blocks that pass outside the window.

All of the confusion. All of the guilt. Now it comes flooding back as I see the girl's face, screaming in wild terror. The dishes smashing to the floor.

I am that monster. I did attack those people. I tried to kill three people. Maybe more. Maybe *her*.

There's a moan caught in the top of my chest. I'm gulping for air. I hit the button for the window and swallow cool air, just trying to breathe in anything new at all.

Devil's hands are tight on the wheel. He's thinking through it, working the angles, making the calculations. Being Devil.

"We need to get you to Pitamont."

I'm lost again. "What the fuck is Pitamont?"

"I thought you were just going crazy, Jim."

"I AM CRAZY!" I scream, frustration and fury exploding up out of my throat like jagged little slivers of glass from the churning misery in my stomach. "I *AM* CRAZY!"

Devil puts a hand on my leg. A simple gesture to hold me in check. The fury turns to a weakness in my bones. The glass turns to sand. I slump. Defeated. Broken, again.

"Livingston said to go to Pitamont. It's a town in the mountains, south of Invermere. He said to go to Pitamont and find his uncle Bob. Works at some garage there. Bob knows the way to Bensonhall."

My eyes are full of water. I'm looking at the road through hot tears. I feel myself trembling, but I don't move. I can't move. Devil sees it. Starts to say something. Clears his throat, and then he falls silent, trying to find his words.

"He was thanking you," he finally offers. "The old man. He was thanking you for his granddaughter's life."

I get a flash of lemon and lilac and the taste of hot blood in my mouth. All I see is the fear in her eyes. I'm the Big Bad Wolf. I'm the monster in the night, so terrible that the villagers thank me for sparing their lives. They leave me offerings and beg me not to pluck the children from their beds. I feel it there, solid and warm inside my fist.

"I swear, I don't know that girl, I never touched . . ."

"You said there was a report about two guys in the park?"

I hear the darkness in my voice. "Attacked without

provocation." *Facial disfigurement . . . mauled by an animal.*

I hold the bauble out in my open hand. I watch the hunk of white jade, reflecting pink in the rising sun. I want to hurl it out the window. I want to jam it into my heart. All I can smell is lilac and lemons, and blood.

"I'm the goddamn monster that people pray to save their children from. Now they leave me offerings, like I'm a fucking demon. Like I'm goddamn King Kong!"

Devil laughs.

"It's a bear, holding an eagle," he explains. "It's a good luck statue. The words for bear and eagle make up the word for *hero*."

Once again, I'm staring with blind eyes at the smartest guy in the room.

Devil's voice is calm and gentle. "The two guys in the park. They were going to rape that girl. You saved her."

Lemons and lilac, fading in the distance, then the blood came.

"You're not the monster, Jim. You're the hero."

Devil opens it up as we pass the city limits, heading west. The engine roars, and the road rumbles beneath us.

"Whatever is happening to you, the answers are out there in the mountains."

Almost on cue, we top the hill and sail out onto the highway, and the Rocky Mountains rise up in the distance ahead of us, a watercolour dream, peeking out above the smoke like castles floating on clouds. Hope sailing on the horizon.

The last of the fury, the frustration, the madness. They fall away in the glow of dawn. Safely away from the city, headed toward my past, and my future. My destiny—whatever the hell that might be.

My only friend is behind the wheel. I feel so very tired and, for the first time in a long time, I feel safe.

"Thank you, Adam."

Devil raises those eyebrows in the rear-view mirror. I half-expect to get my ass handed to me for the slip-of-the-tongue. He smiles.

"Happy to help. Once you figure it out, control it, you let me know. Maybe you give me a little nip on the heel." He grins that old Devil grin. "Maybe I can be a werewolf hero too, eh Jim?"

"Finn," I decide, and it feels right. It feels good. I feel *good*. "Just Finn."

Sunrise breaks behind us, a muted red glow in the rear-view mirror, pushing us onward.

Finn. The hero.

14

I SLEEP. A beautiful dreamless sleep, all the way to the edge of the mountains, where Devil makes his goodbyes.

"Let's just say I wouldn't want to get pulled over anywhere west of here," he tells me.

He gives me a fresh boxed cellular phone out of his trunk, a brotherly slap on the back, and a scrap of paper with Bowmont Livingston's instructions on it.

I'M ALONE AGAIN, but I feel more confident than I have in my whole life. I feel in my pockets as I board the bus, making sure I have the paper, the phone, my wallet . . . the jade figurine.

I take a seat in the back, against the window, gazing out at the mountains as they pass. The smoke is still thick from the forest fires here, but it hovers around the lakes, deflected somehow to wrap around the mountains like sepia-tone skirts that flow and dance in the sun, swallowing up the light and glowing from within.

I've never seen the mountains like this before. Well, I guess I must have, but I don't remember it. All I can remember is the city. The noise, the smells, the lights. A constant barrage of sensory overload. A constant misery of strange places and strange people and, in all that time, the only thing that was ever silent was the judgement on their faces. The mountains were always just a mirage in the distance, a pretty background painting behind glass.

Here, in the back of a Greyhound bus, cutting tiny tracks across these colossal mountains, there was nothing but silence. Calm and natural beauty rising up from the earth. Green and blue and gold. No flashing neon. No screaming tires and no wailing horns. No roaring airplanes overhead. No screaming radios and crying babies in the street. No concrete gods, and no glass temples.

From the south, three sisters fair.

From the East, Finn the hero.

MORE THAN A few times, as we weave our way up and around the mountains, the smoke swallows us whole, sucking us through the haze, lost and unaware, creeping along until we're popped out the other side, fog lifting into daylight again, soft and quiet, as if nothing had happened.

The last of these patches carries us into Pitamont, where heavy rain is pouring down in a torrent, turning everything around us two shades darker. I am deposited, unceremoniously, next to an abandoned Dairy Queen in that strip of highway that I imagine every town must have, the one that runs just parallel to the places where people actually live. It's a ghost town out here on the fringe, in the thru-lane full of gas stations and doughnut shops.

Devil has briefed me extensively on the nature of the town. The population statistics. The ethnic make-up. The various industries that feed the town's coffers. Unlike most of these mountain towns, there isn't much of a tourist trade, there's the odd hiker and cabin vacationer, but the lakes are too hard to get to for the motorboat crowd, and the beaches too rocky for lounging. Likewise, the winter sports are hampered because the trees are too thick and the mountains too rocky for skiing. There's some kind of forestry company that makes up most of the industry. I don't see any bare strips of trees or rough logging roads, but I imagine they'd be further away from the town proper. Now, heading into the fall, it would be quiet. Nowhere more so than here beside the highway, apparently.

The rain has erased the smoke and the fog, but the dark sky and the reflecting sheets of rain make the handful of flickering signs glow with preternatural light. I turn and look through the dark windows of the restaurant behind me—vacant and locked down, the empty tables standing like ghosts behind the tinted glass.

There's a McDonald's across the way, with a blazing red and white sign offering cheap coffee and half-price egg sandwiches. I pass it and wander down the only road that leads inward, presumably into town. No one passes me. Eventually the woods give way to scattered houses and side roads, before I reach what must be Main Street. Every town has one, right? I don't tangibly recall ever being in a place so quiet, so small, and so quaint—but there's *something* about this place, this street.

There's a block-long Army & Navy store, with the same backlit plastic sign that they must have opened the place with sometime in the seventies. It seems oddly familiar, as does the storefront of the restaurant next door. I don't recognize the name, or even the sign, but I get a flash of memory, a medium-rare burger, thick and smothered in ketchup, on a huge Kaiser bun. A chocolate milkshake in an amber plastic tumbler, the kind of milkshake made with chocolate ice cream out of a bucket, mixed with milk and ice cubes, where the foam at the end has little granules, tiny sandy bits of ice. I can taste it, spooning out foam and chocolate grit with the straw, licking it clean. I know that if I go inside, there will be a black chalkboard on one wall, and a long bar, with wooden stools, like in an old western movie.

It looks like a Swiss ski chalet, a log cabin with a wide, heavy roof, sloping down to overhang the sides of the building almost to the ground. I step through the thick oak door as a little bell tinkles overhead.

The place is dead quiet, outside of the sound of tinny pop-country coming softly from speakers echoing somewhere inside of the ceiling.

I sit in a corner, give the place the once-over. Everything is decorated in gingham check and rustic farmhouse kitsch. Paintings of pies and twee messages of faith dot the walls. Not exactly as I was picturing. If I had been here, it was much changed from my memory.

Pleases and Thank Yous Keep the Lord Alive
Love is a Fresh Baked Pie

Happy is as Happy Does
Jesus Loves Us All Equal

I'm pretty sure if there is a Jesus, were he to arrive here on the edge of Pitamont-by-the-lake, this is the kind of place he'd set one foot in, and then head back to the McDonald's. Which is what I'm contemplating when the waitress waddles out of the back, through a swinging double-cowboy door. She's like a troll doll version of Loretta Lynn playing Barbie dress-up at the '50s Dream Diner. Short, fat, and stuffed like a sausage into a frilly, pink, poly-acrylic uniform straight out of a bad TV sitcom. Her hair is teased high and thick, bangs curled down onto her forehead. She stops for a breath, waves to let me know she'll be a minute. She reaches under the counter and comes up with a plate of fries and the world's biggest presumably-cherry Coke. I can smell the sweetness of it, the syrup is in the back of my throat. She leans in, obviously spent, and munches a dozen or more fries, then takes a long sip through the bendy straw before she draws another ragged breath and finally makes her way over to my table.

"I'm sorry, sweetie. Blood sugar. You know how that can be!" she laughs, as if I have any idea what she's talking about. "But the good Lord has spared me from the dia-beet-us. Yes, he has. Every year they check, and every year I am just *fine*."

She waves her arms in the air, praising this Lord Doctor of Diabetes, then plants her pudgy hands down on the table.

"Now. You're not from around here, are you? Never seen you before. You just come in on the bus? It's not tourist season, you know. No skiing around here anyways. And nobody's coming out for the nature this year, on account of the forest fires and all this yucky smoke, hmmm? Maybe you're new in town. No. I would have heard about that. Maybe your car broke down, is that it? Maybe you're visiting someone. No, would have heard *that*." She's breathing hard and sweating. There's a scent to her that I don't like. Cigarettes and tuna fish, but something else.

"Blood sugar," I explain with as polite a smile as I can muster. "Just need a sandwich. Maybe some coffee?"

It's obviously the wrong answer. I must not be worthy of praying at the altar of the *dia-beet-us* saviour.

She sits down in front of me and continues her guessing game, as if I was some strange thing she found on the sidewalk, and not a hungry customer in her greasy spoon.

"Well, that won't do, will it, mister smarty-pants? Come in here and tease a lady about her blood sugar, now will you?"

She glares at me, looking more and more like a troll, and less like Loretta Lynn.

"We don't care for smarty-pants answers here. The good Lord tells us to suffer the fools, and the *Jews*, and the little children . . . Doesn't say *nothin'* about smarty-pants answers."

The scent gets stronger. Something sour and sickly-sweet. It's on her breath like a curdled milkshake.

"You can go and get on out of here, if you're not going to be nice."

I just want her to stop breathing at me.

I lean back in my seat and put my hands up in resignation.

"I'm very sorry. I didn't mean to offend you. I was feeling faint is all. I honestly haven't eaten in a long time. Like, since yesterday."

She looks me up and down. I guess she's trying to discern if I'm a *Jew* or a fool, or something even more offensive to her sensibilities. She heaves herself up out of the seat and waddles back to the counter for another sip of her drink. She finishes it, keeping her eyes on me the whole time. I want to leave, but I'm afraid she'll throw a knife at me, or damn my mortal soul if I try to make a break for the door.

She doesn't bring me a menu. She doesn't take my order. She goes into the kitchen and comes back out almost instantaneously with a cup and a plate.

She drops them unceremoniously on the table in front of me, with a wheeze.

The pie is brown and syrupy. It smells like flies and sugar water. The coffee seems about the same. I'm afraid to touch either one.

"Raisin. All we got left."

She's staring at me, scrutinizing my face. I imagine she's looking for a reason to throw me out into the rain.

"I think I'll just be going." I smile again, as polite as I can muster, and try to slide out of the booth.

She pens me in with her big, pink belly. She leans in close, looking for something in my face. I'm hoping she's not considering it for a snack. Her brow is furrowed, her face twisted into an old man's prune-faced grimace. She's breathing her sour milk stare straight into my ear. I freeze up, looking back at her from the furthest corners of my eyes.

She reaches out a pudgy hand, still sticky with raisin syrup, and grabs my face, twisting my head toward her to examine my eyes. She looks like she wants to pluck them out.

"You've got those eyes, don't you? You one of them? From up the mountain? One of those freaks? Dirty gypsy freaks. Mother lovers and sister fornicators. And those filthy godless Indians, sending their whores up there for those beasts. Drugs, and devil-worship, and *fucking* in the woods."

The words are shocking coming from her pudgy little face. All the talk of Jesus and put-on hominess is gone. The look of disgust twists her face up even more until she has completely transformed into some kind of apple-face demon, shrivelled and terrible. She's a dried-out mummy stinking of ancient dust and spoiled strawberry milkshake.

I nudge her out of the way and step out, carefully, keeping her in front of me as I back toward the door.

"Thanks?" I manage, fumbling the door open and falling out into the driving rain.

She's still staring at me through the foggy glass of the window. She's just standing there, watching me, standing guard against whatever devils she thinks I might unleash on her miserable little pie shop. We're standing there, like gunfighters in the street, separated by a log cabin wall and a deluge of rain.

I RUN ACROSS to the opposite side of the street and duck under the overhang of the roof at the front doors, hoping for a few seconds out of the rain. I fish the scrap of paper out of my pocket. Devil's tightly looping script.

Bob
Vargas Brothers Garage
Pitamont, B.C.

No address, no directions. Fucking Devil. All the answers in the world, except the one thing I need.

I strain to see through the rain and get my bearings. I don't see anything resembling a garage out here in the outskirts. When I look up towards the diner, she's there, at the window, glowering at me. Jesus.

I hustle down the street, despite the rain, hiking my collar, as much to escape her damning eyes as to stop the rain running down my neck.

Still, I feel her eyes on me, and her rancid whipped cream whisper seems stuck to me. *Athwart the gloom.*

15

I WALK THE empty rain-soaked main street of Pitamont like a ghost, until I come to the bottom of the hill and stumble across an ancient yellow tow truck, out in front of what looks like a sixty-year-old gas station and garage. I hear a blaring radio playing Lynyrd Skynyrd and machines buzzing and huffing from an open garage bay, so that's where I head first.

There's somebody buried in the hood of an old truck, coverall-clad legs dangling out over the grill.

"Excuse me?" I say, trying to be polite after my previous encounter in the coffee shop.

The song is picking up steam as is whatever kind of compressed-air-powered tool he's blasting away with in there. I holler louder.

"Excuse me? Are you Bob?"

A head pops up into sight, looking around for the source of interruption, like a chipmunk checking its surroundings.

"Bob?" I yell.

The head turns toward me. He's a native. Indian. First Nations. Ktunaxa? Fat Larry's uncle would be, right?

He has a hound dog face, with baggy eyes, a close-cropped moustache and goatee. His long hair is tied back tight against his head. His thick eyebrows, his hair, and his beard all run the same salt and pepper colours as his grey coveralls and the white t-shirt that shows underneath at the collar. The name tag at his chest says "Bob". I'm praying that this is the place, that this is the guy.

He switches off the machine, hops down from his workspace, and snatches up a tiny remote control under a rag on the workbench, turning down the volume on the big guitar-solo finale on "Freebird".

"Help you?" he says, in a gruff, but not unpleasant voice.

I step up awkwardly and extend a hand.

"Mister Livingston, I presume?" I've been holding that in my pocket since the Chinese restaurant.

"What?" He looks at me, confused, and shuffles past me.

"Sorry," I mumble. "You must get that all the time."

He looks at me over his nose, lifting his head like he should be wearing glasses.

"Not really. My name's Dylan."

He catches me off-guard on that one. I stare like an idiot.

"Bob? Dylan? Your name is *Bob Dylan*?"

"That's me," he says, matter-of-factly, as if he's never heard of that *other* Bob Dylan.

He turns back to the workbench and wipes his hands on the rag before he holds one out to me.

I shake it, still slightly confused.

"You must be Larry's friend."

"I uhm, yeah. We went to school together in Calgary." Still stumbling to put myself back on track.

He climbs back up into the engine of the big truck, talking from inside the chest of the thing, voice clattering around between metal panels and bouncing back at me off of the concrete floor.

"So you a MacTyre, or a Fallon? Have to be both, I guess. Right?"

He pops back up and looks closer at my face. I feel the ghost of sticky raisin-stained fingers on my cheeks.

"Hmm. Got them MacTyre eyes though. Must be Barry's boy, one that moved away . . ."

"My name is Finn," I finally manage. "Larry said you'd know where I needed to go?"

There's a momentary silence. No tools clanging, not even the sound of his breath. "You want to go up the mountain, to your people. Bensonhall. Right?"

A sudden swell of emotion rises up out of my chest and bursts into a warm glow in my face. I feel high.

"Yes! Yeah. Yes. Please."

Bob Dylan laughs from inside the truck. The whole room rings with echoes of joy.

"Been waiting a long time." His salt-and-pepper head pops up again. "Gonna have to wait just a little bit longer. It'll take me another hour or two to finish up this manifold." He pauses, contemplating something.

"You should go see your cousin, Jules."

The look on my face amuses him. A lazy grin forms under his baggy eyes.

"Place is called Victory. Right down the street. Should be going on stage right about now."

"Is he a musician or something?"

His laughter booms out from inside and underneath the truck again. It feels hopeful and warm.

"Something," he says, and turns the volume back up on his stereo, singing along as I hike my jacket up to face the rain.

"Take an umbrella," he says from somewhere inside the truck.

"Sorry?" I look around me for what he's talking about.

"Umbrella."

Still looking.

"I uh, I don't, where is it?"

"Huh?" He finally reappears from underneath the beast this time, rolling out across the floor.

"Umbrella?" I ask again.

"Oh, I don't have one. Thought you might. You should. It's really coming down out there." He slides back under the beast.

"Yeah, thanks," I mumble as I step out into the downpour.

I hear him laughing and singing, even over the roar of the water pouring from the rooftops.

VICTORY TURNS OUT to be a nightclub three blocks away. What anyone would be doing here at noon on a weekday is beyond me. I shake the rain off of my shoulders and my head, shove past a big metal door, and walk down a long dark hallway. I emerge into a red-lit barroom roadhouse, straight out of any biker movie you've ever seen. The place is quiet, except for a few straggling old men at the pool tables and the big bald bastard behind the bar. He is a mountain of a man, with a ripped up Dead Kennedys t-shirt under a well-worn leather vest that reeks of beer, sweat, and weed. He has a long, wide scar running over his bald head and down across the left side of his face.

I order a beer and climb onto a stool, swinging around on my seat to get a better look at the place.

Every wall, every table, every open space is made out of logs, but anathema to the false kitsch of the Jumpin' Jesus coffee shop. This place seems hewn out of the forest itself, so comfortable that it has its own musk—a weird combination of beer and whiskey and wood shavings, man-sweat and oil and something animal. Something wild. There's a stage across the back end of the place, two metal bars propped up at equal space in the middle of it, and a scattering of instruments leaned against the far wall.

The big biker returns with my beer, eclipsed in his giant fist, and pops the cap against the counter, setting it down firm on the scarred oak of the bar.

"I'm looking for Jules," I say.

He smirks, just on one side of his face, the opposite side of the scar, and he nods behind me as the lights dim and guitar fuzz, backed by a solid heartbeat of drums, comes from the big speakers either side of the stage. I recognize AC/DC from the guitar, but can't place the song until Bon Scott starts his plaintive wail.

She said she'd never been . . .

Never been touched before . . .

The girl that creeps out of the darkness is thin and blonde. Athletic. Familiar. That she is attractive goes without saying, but the way she moves is hypnotic, every muscle under her absolute control. Men begin floating toward the stage as if under a spell. By the time the chorus hits, there are a dozen of them, wandered in from the street, standing rapt at the edge of the stage, nodding in unison while she twists and spins, flinging herself around the pole, sliding and swirling around the stage like an acrobat, but so natural, so free, that it becomes less a dance and more a primal call.

The taut muscles of her legs flex and stretch with the beat, as her arms move with the guitar rhythm. Moving faster, smoother, tight ass shaking. Her firm breasts and tight stomach all move in perfect sync with the music. She has a tattoo on her hip—a vintage style portrait of a woman in a headdress, but the headdress is a wolf hide. I can't catch a good look at her face, enshrouded with a mane of thick honey-blonde hair, until she sweeps it aside with a flip of her head and looks directly at me, brilliant emerald eyes gleaming in the dark. I'm as entranced as the men at the stage, one more deer caught in her headlights, swaying like a zombie under her spell.

The song comes to a screeching close, and she is neither out-of-breath nor showing a single bead of sweat. The men at her feet, on the other hand, mop their brows and stand breathless as she scoops up the mountain of ten dollar bills—no coins, no fives. We all watch in quiet awe as she moves off of the stage as mysteriously and suddenly as she appeared.

The men slowly come to their senses, some of them seeming puzzled as to how they ended up in the strip club in the first place. I'm kind of wondering myself.

A phone rings behind me, and the bartender grunts his compliance before hanging up. He checks me out under half-closed lids, measures me up.

"You Finn?"

I nod. It takes me a second to be sure. That is, at least, a part of my name.

"Jules says go on back. Door to the right of the stage."

His eyes are already back on the glass he's quite literally spit-shining with his filthy rag.

I'm halfway across the floor on shaky knees at the thought of this woman when he shouts after me.

"I wouldn't be fucking around if you know what's good for you. She'll tear you to bits, man."

I think he's smiling at me again, just not with the side of his face that he's pointing to. As if my teenage cousin ripped half of his face off.

I wave him off and step to the door, knocking quietly.

16

"HELLO?" I MURMUR, stepping into the dark.

Strong hands grab me and spin me around the door and pin me against it, slamming it hard enough to shake the hinges. She's pressed against me, naked and soft, the heat of her flesh going right through my clothes and into my own skin. Her mouth is on mine, hard, rough kisses. More passion than I've ever felt in my life, her pulling at my hair, nipping at my neck, forcing her tongue into my mouth. Her hand is in my pants, and I'm hard as rock, my cock trembling against her fingers, pulsing with life, ready to explode. I want to let her take me, in absolutely any way she wants.

"Oh god, Finn," she moans. "I've been waiting for you."

"Whoa!" I say, pulling back as far as the door will allow, putting my hands on her shoulders and forcing a space between us. Part of me screaming out in agony. However much I want to taste her, feel her, bury myself in her. I have questions. Questions I've waited my whole life to answer.

"Hang on," I manage, as she continues to force her way back into my mouth, hands pulling and tearing at my clothes. "Hang on!"

She stops, steps back, her naked body barely framed by the edges of a silk kimono. Her eyes are ablaze, and her lips are hungry. I have never been with a woman like this. My experience is all drunken fumbling and shy girls in dark rooms, buried under comforters and duvets. This was like some kind of Penthouse letter. *So I met my cousin for the first time . . .* Cousin.

"Wait," I say, hands out. "You are *Jules*, right? My *cousin*?"

"We share a grandfather, if that's what you mean . . ."

Her voice is deep and seductive, "Don't you want me, Finn?"

God, yes. Can I just say yes? Deal with . . . whatever, later?

But there's this monkey on my back, this wolf. Lurking there in my shadow.

I take a ragged breath and keep my hands in front of me.

Damn she smells good. Familiar. Welcoming. Wet.

"I uh, well I mean. I just got here. We're *cousins*? Isn't that kind of . . ."

"Maybe out there in the city." She purrs. "Around here, with our family, it's survival."

I side-step her and open up some space between us.

"Don't get me wrong, Jules. I really am happy to meet you," I stammer, "and you are . . . very *very* attractive."

She's circling me, ready to pounce.

"Don't you know how this works, Finn? We're mated."

Mated? "I don't know what that means."

She slides up closer, sniffs at me. Closer. Runs her nose up the length of me, breathing deep. She pauses. Steps back. She gives me a sideways look of concern.

"You don't smell right."

"What do you mean, I don't smell right?"

She sniffs at me again. Backs up again.

"He said you'd be ready. That you'd know."

She's circling me again, and it's ceased to be sexy. There's a panic in her voice, in her steps. She pulls the kimono around her and clings to it. She doesn't smell right either. Bye-bye fantasy, hello fury. She smells dangerous. Hairs all over me prickle against the skin and stand at attention, ready to run.

"Do you even know what you are? You're not him, are you? You're not him!"

"I'm sorry, I don't . . ." She keeps circling me. Watching. Curling herself up, more and more, coiled like a snake.

"That lying sack of shit!"

She turns on me, muscles tightening up, her fists balled at her chest.

"Just get the fuck out!" she growls at me, green eyes gleaming with fury.

"Can we . . ."

"Get the fuck out!" she screams. Her teeth are huge and jagged like knives behind her red lips.

She's still screaming as I hightail it out the door. Something heavy crashes into the wall behind me, and it sounds as if she's tearing the place apart. Better the room than me. The big bartender stops me on the way out.

"You didn't pay for the beer."

I know I'd left a ten on the bar when he brought it to me, but I just want a quick exit. I drop another one in front of him with an awkward grin, "Keep the change."

"You'd better fuck off before she finds her way out here, pal." He gives me the lopsided grin.

I glance at the door, fighting a strong urge to go back and give her what she wanted. I feel her hot skin against me, her hands groping, and her mouth pressed against mine. The wall shudders again as something else smashes against it. I remember the fury in her eyes, the white teeth behind blood red lips.

BOB DYLAN IS waiting for me at the garage.

"Have a good time?"

"Not really," I grumble.

"That's weird. She was real excited to meet you."

"Yeah. She *was*. I don't what the hell is going on around here, but the sooner I figure it out the better."

Bob chuckles and slaps me on the back. He leads me out to the parking lot and into the yellow tow truck. It looks and smells as old as the rest of the place. I immediately grab for the hand-crank to roll down the window. It doesn't work. No matter how much I twist and rattle and shove it.

"Sorry," Bob says. "I know you guys like the fresh air. Been meaning to fix that." He leans over me and twists it around with seemingly no effort at all, and the window comes creaking down.

"Thank you."

"No problem, kid," he says.

I stick my head out into the rain-fresh air and close my eyes. When I open them, we're already climbing through the trees, and the black clouds above have cracked, shards of sunlight breaking through. I feel in my pocket for the statue, trying to remember that I'm here to solve my own mystery. Finn's mystery. Jimmy is dead and gone, and I need to leave him in the city, dead and buried.

This is the new me. Finn the hero. Finn the Wolf-man. Clinical Lycanthrope. *Láng rén.* Hero.

Dressed of fur and fierce of tooth.

Whatever that means.

17

"So you're a friend of Larry's, eh?"

I jump at the sound of his voice. It's the first time he's spoken in a half hour of bucking and creaking over the gravel road. This is less a road than a cut through the trees, at a steep enough incline that Bob's tow truck grumbles and whines, without ever making more than maybe twenty kilometres an hour.

"We went to school together," I say quietly.

"You didn't call him Bowfinger."

"Bowmont?"

"Or Professor," Bob continues, ignoring my correction. I'm guessing he doesn't approve of the name change.

Another pause. "You must have known him when he was fat."

I'm not sure what to say to that. "We went to school together."

Bob gives me a sideways glance from where he's hunched over the gigantic steering wheel.

"You the one knocked his brains out his ass?"

So far, the new Finn seems pretty unpopular, though I'm pretty sure this particular crime can't be pinned on me.

"No, sir," I say. "That wasn't me."

Old Bob chews on that for a tense minute or two before he lets me off the hook.

"Too bad. Would have owed you a beer."

I snicker.

Bob laughs. That same hearty laugh that was echoing around

the garage and filling me with warmth.

"Larry was a real asshole before that guy knocked his lights out. He's still a pain-in-the-ass, but he would have been headed straight for jail before that knock in the head. All the worst bullshit people say about Indians, he was it."

"Yeah. That's the Larry I remember. But people change, right?"

People change, Jimmy. You've changed. Try to respect that.

"Guess they do when they get a metal goal post right between the eyes. I hear that other kid rode Larry like a bronco, straight into that goddamn thing."

"That was Devil. My friend, Devil."

"Your friend's name is Devil?"

"Your name is Bob Dylan," I shoot back.

"Yeah, but Bob Dylan's ain't. His name's Zimmerman. I was Bob Dylan before *he* was Bob Dylan."

"Devil's name is Adam." I laugh. "Anything's better than *Bowmont Livingston*, right?"

I'm rewarded with another round of jubilant laughter. I decide that I like Bob Dylan. I like him a lot.

"You always were funny, kid," he says.

I feel my lungs suddenly stop working, like somebody threw the power switch. "Sorry? What . . ."

"When you were little. You were a funny little kid, before your mom took you away."

I swallow a lump in the top of my chest. It feels about the size of my fist, but it goes down eventually, drops into the pit of my stomach and sits there like a rock. I take a shallow breath.

"You knew me?"

"I know you," he says. Nothing more, as if it's all in those three words. No mystery at all. Just a fact. He drives on in silence for what seems like an hour before he slows the rumbling truck and comes to a stop. He shoves down hard on the emergency brake pedal and gets out of the truck, the clunky metal door making a sound I recognize, but don't.

He comes around to my side and opens the door.

"Come on down, little Finn," he says, and something inside me breaks.

I know that voice, those words. It cuts into me, through the centre of me, like a crack in the glass, spreading and ripping a seam through time and space. One more echo from that white room in my dreams, floating out to me through the years. It loosens the dirt, and an army of emotions come wriggling up through my skin, an endless wave of little worms and crawling things, touching their million feet on my every nerve as they climb their way out of me and break onto the surface of my skin. They're pushing that voice, that memory, in front of them. A lifetime of lost days and false lives pushed aside by their digging. The accumulated dust of a millennium falling away. All that's left is bedrock, bare and picked clean. Washed by the wind.

I see him standing there, Bob Dylan who is not Bob Dylan. I see him younger, darker, thinner. He reaches a hand out to me, a hand that smells like oil and gasoline. *Come on down, little Finn.* There is sunlight playing through the trees. Yellow and white, dancing between the boughs of the pines and the firs. I feel so small and so new. Everything is big and wide and full of wonder.

Come on down, little Finn.

I stumble out of the truck, slide down into the mud. There is something trembling inside of me.

"I want to show you something before we get to Bensonhall."

He leads me down an overgrown dirt road, half a block from the truck, through a path in the high trees, the new sunlight teasing its way through the green canopy above us, lighting up the path in a thousand places.

At the end of the road, there's a house. My legs give out, and I'm on my knees, crying, full of relief and despair. A swirling vortex of memory and sensory input tears me into a million little pieces. The rich earthy smell of mouldering leaves and green forest, the light blinking through the boughs of a hundred green trees, the shape and colour of that house. That goddamn house.

I'm homesick for a place I only barely remember in the deepest parts of my bones. I don't know that my eyes have ever seen it before, but something inside of me is weeping for it, as if it's the only place I have ever belonged.

I'm comforted by the voice of a man I don't even know.

"You're all right, kid," he says, hushing me like a grandfather. Like a father. Bob puts an arm around me, helps me up out of the mud, leading me where I need to go.

The past floats across the water on my eyes. Little Finn, little *me,* the *me* from my dreams, comes running through the trees and across the small yard in front of the house. He leaps into a thick black tire, dangling from the arm of the biggest tree skirting the yard. His white-blonde hair long and dancing in the breeze.

"My word, Finn. Be careful!" My mother's voice. Except it's not my mother. The woman that steps out into the afternoon light that plays across the porch, she's so young, so pretty. She looks like my mother, but she can't be—her face is so happy, so *kind* . . . The boy looks at her with love in his green eyes. He's smiling, laughing. So happy, that boy. *Me.* I was never that happy, that free. Was I? I feel it in his face, in his smile, in his beaming green eyes. I yearn for him to truly be some long forgotten part of me.

A shadow looms behind the boy, tall and dark. It reaches for the boy, strong arms breaking through the darkness and into the sun, pushing gently, but firmly on the tire swing. The man inside the shadow steps forward. His hair is long like Little Finn's, a thick, sandy blonde beard and moustache cover his face, but not those eyes. Brilliant emerald eyes catching the sun. He laughs, blows a kiss to the woman on the porch. My mother. No. *His* mother. Little Finn's mother.

The boy, Little Finn, he's so happy. So full of joy. When was I ever like that? What is this place?

My body shudders and rejects the dream. Not me. Never me. I've grown long and old, full of so much hate, and misery, and self-loathing. The misery, and hopelessness, and hate that my mother, *my* mother, Jimmy Finn's mother, fed into me for so many years. It comes festering and bubbling up all through me, until every molecule of my body is soaked in it, steeped and marinated. Lousy with it. Little Finn is gone. Jimmy Finn is broken. And I'm lost somewhere in between.

I feel my feet underneath me again. I'm standing in the now, the here.

Bob Dylan is standing next to me, his sad bulldog face regarding me with something that looks like regret.

"The little boy I knew, he played. He ran. He snuck around all over these woods." Bob says, "Used to have to come coax you out from under that porch there," he points at the rickety wooden stairs, overgrown with brush, "Used to bribe you with them sticks of horehound candy you liked. You and Emma."

"Emma?" The name stirs something else, some twinge of hope. The little lantern is buried, but not quite out. I feel it smouldering in there, deep underneath all of this bullshit I've carried with me all these years. I close my eyes and see Little Finn down there, clinging to it, huddled up next to it, tiny and alone, but brave against the dark, blowing into the flame.

Bob smiles, but it's bittersweet. There's something behind his eyes.

"I dream about a little girl named Emma."

"Bet you do," Bob says. "I bet you do." No mystery. Just fact.

He walks on ahead of me, leaving his comment behind for me to decode. He kicks pinecones out of his path and shuffles through the long grass until he's sitting on the dirty steps at the front of the porch that runs the front of the dilapidated cabin. I take a good look at it through today's eyes, seeing the peeled paint, the bird shit marking the posts, the accumulated dust and dirt piled up along every edge of it. I sneer at the space in my memories where it should have been.

I sit quietly next to Bob and stare out down the road, back to the truck, wondering how long we're going to waste on ghosts.

"I don't remember any of this," I lie. Little Finn is still breathing life into that flame. I feel his father's arms at my back.

"You remember some," he grunts at me. "Can't hide everything, Finn. Sometimes it comes out, whether you want it to or not." Bob puts his big hand across my back, "And with your people, when it finally finds a way out, it ain't gonna be pretty."

"What the fuck does that mean? *Your people?*"

"Means what it means. You can't change what's inside you."

He picks at the weeds in front of us, silently tugging them out from between the grass until he has a half dozen thick round stems of some kind, not unlike sunflower stems. He pops the ends off and begins to weave them together.

"How's your mom?" he asks.

An instant twinge of guilt gnaws at my guts and sends a wave of nausea over me.

"Fine. I guess. We don't talk much."

"Strong woman, your mother."

I huff and slide across the stair without even realizing I've done it.

Bob's hands twist and knot at the stems, slowly and purposefully, the same way he talks.

"You don't think she was strong? All alone out there, being

what she is . . . what you are?"

"I don't know what the fuck you're talking about. My mother was a selfish bitch."

"Hmm. Mixed-up maybe. She was trying to protect you."

"Well, she did a shit job. Dumped me on anybody else first chance she got, so she could go out and pick up random assholes."

Bob's fingers keep working. He nods as I speak, as if he's agreeing with me.

"Probably confused and lonely. Same as you. Needed something she couldn't get so easy out there."

"What? A parade of shitty boyfriends, and a kid she couldn't bother with?"

"You got a lot of sour piss in you." Bob's hands keep moving, slow and steady.

I sit silent for a minute, trying to work up something resembling sympathy for the woman that called herself my mother.

I stand and walk, leaving him to whatever the hell he's making out of his chunks of weeds.

I wander slowly around the house, the rest of it just as worn and neglected as the front, holes in windows, the wood stained and faded, a procession of deserted hornet nests in the eaves above me. I step around the back, into a larger yard, a small field, really, that resonates in my memory, despite the overgrown brush and rotten posts trailing a rusty laundry line.

It flows over top of me, just like in my dreams, but clearer now.

Sheets. White sheets, flowing in the wind. They twist and cascade around me as I walk, hands out to the past, willing myself to touch them, and giddy when I feel them flutter against my fingertips.

Now hearing the voices, high and small, little voices from all around me, laughing, bouncing with the little bodies that they spill from. Little Finn, his pale hair, almost as white as the sheets, running past my legs, followed by the girl, dark braids and freckled face, those olive green eyes. Emma. I drop to my knees and throw my arms around her, around nothing, as she passes through me, running after a memory. They jump and spin and yell, chasing each other through the white walls flapping like wings on the wind. They stop suddenly. They freeze, then turn together to stare wide-eyed, right at me. Through me.

There is a scream from behind me. A hideous, tortured cry of agony, and all of a sudden, the sky is dark and moving. The birds screech as they come, swirling down onto me, onto them, onto the two children. The children are screaming, running for the cover of the house. The birds swarm toward the house, landing in a black mass across the roof, cawing down to the stragglers on the ground. The sheets are torn and mangled, twisted in the dirt beneath them.

The cry comes again, animal and terrible, some creature caught in a trap, screaming for salvation as it gnaws its own limbs off. My mother. No, not my mother. *His* mother. Finn's mother. She's running, a look of panicked terror on her face. She grabs the children by the hands; they are running for the road, away from the woods.

"Run, Finn!" she says. She pleads.

"Run away home, Emma. Run fast and run now.

"Finn. You go with Emma. Right now. And don't you look back, baby."

She holds him. She kisses him. Not my mother. His mother.

The two children run. They run fast, and they don't look back.

Little Finn doesn't look back. Me. I don't look back.

The scream turns into a howl.

It's behind me, fierce and angry.

Some animal, growling with hunger and rage.

It wants my blood on its tongue.

Something stands between us. Some*one*.

I can hear them, feel them. I know them.

I can't look back.

There's hot breath rumbling at my neck.

I don't dare look back.

Run, Finn.

My mother's voice.

And don't you look back, baby.

"YOU OKAY, FINN?"

Yesterday fades, the teeth at my back are gone. All that's left is confusion. Again.

I'm standing in the front yard, staring down the road. Bob is still sitting on the step, working the weeds in his hands.

"What happened here?" I ask him.

The phantoms of it must still be there on my face. Bob leaves off his weaving. Tossing his project into the tall grass to fade into the earth, he steps across to me.

"A man goes out to hunt, he has to listen to the forest around him," Bob says, taking a deep breath and raising his hands around him as he continues.

"He has to listen when the birds call, and it echoes off of the mountain. He has to hear the wind when it rustles through the trees at night and tells him if it's gonna bring rain."

He takes my hands. He chants something in some language I don't understand.

He puts a hand flat against my chest, over my heart.

"None of that means a goddamn thing if that man don't know *whose* ears he's listening with."

And he walks away, back to his tow truck waiting in the road.

18

THE REST OF the drive is more of the same, more green tumbling by as we rumble up the mountain road.

Bob hasn't said another word.

I want to ask him about my father. When can I see him? What did he become? Why didn't he try to find me? Where the fuck has he been all my life? Most importantly, what the fuck kind of *thing* is he, this demon from my nightmares, and am I just the same? Did he lose his mind? Did he turn into the fucking wolfman and run off into the dark of the forest? A *láng rén?* I think about the Chinese girl and I wonder what Bob's people call it. Would they call me a hero? Or would I be a monster in the night? Three monster sisters speared by some jackass playing a harp.

I came here for answers and, so far, only have a thousand more damn questions.

We crest a hill and break through the trees into the full power of a late afternoon sun. Down through the trees, in the shadow of the mountain, is a wide plateau of green grass and mountain streams, dotted with small cabins.

This place feels familiar. Feels *safe*. The big manor-style house that fills the far end of the clearing, it looks as big as a hotel. The sight of it fills me with music, the smell of pine trees. The word comes to my lips without warning.

"Bensonhall."

I want to pounce through the windshield and run. I want to

feel the ground beneath my feet as I bound, faster and faster, sliding and falling toward it. I need to be inside of that place, safe and warm and welcome. It's at the end of a very long road. The end of my road. Here's hoping.

"*From the south, three sisters fair ran athwart the gloom*," I mumble.

"Guess you're starting to remember now, eh? That's good. But listen, kid . . ."

"Stop!" I shout, already opening the door before he slows the yellow tow truck, falling out into the dirt and scrambling over myself in the grass.

It's a statue, beside the road. A tall, strong wolf, with its cub beside it. The workmanship is rough, but there's something pure and natural about it. Something real. I turn the hero stone in my hand inside my pocket.

"Your dad made that," Bob says, sadness gluing together the gravel in his voice.

"Where is he, Bob? I need to see him." I can hear the tears in my words before I feel them pushing at my eyes.

Bob's hand is on my shoulder. I know what the answer is going to be. I don't want to hear it. I keep talking.

"There was a man, in the city, he told me to come here. He told me where. He said my father would be here. That I should come and see him . . ."

Bob's face doesn't change, but his eyes narrow, so slightly that I almost miss it.

"Bob. Where is my father?" I still know what the answer is going to be.

Bob steps past me and runs a hand across the statue of the wolf.

"My great-grandfather, he was the one who met you in the woods. Not *you*, you understand. Your people. *Ḱat ʔa·kisqƚiƚ, Two-Eyes-of-a-Blackbird*, he was called. He was lost in the snowstorm, out here in the woods. A hundred and fifty years ago. So they say. He met *your* great-grandfather, Connor MacTyre, hunting in his fur. They were the first of friends between the Ktunaxa and the Strong Wolves."

His eyes are misty and far-off as he tells his story. I'm staring at the wolf cub. I don't know what it means.

"Me and your dad, we were the same. Friends. Ktunaxa and

Strong Wolf. What he did, he was trying to do for you. I told him. No use in trying to change what you're born with. Might as well wish you had flippers for feet just because you take a bath once a week." Nothing Bob says seems to make any sense.

"What he did? For me? What does that mean?"

"A father always wants to change the world for his son, make it better. Make it easier. Not always the right thing to do, but love makes us weak, Finn. Love makes us do strange things. Like your mother, running away with you, hiding you away."

"Where is he, Bob?"

"He made that statue for you, Finn. Out of guilt. Out of love. That guilt and love ate him alive for a long time. He made me promise."

"Promise what? Where the fuck is he?" I know the answer. I'm looking at him. "He didn't send for me, did he?"

Bob seems lost in his own reminiscence. There are tears in the corners of his eyes. His voice begins to crack.

"Made no sense to bury him here. Makes no sense to bury anybody anywhere. Should feed them to the world, like any other animal. But I did it anyways, because of guilt. Because of love. Because I promised him."

There it is. The answer I already had. I just needed somebody else to say the words. I try to muster any recollection of my father outside of the absolute fear I've lived with for my entire life, the nightmare creature chasing me in my dreams. The boogeyman my mother let haunt every shadow. I try to call back the image of him, tall and blonde, smiling, pushing me on that tire swing in front of a house I barely recognized.

"Why can't I remember anything about him?" More to myself, to the ether, than to Bob.

He answers anyways, wiping at his eyes. "Funny thing, brains. Delicate machinery. Easy to mess up. Hard to fix."

"Delicate machinery, that's exactly what Devil called it."

"Guess he'd know." Bob says, "He's the one used the right tool for Larry. Sounds like a smart man, your Devil." Bob winks and leaves me standing in front of my father. I feel like I should say something. Do something.

"Day's wasting, little Finn," he calls from the truck. "Time to get you home."

He's grinning at me again with his sad eyes when I climb up

beside him.

I look out across the green valley. The houses look worn, but well-kept. Wood cabins, three of them along the right treeline, on this side of a stream leading from the opposite mountain, and out to a small lake in the distance, in front of the biggest house, the one that looks like a hotel. There's a little wooden bridge over the creek that leads to that house.

"Who lives here?" I ask, pointing to the cabins as we pass them.

"Used to be everybody lived together in the big house, whole family. Over the years, people wanted their own space. Some of 'em moved away completely. Your dad, he built your place up the mountain to get away from your grandfather. Hard man, your grandfather.

"Now there's hardly none of you left. Jules lives there," he says, pointing to the first cabin. "The rest of hers live in that one, just Jamie and Kev left. Your Aunt Siobhan's gone a few months now. Lot of people dying up here the last year." There's something suspicious in his voice. For once it doesn't sound like a simple fact.

"That one there was Sean and Oonagh's, Emma's house." He says, pointing at the last little cabin, "None of the rest wanted anything to do with that place after . . ." he lets the thought trail off. "The hunter is in there now."

"The hunter?"

"McQueen."

I catch a strong stink of animal as we pass. Strong and ripe, something I've had stuck in my nostrils before.

"Another cousin?"

Bob's craggy face hardens into rock.

"He ain't nothing to nobody."

The truck rattles as we cross the tiny bridge over the stream, and the big house is laid out in front of us.

It's actually three houses. Three buildings, anyways. The centre building is wide and massive, two stories of warm looking pine, with big, inviting windows on both floors. The place looks sturdy, strong. To one side is a flat wide building, maybe a garage or a workshop. To the other side is another small cabin, a worn drive and several vehicles, all utility-type vehicles—SUVs and Jeeps—much newer and much nicer than Bob's truck. The stream runs in front of the buildings, to a wide blue pool, with a small gazebo on its shore, made from the same soft, yellow pine as the rest. There's another stream branched off from the far side of the little lake, and I notice white conduits hidden just in the trees, leading up into the small cabin, where there's the definite hum of machinery.

"What's that?" I ask him, pointing to the shed.

"Water pumps, sewage treatment, that kind of stuff. Barry designed all that."

Bob pulls into the drive and turns around to park, pointed out the way we came. I hop out into the grass, take a deep breath of mountain air. I'm about to ask Bob more about the machines and the piping, when a cheery voice, carrying the trace of an accent, comes from behind us.

"Well! This is a lovely surprise. What brings you all the way up the mountain, Robert? And who is your friend?"

Something about that voice vibrates through my bones and strikes that tiny lantern in the deep of me, stronger and brighter, lighting the cavern in my soul. Little Finn stands up in the dark, searching the space above him.

The old man is sniffing at the air when I step out from behind the truck. He's a natty gentleman, tweed coat, vest, even a goddamn bowtie. He's leaning on a cane. He has a wild mop of snow white curls.

"Bob?" The old man's watery eyes, olive green and deep like the ocean, turn from Bob to me, and back again. He pats Bob on both shoulders with a hearty laugh and turns toward me, arms wide open.

"Oh my goodness! Finn! Come here, my boy!" His eyes are wide and intense, and his smile is full of mischief and life.

Part of me is surprised that there is no hesitation. I fall into this strange old man's embrace and that little lantern light burns fierce and hot and bright, and every shadow inside me is torn away, as if I had walked directly into the centre of the sun.

"Ahh! Finn, my boy!" He's laughing, squeezing the life out of me. "Welcome home, lad!" And I believe him.

I look at Bob through wet eyes and catch a rare glimpse of teeth under his wide smile. I can feel my heart, pounding and huge, lodged at the bottom of my throat.

"Finn, this here is your Uncle Arthur."

19

"OH, MY BOY! My boy!" The old man is laughing, spinning me around with much more strength than I would have expected in a man half his age.

"Take it easy on him, Artie," Bob says to the old man. "He doesn't remember too much. And he only just found out about Barry."

"Well now," he says, setting me down on my feet and fixing me with his wild stare, "let us not dwell on sad things. Today is a joyous day! At long last we have found you, and you are back home where you belong."

I want to ask about my father, about Bensonhall, about everything, but I'm so entranced by the positive energy of this old man. Uncle Arthur. Family. I've never had family—outside of my mother—and I've never even really known somebody with the kind of family that I saw on TV or in the movies. Some big group of people who loved you just for being a part of them, and they looked out for you, protected you, like you were one of their own limbs. Is that what this place was? Bensonhall? A family?

Arthur puts a finger to the side of his nose and leans in with a wink, reading my mind somehow.

"Plenty of time for questions, Finn. Plenty of time, indeed."

He slides his arm inside mine, leaning on his cane, and pulls me along beside him.

"Now, shall we go and explore? You have a lot to catch up on, and there are, doubtless, a great many things to rekindle that memory here, yes?"

"Sure," I say, though every atom of me is rattling around confused and unsure. I'm giddy. It's Christmas morning, and my stocking is finally filled.

I throw a glance to say as much to Bob, but he shakes his head and gives me a tired grin.

"I gotta get back down the mountain. Work to do. I'll come back in the morning."

He waves as he rattles back across the little wooden bridge and disappears into a cloud of dust just before the trees.

"Now then," Uncle Arthur says, pulling me toward the big house, "shall we?"

THERE IS SO much inside this house that I remember. Certainly not the big screen television, or the gleaming chrome fixtures in the very modern kitchen, but the wood of the staircase, the plaster mouldings, the high ceilings like some Victorian mansion. The floors especially, the grain of wood, the vast open spaces of wood floor, real hardwood floor, polished to gleaming. I get down on my knees and put my face close to it. The smell of pine is everywhere. I look across the floor, eyes level, making it as big and wide and endless as possible. I remember this floor.

"You used to bring your little toy cars here and skate them across the floors as if it was your very own racing track. Quite a rambunctious boy you were. A pair, really, you and my Emma."

I betray myself again at the sound of her name.

"Ah, so we come to it!" He laughs, "Some things are much harder to forget than others."

A streak of late afternoon sun cuts through the big room, landing just in front of my face, almost touching me. I can feel the warmth of it just out of my reach.

"Time enough, my boy. Time enough." Arthur puts a hand under my arm to help me to my feet. Again, I wonder at the strength in this little old man.

He leads me down hallways and up a wide staircase, past mounted heads of deer bucks and antelope, past paintings and photographs of people I should know, but don't.

There's a painting of a tall, broad-shouldered man, sandy

blonde hair with mutton chops grown thick around his jaw. He's standing with an Indian . . . Native . . . a brave in buckskins with long braided black hair.

"This is Connor MacTyre. The one who led our families here to Bensonhall."

"And Bob's great-grandfather?"

Arthur nods.

"Bensonhall." I ask, remembering Devil's history lesson, "Is that a misappropriation? *Binn Connall*?"

Arthur turns, beaming at me. "Yes! Yes indeed! Very good, Finn! Excellent!"

He continues down the hall slowly, leaning on his cane again.

"We came here more than a hundred and fifty years ago. Persecuted as we were—as were many, shall we say *ethnic* groups—in those days. Connor—your great-grandfather—was something of an explorer. He came north from San Francisco, up the coast and to Vancouver, what is now known as British Columbia, ironically enough. You see, originally. . ." he turned to face me, to be sure I understood, ". . . originally, my boy, we were the oldest of families from what is now called Ireland."

"I know that much. When we left here, my mother changed my name to Jimmy. Jimmy Finn. And she would sometimes get a trace of an accent when she was angry, or upset."

I catch the slightest of furrows in his brow, but I am distracted, looking around the halls, at the accumulated history of my family, my *family*, and I have the strangest need to have her beside me, holding my hand like she did when I was small.

"Bless her for that. You can take the girl from the village, hmm? Not so easy to take the village out of the girl."

I run a hand through the fur of a bear standing angry guard next to a doorway. It's real, and four times my size, and even in death, looks like it could tear me to ribbons of pink flesh for its dinner.

"What are we?"

I need that answer.

More than anything else. I need *that* answer.

Arthur pauses and fixes me with his rheumy eyes, that mad hatter smile creeping back across his lips.

"We are family, Finn. The last of a great family that once held the green hills and great halls of the land of wolves. *Laignech*

Faelad. Ireland. We were driven from our ancestral home by the Roman Catholics, chased across this New World by the further followers of Christ, and finally came to rest in this sanctuary in the mountains, mountains far higher, far greater, than any in our own past. This is *Binn Connall*, Mountain of the Strong Wolf, and we are the wolves, Finn. You are the last of us. All that remains of the thousands of years of our families. MacTyre and Fallon, and many others now lost to us. You are the last. Well, there are Jules and James and Kevin, yes. But you, Finn. You and Emma . . ."

"I dream about her."

Arthur stops, a look equal parts surprise and pleasure making its way across his face.

"Oh yes? Isn't that interesting? Tell me about these dreams, my boy."

He hooks his arms in mine again, shuffling close, conspiring.

An odd little man, but I feel a warmth for him that I didn't think I was even capable of. A warmth that opens me up to him, and I tell him the whole thing, the dreams, the running in white, the blood, the teeth, my mother calling us away. And how it's the same dream I'd had every night of my life, for as long as I could remember.

"That was an unfortunate day," is all he says.

The warmth inside me doesn't stem the fury at being denied a real answer for the millionth time in a lifetime.

"What the fuck does that mean? An unfortunate day? What happened to me? I was taken away from this place, from my life. I've been poked, prodded, locked up like a fucking animal! I've had pills crammed down my goddamn throat for thirty years! This dream has haunted me every day of my life! You say that there are advantages to being in this family? I'm not part of this family! I grew up without a family. I don't know you. I don't know this place. I have some kind of monster inside of me! And all you can say is that it was an *unfortunate* day?"

I'm backed against the wall, fists clenched, nails curling into my palms, digging deep enough that I can feel it. I want to draw blood and feel it dripping from my fingers.

He sees my rage, and his face drops, flushed and sad.

"I'm sorry, Finn. You have every reason to be angry, every right to know. I'm only sorry that your mother never . . ."

That doubles the rage into the red zone. I feel my heart

pounding in my head. I see the demons behind my eyes, the teeth, the blood. I hear the screams somewhere inside of me.

"She's the one that locked me up!" I trail off into a garbled approximation of actual words and rise to a scream. I can't hold it back anymore. The scream fills me up, then bursts out of me, blasting out of every pore. My fists, like wrecking balls, thrown wild from my sides, one hand smashing through the railing at my hip, the other landing somewhere inside the wall. They return to my face, pounding into my forehead, trying to drive back the ghosts I've unleashed there. I drop to my knees, hammer my fists into the floor, again and again.

Still, the screaming won't stop.

It becomes a howl, wild and untethered from reality. Pure, and primal, and more animal than man. I let it come. I can't fight it anymore. If I'm some kind of monster, just let it come out and take me. No more games. No more riddles, no more fucking mystery. Come what may.

Arthur falls to his knees in front of me, adds his voice, his pain, to mine. We're howling, calling out to the woods around us. The pain, the misery, the terror of my life left behind.

I hear other voices join in, from beneath us, from outside, far away. A terrible orchestra of pain and abandon. I hear it, and I feel it in my bones, reverberating there like a tuning fork, vibrating with life, and the pain is replaced with power. The misery becomes a song of victory. The ghosts become tame. Tethered in front of me, guiding me into the night, instead of swirling in mad chaos around me. The birds scream and call, cutting through the howls in a dark symphony of wild fury.

The other voices rise and cut through the ether, adding their strength to mine, holding me up, charging me full. They fill all of those empty spaces inside of me. They call with me. I'm not alone. For the first time. I am not alone.

I am home.

20

ARTHUR RUSHES FORWARD and embraces me again, tears rolling down his cheeks.

"Oh my boy! My boy!"

I feel a new strength in my muscles, a new hardness in my bones.

"I've not called like that in years!" He slaps my back and beckons me past him into a large, open parlour of some kind. The smell of it opens something in the back of my mind. The outside walls are lined with white linen curtains that run the length of the walls, the whole room is white. The drapes are open slightly, and I can see the windowed doors open to the afternoon air. The strong smell of pines and fresh water. I can hear the water running outside, babbling over the rocks in the stream bed. I can hear the birds and squirrels running through the branches. Everything echoes inside this room. Echoes in white.

The far side of the room holds a wide white piano. What I think they call a *Baby Grand*. Arthur sits in front of it and begins to tinkle on the keys, a soft beautiful melody echoing off of the walls and circling me.

"You have to understand, Finn. Emma has lost her family also. These are the things you have confused in your mind. Your grandfather was the first. His name was Fionn Bharr. You are, in fact, named for him. My brother. He was the first to rail against the change. Thinking he could master it as he mastered so many other things." Arthur continues to tinkle away at the piano, the lovely tune spinning me with it, and I'm dancing, enveloped in white.

"A veritable genius of a man, your grandfather. Fionn Bharr brought so much to all of us and to the town below. He and I were the first to leave this place, to adventure in the wider world, always with the promise to return to our home, always with the promise to manage our *gifts* when away from Bensonhall.

"Fionn Bharr and I, we attended University in the East, we fought in the second Great War, much to the chagrin of our own father. We both returned without having revealed our true nature to the world. We would take turns, affecting the change, when necessary, whilst the other kept a close eye to keep the wild one out of harm's way.

"Your grandfather, as I say, was quite an intelligent man, a man of science. When we returned, it was with technology and modernization, the promise of wealth and prosperity from the land around us, without despoiling the nature we so cling to. He created a way to extract the essence of the trees, without destroying them, to create a copious amount of pine essence with the most minimal of effort. Something we have long exported throughout the world to great success from our little hamlet to little or no investigation. It allowed us to build this place for the family, to provide for ourselves, for the town of Pitamont below.

"Being a scientist, and a man of rational mind, Fionn Bharr long sought an answer to what he called our *curse*, what I call our *gift*. He was a hard man, and cold in some ways. He and your father, Bairre, especially. Always at each other's throats, as it were. Your father took his wife, fat with child, with *you,* and built that little house out in the woods, the house you recall from your dreams. They were happy there. You, my boy, were very happy there."

I see it in my mind, swirling with the music, dancing through the white curtains, imagining the yard, thick with grass, white sheets flapping all around me. Around us. Little Emma and Little Finn.

"Fionn Bharr," Arthur continues, still playing his soft melody, "was quite taken with a girl from the town. She worked with us at the factory, for all it was a factory, as your grandfather's assistant.

Secretary, if you will. She was a lovely girl, soft and pale, gamine legs and luxurious chestnut hair. Your grandmother had passed two winters earlier from a rare case of the pox. Fionn Bharr and the girl from town—Nancy, I believe her name was—planned to run away together. Fionn Bharr was mad with lust, and fighting his natural proclivities did nothing to stem the furies building in his system. One night he changed, mid-coitus, you understand, and tore the poor girl to ribbons. Fionn Bharr was mortified at what he had done and took his own life. Your father found them the next morning."

His voice had flattened, and the tune had taken an ominous turn, each pinging note echoing around the chamber, ghosts floating after his words.

"We secreted the bodies, spread word that they had run away together. Still, gossip spread throughout the town. Monsters in the woods, it was said. Evil loose in the night. That sort of thing. The children were most affected. Your father and his sister Oonagh, Emma's mother, were especially distraught. They, and Oonagh's husband, my own son, Sean . . . they forged a pact. For your sake, for the sake of Emma, they would fight the change and learn to rule their baser instincts. So as to teach you the secret of living a purer life, such was their rhetoric. It did not end well."

THE MUSIC COMES to an abrupt stop, as a new voice, dark and velvet, enters the room.

"No. Didn't end well at all, did it?"

I'm afraid to turn around. I know who it is. Somehow I know. Something about her smell, the timbre of her voice. I know. I've seen her almost every night of my life, a little girl with olive green eyes and dark pigtails, the only thing tethering me to this place, this life, and my own history. The rainbow in the dark, leading me here. She can't possibly be that after so many years, can she? What if it breaks the spell? What if it sends me careening back to that other place, that other me? To Jimmy Finn, swallowed up in black.

"So you're Finn?"

She leans in the doorway, arms crossed tightly at her chest, a small grin curling at one corner of her thick pink lips. A wrinkle forms at a tiny scar above the right side of her mouth as the grin evolves into a sneer. Her eyes, the same eyes from my dreams, wide set and lined in black. They're harder and full of years, but still that same olive green—deep as the forest around us, gleaming in the pale moonlight of the whites that surround them. Her dark hair is no longer in pigtails, it is cut to her jaw, and surrounds her face with thick, dark curls.

"What the hell are you doing?" she asks, stepping into the room, her heels clacking against the hardwood floor. Slim legs, sheathed in dark blue denim, stomp past me and carry her to the bench where Arthur sits.

She whispers something into his ear, keeping her eyes on me, intense and unforgiving.

Arthur turns on the piano bench and takes her hand. "I fear our young Finn has had a hard time of discovering himself, all alone out there in the world," Arthur says. "He has a right to know, Emma."

She crosses her arms again, the black leather of her sleeves creaking.

"But what is he doing here? Now. After thirty years." Then, directly to me, "What the fuck are you doing here?"

It hits like a bullet right between my ribs.

"I . . ."

Arthur leans back from the piano and gives her solemn look.

"Language, please, Emma! We do not disparage or disallow the misfortune of family."

"We have enough misfortune in this family without him."

She stomps past me again. There is something false about her rage, something off about the smell of her. Something delicious and enticing. I close my eyes and see bare legs running with fresh blood, I feel some new fire rage through me, some new hunger, something bubbling and roiling from the middle of me. I want to reach up and grab those legs. I want to pull her to the floor and melt into her. Instead, I watch her disappear through the door and around the corner, totally disregarding the giant bear looming outside, ready to strike.

Arthur is at my side, a hand on my shoulder to warn me back.

"I apologize, my boy. Emma is the jewel of my existence, but she is also a very strong-willed young lady."

"We're not so young anymore, you know. If I'm thirty-five . . ."

Arthur unleashes his wide, maniacal smile again.

"That would depend on how long you live then, hmm?"

Those wild eyes are dancing, waiting to unleash one more secret.

"How old are you, Arthur?" He's spry for a great-uncle, or a grandfather to a thirty-something. A spry seventy-something?

"I am one hundred and twenty-six years old."

The number of teeth behind his lips seems to double. My own teeth feel like they've dropped out of my mouth *en masse* and lodged in my throat.

"There are many advantages to being a member of this family, Finn. Many advantages."

He pats my shoulder and leads me back to the piano.

"You mustn't let Emma bother you. She was very fond of you when you were children and heartbroken when you were taken from us. You had a special bond. Very best of friends."

"Finish the story. What happened to my father?"

"Your father is the least of the story, my boy. He eventually came to his senses. Too late, I'm afraid, to mend broken fences, but he at least survived his madness. You see, if we deny our nature, if we don't embrace the change, it will take us regardless of our will. By my own estimation, every seven years or so. We are overcome with our animal urges and succumb to a fever of the mind. Violence, misery, and terrible misfortune are bound to follow. Oonagh and Sean, they succumbed. Your father? He was never the same, but he survived to learn that lesson."

Madness. Monsters in the woods. Evil loose in the night. *Dressed of fur. Fierce of tooth.*

Monsters. Not heroes.

21

"GET OUT HERE, bitch!"

Arthur stops playing again.

"NOW, Emma!"

I know the voice. I feel the heat in my crotch and remember the anger, the eyes so much like my own.

Arthur pops up from the piano bench, a look of outrage on his face.

"My word!" He growls, reaching for his cane and limping off into the hallway faster than I can follow, "What on Earth has gotten into this family today!"

I join him at the wide window, overlooking the front of the house, where cousin Jules, fully dressed but no less furious than when I'd last seen her, is screaming profanities. There are two younger male versions of her—lithe, blonde—standing on either side, twelve years old, maybe. Twins. They could be photocopies of my own younger self. Black birds—ravens, starlings—dot the lawn around them, scrambling, pecking at the ground.

"Your cousins," Arthur whispers over his shoulder.

"Yeah, we've met. Jules, anyways. Very . . . umm . . ."

"Quite forceful, that one. Much wilder than the rest."

"That's Kevin and Jamie? The brothers?"

The two boys stand, quietly curious more than anything else, their heads moving in unison as they regard their surroundings, on the lookout for something. Sniffing at the air, eyes bouncing to their periphery.

"Indeed. Good boys. Quite unlike their sister, dare I say, much less *malevolent*. Quiet. Especially since their mother's passing."

Where the hell was I that everyone was dropping like flies, going mad, and ravaging townspeople? It's like a goddamn Frankenstein movie. Next thing I knew there'd be fat, pink waitresses with torches and pitchforks coming over the hill, shouting religious motivational slogans. *God Hates Clinical Lycanthropy*

"I'm going out there."

Arthur lays his cane across my path.

"I would not, Finn. No good can come of it."

"She's nuts. Somebody has to talk her down."

Arthur nods toward the window, where the top of Emma's head pops into sight on the veranda.

The brothers suddenly stand a little straighter, widening their shoulders and fluffing at their hair. Cute.

"What do you want, Julie?"

"What did you call me, *cunt*?" Jules shouts.

"Well, I didn't call you a cunt, did I, *Julie*?"

Jules' eyes widen with rage, her fists balled at her sides, shoulders hunched. I've seen this stance before.

I'm not about to let Emma get tossed around like a piece of furniture in a strip club store room.

I bounce down the stairs before Arthur can get another word out.

As I hit the doorway, Emma framed in harsh daylight in front of me, there comes another voice, deeper, refined. Calm and soft, yet darkly commanding. Properly English.

"Now, ladies," it says. "Let us not say something we might regret."

Jules shouts across the yard, "You said he was mine! What the fuck, Simon? You said he was meant to be my mate, not hers!"

Jules swings a manicured nail toward Emma, "You hear that, bitch? He's mine! You're not the fucking Alpha around here anymore."

The birds take flight and swirl overhead, scared by the noise or stirred by her fury. I can't tell.

"Jules," the stranger coos, "I am sure that we can address this matter in private. Why don't you and the boys head home now, and allow me a few moments with my wife?"

Wife? Who? *Emma?*

I step out into the light, blinking against the glare and quietly present myself, more to get a look at this new player than anything else.

"Ah! At long last," he says, stepping up to wrap an arm around Emma, whose arms immediately drop to her sides, limp, before reanimating and climbing like snakes to wrap around this man.

"Simon!" Jules is hollering. Nobody is paying attention.

He is especially tall and thin, draped in a long black coat, tailored to fit close, making him look even taller. He has a wild mane of black curls and a long face. His nose and lips seem large, but they give his face a plasticine kindness. He's like an overgrown Goth kid, all gangly limbs and black Doc Martens.

"Mister MacTyre," he says to me, extending a hand full of long, bony fingers. "Allow me to introduce myself. I am Simon Magus, Master of Bensonhall."

"Another cousin?" I ask, staring at the narrow palm of his hand, noticing that there are rings on every one of his fingers.

"Not quite. Not in the biblical sense, if you will." He laughs, a genuine and gentle sound that puts me off guard. "I am Emma's husband and, thereby, lord of the manor, as it were."

My heart sinks, but something else takes its place, something hot and prickly, spikes piercing the skin and forcing their way out into the air, radiating the heat from inside me. The human part of my brain wants to like this man, wants to immediately accept him, but the other part of me . . . I look into his dark eyes and past the unassuming face. I sniff at the air round him. I smell it, hidden and secret. He smells like death, and rot.

I take the hand, holding firm, letting my new-found power find its way into my fingers.

"Quite a grip you have there, Finn," he says.

I flash the family smile, mad and toothy. I want this man's life draining at my teeth.

I see a glint of doubt behind his black eyes. He backs away, still gripping Emma to him.

"Well, where are my manners? Welcome, Finn. Welcome!" he says, waving his free arm around the place. "I hope you'll be comfortable here with us. I believe you'll find we've provided every amenity." He smiles, a quiet, unassuming smile.

"Hey! Motherfucker! What are you going to do about this? You lying sack of shit!"

The birds are still whirling overhead, but they don't seem to come any closer to the house than the edge of the drive.

He keeps an unsure eye on me as he turns to Jules, still fuming in the driveway, still flanked by her brothers, silent eyes shooting daggers at the thin man.

He waves a long hand at Jules, and the rage seems to dissolve from her, into the air.

"Jules, please. Do behave yourself and show some regard for your long lost cousin?"

"Oh, we already met in town," I say, letting the words drip off of my longest teeth, willing him to see what I see, his throat torn open on the ground in front of me.

"Ah!" He laughs, regaining his smooth composure. "Then I suppose you have already borne witness to her . . . precociousness?"

Jules is still standing expressionless, like she's sleepwalking. Her brothers look confused. The birds swirl higher and then disperse, winging off in all directions.

Magus calls out, "Mister McQueen!"

A wild-looking man pops up from behind the SUV furthest from the drive, a small crossbow in his hands, which he swings onto his shoulder, casually. I know this man. I know his stench.

He smiles at me through the dark scrub that covers his face, tosses me a salute. His long dark hair, pulled back in a loose ponytail. He's no longer covered in hospital blue, but filthy jeans and a leather vest over brown skin covered with dirt and hair.

"Hiya mate," he winks. "Looks like you made it out of there before they roasted your ol' chestnuts, hey?"

"McQueen," Magus cuts him off. "Would you be so kind as to take Jules and the boys back home?"

"How long'll she be *out*, boss?"

"Long enough, I would imagine," he replies over his shoulder, grinning amiably at me.

McQueen moves off, with his crossbow on the two boys, herding them ahead of him, as he carries cousin Jules over his shoulder like a dead trophy.

The thin man laughs and steps past me with Emma still

wrapped around him, like a little girl hugging her daddy. He stops, turns her face toward him, sleepy and strange.

She moans softly and presses her lips to his. I cringe.

Simon Magus turns to me, raises one thin eyebrow, and lets one side of his lips curl up.

"Welcome home, *little Finn.*"

22

I'M ABOUT TO tackle mister tall, dark, and full-of-himself and rip him apart, when Arthur's cane crosses my chest, the thick, silver handle pressed into the tiny patch of exposed skin at the nape of my neck. A cool breeze seems to roll through my veins, moving out from my chest into my head and out to my extremities. My fists unclench, and the rage and the bloodthirst leave me in a heartbeat. My head clears, and I'm looking down into the face of my great-uncle, who quickly ushers me down the stairs and across the drive, out into the grass. I can see McQueen driving his captives across the little bridge and toward the cabins on the other side.

"We should help them."

He shushes me with his stick, pressing it to my lips. The metal is cool and immediately calming in a way I can't explain.

"Not now, Finn. Not now. The time will come, my boy."

"But Jules . . . That fucking ape, he's going to . . ."

Arthur grips my arm. Pulls me close to whisper in my ear.

"He is watching us, my boy. If he suspects anything, if he chances to guess that you know more than he is comfortable with . . . nothing will save our Jules, or poor Emma. We must play along. For now."

I glance up at a figure in the big window in the top floor of the house. Magus is watching.

"What the fuck is going on around here?"

"All will be revealed soon enough. He has, no doubt, summoned you here for his own nefarious purposes. Little does he understand what he's actually dealing with. Strong Wolves, Finn. *Strong* Wolves. And a strong wolf leads from behind the pack."

"Dressed of fur and fierce of teeth . . ." I add, almost by reflex.

Arthur steps back, looks to the window, and then pulls me along beside him as he walks, stumping along on his cane. I see it now. It's a show for Magus. The crippled old man.

"Where did you hear that?" Arthur asks.

"Hear what?"

"That phrase—*dressed of fur, fierce of tooth*."

I shrug, "My mother used to say it, I think. It's been caught in my head for the last long while. I can't seem to get rid of it. What is it?"

"It's an ancient story, Finn. Ancient indeed."

"King Airitech."

Arthur stops again, glances around nervously.

"Yes. But what does it mean, Finn?"

"It's a story, right? A myth? The king had three daughters who became wolves. They were speared by the hunters for eating the sheep. They lured them out with harp music? My friend Devil told me."

"Bless your mother," he says, pulling me closer. "And bless your Devil." It's the first time I've ever mentioned his name and haven't gotten a sideways glance.

"REMEMBER," ARTHUR WARNS as we step back onto the porch of the big house. "Not a word. We mustn't raise any suspicion. But keep your eyes and ears aware, my boy. Always aware."

He shows me to a room at the top of the house, a loft space turned into a wide, low-ceilinged room. There's another wide, flat television, mounted to the wall. Bigger than anything I've ever owned. A long cabinet, covered with various bottles of liquor, dressers full of clothes that are somehow my size. New clothes.

There's a wide bed, with the softest mattress I've ever laid on. There's even a small *en suite* bathroom with a sink and a toilet and a shower stall. Every amenity, just like the man said. I can't help but think of the jail cell Officer Friendly dropped me in, or the hospital room where I first met McQueen. Or the hospital rooms I spent months at a time in, thanks to Doctor Rhodes.

Rhodes. *Shit.* I haven't taken my meds in days. I pat at my pockets and realize they're empty, except for my wallet and the little jade statue. I take them out and set them on top of the dresser, like I'm moving into a motel room for the night. Staking my claim.

I also realize that I haven't washed in days.

I peel off my clothes and stand in front of the mirror, looking for wounds. Maybe looking for spots where the fur shows through. There's a huge yellow stain around my ribs, where the pain used to be. By all accounts, I should probably be dead. If not dead, I should be black and blue and barely moving. There's a pale white line on my leg. When I look at it I feel a twinge of heat, and I smell blood, I taste raw flesh. I taste that raw steak, fresh out of the package, bursting with red juices.

I stare deep into those emerald green eyes in the mirror.

"Are you in there?" I ask them. "What are you? Huh?"

Man? Monster? *Láng rén?*

Hero?

Say it.

Say it, asshole.

"Werewolf."

It still sounds like a joke.

THEY ARE ALL sitting at the long wood table when I come into the room. Arthur and Emma on the sides. Magus at the head of the table, a long way down. He waves me into the chair on the opposite end, half-standing as I sit, still playing the gentleman.

"Please, James." He smirks.

"Finn," I growl, fingers gripping the arms of the chair. I can feel the wood splintering in my fingers. I can hear it creaking and cracking in my grip.

"Of course. *Finn,*" he says, setting himself softly on his seat, folding his fingers in front of himself and raising an eyebrow. "I apologize. It took quite a while to find you, and all of the records, all of the information, showed you as having been called *James Finn.*"

"Jimmy Finn is dead."

"I completely understand, Finn. I've seen many names and

many lives in my own time," Magus replies. "We can't all be so fortunate as Arthur here and spend our whole lives as master of our own domain."

I look at Arthur. He's sitting stoic in his place, fingers tight around the head of his cane, staring straight ahead at Emma, who is staring at her plate. She is lovely, shoulders bare and slender arms at her sides, hands folded out-of-sight under the table. Her dark hair is tucked behind one elfin ear, spilling around her face like a tangle of black tentacles. Lovely, but semi-conscious.

"I trust you found your room satisfactory." Magus continues, "I'm glad you found the bath. Frankly, you were almost rivalling Mister McQueen's prodigious musk."

Magus laughs. No one joins him in his merriment.

I regard him carefully, trying to keep Arthur's warnings in the front of my mind, but my curiosity gets the better of me.

"So what's your deal?" I ask him, playing it casual, picking up the wine glass and sniffing deep. "Is it in the wine, or what?"

"I beg your pardon?" he says, in that prim accent. "Is *what* in the wine?"

"Whatever you're doping everybody with. Or maybe it's in the food? The water?"

He snuffs that one off, cracks his fingers into fists.

"I assure you, Finn, there is nothing wrong with the wine." He says, standing to his full height and pushing his chair back, "It was quite expensive and very difficult to acquire."

He struts past Emma, trailing a hand across her shoulders, caressing her, but keeping his eyes locked on mine as he creeps up, leans in close to me, lifts my glass, sniffs, swirls the drink inside, then brings it to his lips and drains it dry.

He puts his long fingers on my shoulder.

"Whatever, I wonder, would give you the notion that I'm poisoning my own family?" He darts a glance at Arthur, then gives me the same look Devil gives me when I'm not catching on fast enough. Except this time, I'm not intimidated by the smartest guy in the room.

"Family?" I ask as he moves back to his own seat, watching him as he seems to float to the other end of the room. "How, *exactly*, did you come to be *Lord of Bensonhall*?"

He laughs, sits calmly, chair still away from the table, and flips out a napkin across his folded legs.

"Please," he says, gesturing to the wine. "Surely you trust me now?"

"I'm fine, thanks."

"*Quel dommage*," he shrugs, lifting his own glass. "To the return of the prodigal son."

"You were saying?"

"Emma, my love, tell Finn our story." He smiles, waving that hand full of long fingers in her direction.

She turns and smiles at me, the fog in her eyes lightening, but not entirely lifting.

"Finn," she says, dreamily. "Have some wine."

I almost give in. I really could use a fucking drink. It took everything I had not to crack at least one of the thirty bottles lining the cabinet in my room.

I chance a look at Arthur. "The wine is lovely, Finn," he says, winking and gripping his cane.

I take the bottle in front of me and pour a half cup. I raise it to my host, pretend a sip, and make a little sound of approval.

"How did you two meet?" I ask Emma directly.

She looks confused. She turns to Magus, then Arthur, then back to me, before Magus speaks up.

"You remember, love. We met when you were in Seattle. We shared coffee in the rain."

"Coffee *and* rain in Seattle, huh? Sounds like it was meant to be."

Magus turns his thin smile on me again.

"I do believe I'm sensing some hostility, Cousin Finn."

"I'm not your fucking cousin."

Arthur's eyes widen, just a shade. Warning me off.

Magus strokes at his bottom lip.

"Nonetheless, my friend. If not for me, you would never have found your family. You would, instead, still be locked up in a hospital, taken for a maniac, would you not?"

"I'm not entirely sure it wasn't your man that put me in there. I smelled him following me for a week."

Magus laughs, a deep, maniacal laugh.

"He does have quite a stench."

I keep my eyes on his hands. There's something I don't like about those long fingers.

"Well, you know how easy it is to pick up a scent, right?"

The laugh dies in his throat and is replaced with darkness.

"Whatever do you mean?"

"I mean, if you're part of the *family*, if you're one of us . . ."

His teeth come out under those thin lips. The bottom teeth crammed together on one side, crooked and jagged. At least one of them is gold and catches the light from the candle like a glowing ember inside his mouth.

"You mean a *loup garou?* A Were-wolf," he says in that maddening accent. "*Dressed of fur, and long of tooth*?"

It must show in my face. I can see the look reflected in his coal black eyes.

He's got me. Gambit lost. Arthur hangs his head.

"A wolf, like you. Of course."

Magus swallows what's left in his glass, then pats the table.

"Emma, darling, would you mind bringing out our repast? Our guest must be famished."

Then, to me, "Finn, I trust this will meet with your approval."

His crooked teeth hiding under that smile.

I watch Emma push herself away from the table and rise silently, stepping out of the room, her bare feet barely making a sound on the wooden floor.

I ask him again.

"So what did you do to her, then? If you're not drugging the food?"

Magus spins his long fingers out from his hands, the ten rings dancing in the candlelight. He shows me his empty palms, spins the fingers, into his palm, back out again. Now his hands hold two lush red roses. No stems, just the blood red crests, each one a perfect arrangement of endless red lips. He spins the fingers again, crushing the petals in his fists. His fingers spin, in and out. Open, closed. Full, empty. Then he closes the fists once more, shows those crooked teeth, and flicks the long fingers toward me, with bursts of flame exploding from each palm. He catches the balls of fire, rolls them around his hands like they were little foam balls, over, under, spinning and rolling them from hand to hand, top to bottom, fingers to palm. It doesn't burn, but it looks so real, those blue flames, roiling to orange and reflecting off of his black eyes and his gold teeth. Then he rolls them out to the ends of his fingers, and the two fireballs split into jets of flame, spurting from the ends of each finger, a candelabra of flesh and bone.

"Nice trick," I snarl.

He snaps his fingers and the lights go out. Just the long fingers of empty hands.

Emma comes in behind me. I smell the dark chocolate and vanilla of her footsteps. She moves past me, placing Magus' plate in front of him, for which he thanks her with a wink and a kiss, blown across the table as she drops Arthur's next to his cup.

"*Bon apetit*," Magus says as she slides the plate in front of me.

It's four fingers, bloody and ragged at the stumps, arranged on the plate in a fan, with a few sprigs of parsley. I stare at them. I hear McQueen in my head.

That must have been a bitch to bring up!

I'm about to scream. About to run. I feel my gorge rise. I hear Magus laughing.

Then my head clears. I feel something against my arm, something cold and calm.

I look at Arthur. He nods and holds up a carrot on his fork. The cane, in his other hand, beneath the table, somehow breaking Simon's spell.

I look down at my plate—a small breast of chicken in some kind of white sauce, carrots fanned out next to a sprig of parsley, mashed potatoes.

"Nice trick." I swallow the lump in my throat and reach for the glass of water.

THE REST OF the dinner is more of the same. I am famished, so I eat, despite my instincts, or maybe because of them. I wolf down two plates of the chicken and vegetables. I stay away from the wine.

After we eat, more of Magus' bullshit, while he tells me some story of how he was just a sailor on leave, never thought he'd meet someone else like him, until he came across Emma, followed her scent through the Pike Place Market, chased her down and begged her to talk to him. It's all bullshit. Nobody like us could choose a life out on a boat, with so little room to run, so little green around us, no earth under our feet. Even I know that much, and for all of his talk of following scents, I haven't seen him sniff at the air, even widen a nostril, not even when Emma came into the room. How is that possible?

He tells his story with Emma on his lap, nuzzling at his neck, while Arthur sits silently beside me.

When I finally excuse myself, Magus cuts Arthur loose to show me to my room. Emma stays wrapped around him, oblivious to everything else around her.

"So, what?" I ask Arthur as we crest the stairs, presumably out of earshot. "He's some kind of magician?"

Arthur whispers, "Some foul sorcerer, yes. He is the player of the harp. Many of us have already fallen prey to them. I'm not entirely sure of his endgame, but you are certainly a part of it. Be wary, Finn. Be strong."

23

"COME ON, FINN! Run with me!"

Back in the room with no walls. Now I see it. It's not that there are no walls, it's that the walls are moving. White flowing from the edges of this place, fluid, shifting. The white curtains flowing in the room full of echoes.

The piano is singing to us, to me and Emma. She's spinning, twirling. Each time she turns, she becomes something new. Little girl into woman into wolf. The little girl laughs, and it echoes from nowhere, climbing and falling with the notes of the song. She's singing. Emma is singing, and Little Finn is laughing beside her.

I'm watching them spin together. Spin, and sing, and laugh. I'm me. I'm full-grown Finn. Long and old and confused, but for once, I'm not that scared little boy.

"Emma!" The voice I hear is not my mother's.

Emma stops spinning in her little girl form. Little Finn is holding her hand. They both stop spinning and stare down the long hall. Two sets of green eyes, different, but the same. Both look terrified.

The children cling to each other. The room changes, white to brown.

"Finn. Hide," she says.

Little Emma pulls little Finn under a long couch, the world

close on top of them, dark and solid.

Out in the light of the room, feet stomp the floor.

"Emma! Finn! EMMA!"

There is something very wrong with that voice.

It's cracking, full of static, like a radio station not quite tuned in.

It fills with gravel and rage.

"Finn!"

Another pair of feet. Two people. Naked. A man and a woman. She is beautiful. Like the little girl, dark hair and olive eyes. He is tall and thick with muscle, covered with thick hair.

She claws at his face as he grips her arms, both drawing crimson trails beneath their fingertips. Their faces are twisting, breaking, falling apart in front of me, faces falling away to reveal gnashing fangs beneath. Nothing but teeth. So many teeth.

And then the people are gone.

Two dogs—two wolves—are tearing each other to pieces. Blood and fur and terrible noises.

I hear screaming. Loud and piercing. Like a thousand crows calling in unison, screeching with all their might. It's coming from inside me. I feel a touch against my hand. I don't recoil. I don't start. It's warm, comforting. Tiny fingers wrapping around mine. She is beside me. I turn and look into those olive eyes, so deep and calm. There are vast forests inside the green of those eyes.

"It's okay, Finn," she says. "We can go home."

I WAKE UP wet. I've sweat through my clothes, through the sheets. The window is open to the night, and a cold autumn wind has laid icy fingers on the room.

I'm up shutting the window and into the bathroom on instinct, stripping off cold, wet clothes, firing up a hot shower. I wipe the steam from the mirror and look into a haggard face, new beard peppered with grey, dark caves hiding my eyes. I stare into those eyes trying to see what everyone else sees. Some strange birthright, some familiarity. I wonder if my father's eyes were the same.

I need some air.

THE NIGHT AIR is cool and crisp and clean. I can hear the water running its course down the stream, mumbling to itself as it goes. I hear more water, rushing fast and hard, somewhere behind the curtain of trees. I take a deep breath and let it tingle out to my hands and my feet, curling the grass up under my bare toes.

The sky is obsidian bright, a thousand pinpoints of light, alive and dancing, a million miles away. The moon glows silver and wide, nearly-full. It pulls at me, deep inside, so hard that I expect to fold in on myself and turn inside-out, flip-turning into some new, better, version of myself. There's nothing but potential in that moon, in the clear black sky, waiting to be filled.

I smell smoke off in the direction of the smaller cabins. Smoke, and something else. I strain to hear it, but there are voices, one deeper, rougher—McQueen, grunting. Swearing under his breath, whispering.

The other voice is muffled, not much more than a sleepy whine. Judging by how they left in the afternoon, and how Jules had acted earlier, I'm imagining any number of situations, none of them comforting.

My suppositions are interrupted by a rustle from behind me, something moving in the trees.

I turn to face two small wolves, seemingly identical, brown and grey. They stand on thin-looking ankles and stare past me with their green eyes, watching where I had been listening. Looking from the cabin to me, then back to the cabin, almost expectantly. It doesn't even seem strange to me, there's no question in my mind. Two twelve-year-old boys, blood of my blood. They just happen to be wolves right now.

"The fuck do you want me to do? Go fight some psycho with a crossbow? She's *your* sister. Besides, it doesn't sound like she minds." I'm already averting my eyes as the words come out of my mouth. I know it's not true.

They keep staring at me, turning their heads in synch, slightly to one side, regarding me with curiosity. They are silent and still, judging me from the safety of the treeline.

"What? I don't know what to do. I don't even understand what the hell is going on around here. What do you want from me?"

The two little wolves keep their eyes locked on me, but swing their heads in unison toward the trees.

They want me to go with them.

"I can't," I finally admit, as much to myself as to them. "I don't know how."

McQueen's voice echoes through the little valley, howling. It's not the sound of an animal, it's the sound of a party. There's a crash and the crack of wood as he steps out into the night, slamming the door open in front of him. I turn to see him stumble out in front of the cabin, naked except for the natural scrub of thick, black, and wiry hair that covers almost every inch of his body. He leans, drunk, against the logs of the cabin wall and pisses a hot stream into the grass. Marking his territory, I guess. The smell of it turns my stomach.

I step into the shadow of the big house, hoping he hasn't seen me, or my companions.

McQueen finishes his gardening and crashes back through his front door, and I look to the trees, finding myself alone again. Jamie and Kevin are gone.

FOUR HOURS LATER, the sun is up, streaming through the windows of the big house, and McQueen is awake and fresh, or as fresh as a stinking creep like him can get, grinning at me as I enter the vast kitchen to the smell of hot, fresh coffee. The coffee and the smell of frying bacon are almost enough to cover McQueen's stink. Almost.

"Help y'self, mate. Boss'll be down in a jiff. He's likely worn out," he says, hopping down from his counter perch, ". . . if he and the missus had a night like I did."

I cringe and reach past him for the carafe and a cup.

Arthur is sitting in a bright corner, cradling a cup of tea in one hand, the silver head of his cane in the other.

"You're going to have to explain how that thing works," I whisper as I sit, eyeballing McQueen across the room to make sure he's out of earshot.

"A gift," Arthur winks, "from my sister. She worked it herself. It is engraved with the ancient markings of our clans. Quite wonderful, is it not?"

"Silver, right?" I say, making small talk to throw off any suspicion from the lurking presence of McQueen. "I thought silver was a no-no. The only thing that can kill a werewolf."

"Oh, my boy. You mustn't believe all that poppycock. The things that writers and old women create in their minds. You should know there are other kinds of wolves, all with specific

Achilles heels as it were. We are fortunate to be blessed in many ways, much improved strength and vigour over our fellow man, speed and heightened senses, you know. Long life if we embrace our nature."

"But all the family that's died . . ."

"What we are not blessed with is impervious skin, nor immortality, my boy. There is also the madness, which, of all of our curses, is the worst."

"So, my father . . ."

Arthur shushes me, nods toward McQueen and the sound of approaching footsteps.

"Another time, Finn. A conversation for another time."

McQueen leans toward the hallway, trying to listen in as their voices approach us. I have an easier time of eavesdropping.

"I will not. What the hell is wrong with you? You are my husband, aren't you? How do you even ask me to do something like that? You asshole!"

Magus' voice is quieter, more restrained, but it holds a more threatening tone.

"You *will* do it, Emma. You will do it because I command it. Or do you think you can refuse me?"

I smell the aggression, not his, but hers. Hot and furious, something close to the smell of blood.

Even the bacon grease and coffee can't hide it.

By the time they enter the room, the conversation is ended. Emma shoves McQueen out of her way, sending him toppling into a chair on the opposite end of the table. He immediately jumps up toward her, but Magus raises a hand to call him off, and McQueen hunches his shoulders, picks up his cup, and stomps off toward the front door, slamming it open on his way out, as is obviously his hallmark.

I watch Magus slink up behind Emma, teasing his fingers across her shoulders as he did the night before. I see it again, in my mind's wishful eye, his pale, thin neck stretched out in the dirt, the red bubbling forth like a river under my teeth.

"Now, Em," he coos at her, pulling her hair aside and stroking her neck. She straightens, almost imperceptibly, and opens herself to him. "Be nice, hmm? Say good morning to cousin Finn."

"Good morning, cousin Finn," she says, dreamily, swaying lightly in the sunlight.

Magus is dressed all in black, thin and pale wherever he pokes out of dark cloth. He spins on his heel and approaches the table, eyes locked on mine as he does. Without even looking at it, he spins a chair out toward him, straddles the seat, and folds his hands on the table in front of him. He is graceful, I'll give him that. Like a snake.

He makes his eyebrows jump, twists his hands, and somehow produces a deck of cards, fanning them out across the table in front of him, as if out of thin air.

Emma quietly places a cup of coffee beside him and kisses his face. I take note of the necklace for the first time. It looks like silver, same as the head of Arthur's cane, but this is a locket, or some kind of amulet, round and pocked like the moon itself. It swings between her breasts as she leans in to him, then disappears into her shirt as she stands, regards me with those olive green eyes, even deeper under accents of brown and grey on her eyelids.

Magus twirls a card across his fingers. "Have I ever told you, Arthur, how I spent my youth in New Orleans, learning the ways of the cardsharp?"

Arthur looks at him with quiet eyes.

"Let me show you a trick, Finn," Magus says, turning to me. He fans the cards in front of him, a seemingly perfect spacing of fifty-two, every card laid with absolute precision.

I humour him. I pull a card. The backs of the cards are decorated with Victorian flourishes and strange symbols. I flip it to find the King of Hearts. The King has a wolf's head in profile, howling at the letter K in the nearest corner.

"Very good. Very good, indeed." His voice drips with poison.

He takes the card, slides it back into the fan, and scoops them all together with a flourish, cupping them between his palms. He mutters something in Latin and opens his hands. The cards burst into flame, so instantaneously hot that we all back away from the table. The cards incinerate in the air, falling to ash in a pile in front of him. He's still watching me. Those gold and crooked teeth peeking out under that sly grin.

He raises an eyebrow again and snaps his fingers. The grey dust and smoke swirl into the air in front of me, reconstituting into the shape of a single card, which flutters across the table, as if on the ashen wings of a moth. It comes to a stop on top of my cup, face down, the back of the card identical to the one I had picked from his hand.

He nods for me to look at the card.

It's the King of Hearts. The King no longer has a wolf's head. Now he's just a skull.

"Nice trick," is all I offer him. I drop the card on the table and slurp at my coffee, keeping my eyes locked on his.

Magus' smile widens to the sides of his long face. He plants his hands on the table and pushes himself up, as if his business is done.

"You may keep that."

He bows to us, having finished his performance.

"Arthur," he says, then turns to Emma. "My love."

He blows her a kiss as he turns to leave.

And then all of his grace is lost as he walks straight into the barrel chest of Bob Dylan, standing in the doorway.

"*Skinkuk,*" Bob says, flat and nonchalant.

Magus sneers, all of his elegance and poison wasted. He's flustered, for the first time since I met him.

"*Kyanukxu,*" Magus hisses, and shoves past Bob like an angry child. I hear him follow McQueen out of the house with the slamming of the door.

I look to Emma, who's regarding me oddly. The clouds have lifted from her eyes again, and she's looking at me as if she's seeing me for the first time.

"Finn?" she asks. Her eyes dance as she smiles at me, the deep olive green glowing from within, eerie with a light I haven't seen there before, except in my dreams.

In my mind, she runs to me, throws her arms around me, filling my senses with chocolate and vanilla and heat.

What she actually does is shake the cobwebs from her head, smile politely, and then kiss Arthur on the forehead, before she turns and follows Magus out of the house, the door closing quietly this time.

Bob looks around the kitchen, sniffs at the air.

"Bacon's burnin'." He goes to the stove and tosses the pan into the sink, blasting the water and creating a cloud of steam.

"That's a shame. Was lookin' forward to some breakfast. You

comin' into town, Finn?"

I place a hand on Arthur's shoulder, suddenly reticent to leave him in this place. I can still smell McQueen's stink nearby.

"Go on then," Arthur says. "You've only just arrived, my boy. Take the day and set yourself in order."

I nod, then look to Bob. "Give me a couple of minutes?"

24

SHE'S STANDING OUT on the wide veranda, staring off into the distance, maybe at her abandoned childhood home, maybe at a rabbit on the edge of the woods.

"Did you really meet David Copperfield in Seattle?"

"I left here as soon as I was old enough. Ran away to college. Not far enough I guess."

"Listen, I don't want to . . ."

"Why did you come back here?" Her voice is flat and full of regret. Or maybe it's resentment. Maybe she just doesn't like me.

"This is my home."

She laughs at that. The sarcastic chuckle of a perturbed cheerleader.

"You left a lifetime ago, Finn. You don't belong here. Not that there's much *here* left."

She hugs herself, shivering against the morning chill. I pull off my sweater and wrap it around her shoulders. It gets me a dagger between the eyes, but then she softens enough to shove her arms into the sleeves and stuff her hands down into the pockets.

"Thanks."

"I've never fit in anywhere, Emma. Coming back here, it's been . . ."

"Weird?"

"To say the least. I didn't even know what I was, what we are, until a few days ago."

That stops her. She turns to me with those olive green eyes from my dreams, as dark and deep as the sea.

"How could you not know?" Her voice finally softening, and my heart nearly breaking at the sound of it. That little lantern in my soul swells and glows warm. Little Finn hollers in triumph in his cave.

I swallow hard and feel the weight of a lifetime of confusion sitting focused on the top vertebrae of my neck, right at the base of my head. It threatens to crush me any second.

"I . . . I always thought I was crazy. My mother never told me about any of this. It's all like some acid-trip fever dream."

"Tell me about it. Imagine getting your first period the same night that you wake from a nightmare and find yourself out in the woods, covered with what's left of the deer you just tore apart, not knowing whose blood is whose."

"Jesus."

"Aunty Siobhan tried to help with the girl stuff, but she wasn't my mom. She had Jules to take care of. I love my grandfather, and he's always treated me well and taken care of me, but I've always been . . ."

"Alone?"

Her eyes harden again and she turns back to staring at the empty cabin across the meadow.

"Whatever we were supposed to be, whatever friendship we had when we were five, it's ancient history. You don't belong here."

She strips the hoodie off and drops it on the wood-plank floor and walks away, stomping down the stairs and across the grass, and she is as beautiful as anything I have ever seen.

She almost makes me believe the anger, the hurt, until she glances up once—just once—as she backs out of the drive in her white SUV. She has tears in her eyes. Those beautiful olive green eyes, as deep and as dark as the sea.

25

THE RIDE DOWN to Pitamont is no less rough and no less numbing than the ride up. The air is clearer than I've breathed in months, maybe in my life, certainly in my memory. The vanilla and chocolate perfume of Emma is clinging to me, now soaked into my sweater and following me like a ghost. I know it's ridiculous to think there's something between us, after decades apart. We're total strangers. Still, there's something. Something that makes that little lantern rage like the sun.

Bob hunches over the wheel, his usual hangdog expression even more dour than the day before.

"What did you say to Magus?" I finally ask.

Bob chuckles. "Really shook him up there, hey? Dark bastard."

"It broke whatever spell he had on everybody. Maybe only for a minute, but it did."

Bob straightens up, stretching out his spine, before he answers, slowly.

"He's a dangerous one. You be careful."

He cracks his neck to one side, and then the other, still taking his time.

"What I called him was *Skinkuk,* means Coyote, in my language."

"Like the trickster, right? Isn't that what Coyote is in Indian . . ." I catch myself, "I mean, *native* mythology?"

Bob turns and gives me a wink. "I think they call us *First Nations* now. But that's the same as lumping you together with every other white guy, no matter where your ancestors came from. I'm a Ktunaxa."

I shrink back in the seat and Bob laughs.

"It's ok, kid. You can say Indian. I'm not gonna sue you, or scalp you."

He takes another minute, chewing on something, before he finishes his thought.

"I can't tell you about anybody else, but the Ktunaxa, we're a small tribe, always worked as a community, and looked out for each other. That's probably why we got along with your type so well. The Europeans came and penned us up in reservations, took the land for themselves, sure. But they did the same to your tribe back in Ireland. We're family, Ktunaxa and the Strong Wolves. We've always worked together." He continues, "But *Skinkuk*, he's always out for himself, stealing, manipulating. He's a troublemaker."

"That guy seems like more than a troublemaker."

"Yup."

"How is he controlling them? Emma and Jules?"

Bob shrugs.

"Arthur's cane. Do you know about that?"

Bob shrugs again.

"Come on! You must know something about what's going on."

Bob takes a deep breath and lets it out in a long sigh.

"Your father wants me to keep you safe."

"My father is dead. My family needs me."

Bob's poker-face slips, he smiles on the far side of his mouth. He doesn't think I can see it, but there's a twitch in his chin and a twinkle in his eye.

"What did Simon say to you, when you called him Coyote?"

"Called me a goat."

"That's a pretty lame insult," I offer.

"Depends how much you like goats." He laughs. That raucous laugh that fills the cab of the truck with light.

BOB PULLS IN at the garage, where three dark haired dudes in matching coveralls all turn from what they're doing and offer a unified nod toward him. The tallest one saunters over to us as we're climbing down.

"Bob." He says, "This the kid from up the mountain?"

Kid. Like he's any more than a couple years older than me. I put a hand out, "My name is Finn." It's like an afterthought, realizing that's my first name. "Finn *MacTyre*." The man is dark, not as dark as Bob, but could easily be part Ktunaxa, or some other tribe. Dark hair, dark eyes. The same measured economy that Bob shows, taking his time, sure of every move, every word.

He looks at my hand, looks at my face. He wipes his fingers with the rag in his fist. He slaps his hand in mine and shakes with a firm grip. He smiles, a handsome, friendly smile.

"I guessed that. It's the eyes," he says, pointing two fingers at his own eyes.

"I'm Jericho. Jerry." He says, "That's my brother Jedediah. Call him Jed." The second brother waves from under the hood of the same truck Bob had been working on the day before. "And that's Jonah back in the office." A hand pops up in the window, despite it being too far for him to have heard us. "Mom was a little religious," he offers with a blush.

"Nice to meet you." I nod, feeling oddly comfortable with this man.

He turns to Bob and goes into depth about a bunch of work that's waiting. A hundred words I don't understand, a few that I've heard before. Bob turns back to me.

"Look, I gotta get some work done here. Try not to get in any trouble." He pulls me aside and whispers the rest. "Magus and his hunter aren't likely to come down the mountain. Who knows what the hell they do up there all day, but they don't show their faces down here too much. I think he needs to stay up there to keep his dark magic in place."

The brothers all turn and wave as I walk away, tuned into the same station somehow, all three nodding in unison, same as when we pulled in.

I WALK DOWN past the Victory, half expecting to feel that strange compulsion to go in and stare at the stage, give cousin Jules all of my money . . . Jules. There's a gnawing taste of guilt twisting in the pit of my stomach. What if she wasn't under her own free will? What if she was brainwashed or hypnotized or under some kind of spell, like Emma? And I just stood and watched that creep piss on the lawn in the middle of the night and didn't do anything to help her? *She'll tear you to bits, man.* Isn't that what the scar-faced barkeep said? Followed by the sound of furniture being turned into kindling in the back room of the Victory.

I walk on, past wide paved streets with small houses on big lots, plenty of grass, plenty of room. In the city, each of these lots would hold three houses, tall and thin, mere inches away from each other, and every one a carbon copy. These houses are all sizes and shapes, some with perfect green lawns, some with rock gardens, flower beds, or assorted toys strewn all over. A few have cars junked out and propped up on blocks. The overall effect being that it feels like a new city neighbourhood every hundred feet, but they all blend one into the next, none of them seeming out-of-place here, despite the differences. The trees are tall and thick and healthy, in every single yard. After a barely five-minute walk, I'm back on Main Street.

I pull Devil's cell phone out of my pocket, waving it around in the air like an idiot while I try to get the best signal. Is that even how these goddamn things work anymore?

I walk to the end of the street and up a steep hill, a handful of people staring at me as I pass, a couple of dirty old trucks rumbling in the opposite direction in the middle of the road. No lanes here.

I crest the hill and look out over the rest of town—more little houses and wide yards, a million treetops in between. In the distance, the lake sits like a puddle of silver, reflecting the sky like a mirror. I check the phone screen again, then decide that if I can't get a call out from up here at the top of the world, I'm not making one at all.

The first number I call is my mother's, more out of guilt than concern, more out of ingrained obligation than any real wish to share my new situation with her. Besides, I'd still rather deal with her misery and guilt than try to explain myself to that pretentious moron Rhodes.

"Ma?" I say as the line clicks open.

"Jimmy? Oh my god, Jimmy! What have you done? Where are you?" She's practically screaming into the phone. I hold the receiver away from my head, trying to shout at her to calm down and listen. Once the furor dies off on her end, I bring the phone back to my ear and try to explain, suddenly eager and excited to share everything about the whirlwind that's enveloped me. I'm all of a sudden five years old and bouncing off the walls to brag to Mommy.

"Ma. I found it. I found *her*."

"Her who? What are you talking about, Jimmy? Where are you? Doctor Rhodes . . . the police. The police, Jimmy. The police have been here asking questions. What am I supposed to say?"

"Ma, would you just listen. I'm here. I found Bensonhall."

Silence. Dead and absolute silence.

"Ma?"

"I told you to forget that nonsense."

"Ma. Listen—"

"Did your father put you up to this? Has he contacted you somehow? He promised me to leave you alone. You can't live that way, Jimmy. You can't."

"Live what way? With my family? As what I am? Say it, Ma. We're fucking wolves. Strong Wolves. *Dressed of fur and fierce of tooth*. You told me that."

"I never . . . I took you away from that place because they were all insane. They were going to . . . your father . . . he tried to kill you! Did you know that? Did you?"

"I don't think he did. I remember now. He lost control, sure. But he didn't hurt you, did he? He wouldn't have hurt me either. You just took the excuse to run away, didn't you, Ma? Dad's dead. Did *you* know *that*? Did you? Is that one more thing you've been hiding from me?"

There's a pause. A hitch in her voice. "Your father . . ."

"Is dead."

Silence again. A long silence. I can hear something, sobs maybe. She's covering the receiver with her hand so I don't hear her crying for him. For the monster she's pretended to hate for thirty years.

"Ma."

She clears her throat. I can see her composing herself. One hand holding the phone to her chest, the other straightening her shirt, her face, her hair.

"James Finn, you listen to me . . ."

"No, Ma. My name is Finn Bar MacTyre. Right? Isn't it? Don't you fucking call me *James*. Never again. Lies, Ma, all of it!"

"Jimmy!"

"And tell Doctor Rhodes I don't need his help, his medicine, or his shitty fucking chairs."

"Jimmy!"

"Thirty years, Ma. Thirty fucking years I let you treat me like I was sick. Convince me that I was crazy, that there was something wrong with me."

There's a tiny crowd gathered a half-block away, staring and mumbling, judging me from a distance. I see teased-up hair on a fat little troll doll of a woman in the middle of it, whispering to her equally fat and judgmental friends. She's clutching at her neck, something in her fist, eyes to the sky, begging her imaginary friend to save her from this spectacle in the street.

I turn around and throw a finger her way.

"Fuck you, lady!" I holler. "Get a TV."

I can hear my mother sobbing on the other end of the phone. Part of my heart breaks off and lodges itself at the base of my spine, sending a tingle of pain through my body and buckling me at the knees, but it's only for a second, then I'm filling with rage again. Ready to rip and tear and bite at the world.

"Jimmy, please."

"No, Ma. That's it," I say softly, quietly, but with absolute surety.

"Jimmy."

"I am home, Ma. You know where to find me if you ever need me but, *please*, don't."

"Jimmy, they'll destroy you. Just like they destroyed your father. They ruined my life!" she caterwauls. I can see her, clear as day, on her knees, clutching at the phone cord, wailing to the heavens. Elizabeth Taylor groaning for salvation, for a hero to come and take her away. More melodrama. More guilt.

Not for me. I'm done living her lie.

"Goodbye, Ma."

I don't even wait for a reply. The phone clicks, and I'm free. The miserable troll is tut-tutting from her street corner, and it rolls right past me.

Serenity.

I wander down the other side of the hill and veer off on a side street until I find a quiet corner, under the shade of a tall tree. It's high enough that I can look out across the groves of deciduous trees skirting the town. Orange and yellow and green so dark that it looks black. Halloween colours, just beginning to fill up the world.

I feel calm, and easy, and for the first time, peaceful.

The rollercoaster comes to a stop, and I can look back at the tracks and see every rise and drop and loop-de-fucking-loop that's brought me home. I don't even realize the phone is in my hand until I've hit the button and lifted it to my ear again. The line buzzes, waiting impatiently for its turn.

"Yeah?"

"Devil. It's Finn. Jimmy."

"Jimbo! You okay?"

"Yeah, man. I think so."

"Good. Cool beans, right?"

I start walking, back in toward Main Street.

"There's some weird shit going on up here, man."

"Family is always weird. You find your dad?"

"He's dead."

Silence, but only for a second. Unlike with my mother, I feel the emotion behind the pause. I can hear Adam DeVille's heart crack, one little drop of blood and sympathy for a friend.

"I'm sorry, Finn."

I feel my lips curl, and that little dagger in my spine dissolves, reassembling itself where it belongs, pumping, beating, solidifying into something warm and alive. That single drop of sympathy from Devil patching a lifetime of misery and disappointment from my mother.

"Thanks, but it's okay. I'm okay."

"Of course you are, dude. Big Bad Wolf, right?"

I'm over the hill, past where the troll doll and her friends had convened. Now the street is empty.

"You figure that shit out yet, hero?" Devil asks.

"Kind of?"

"I've been thinking. Remember Terry Halloran, from gym class?"

"You've been thinking about Terry Halloran?"

"He was, what? Six-three and three hundred pounds in the tenth grade? There was that time in wrestling. He belly-flopped on top of you, folded you up like an accordion. I thought you'd be paralyzed."

Where the fuck was this going? "Yeah, and?"

"And you tossed big Terry off of you and across the room. Everybody joked that it was adrenaline fury, like those people you hear urban legends about—lift buses off of their kids and stuff . . ."

"What does that have to do with anything?"

"Maybe this isn't something new, something happening to you in the now. Maybe you've always been this, and you're just waking up to it."

"Yeah," I say with a smile, finally one step ahead of Devil DeVille. "I've already figured that much out, Professor."

There's a moment of silence, and I imagine Devil swallowing a little lump of karma. Then he clears his throat. "What about the dream girl?"

It's like we're fourteen again, busting balls and gabbing about crushes. Talking about Amanda Sorenson's rack, or how the MacDonald twins always smelled like Hubba Bubba grape.

I realize I've never had a friend other than Devil DeVille.

"She's married. Some kind of fucking magician. He's this Goth dude, can control people."

"Goth, like a Visigoth German Viking of the middle ages, or a Neil Gaiman-looking, Robert Smith, make-up-and-moonbeams Cure fan?"

"What's a Neil Gaiman?"

"You're an idiot."

I laugh out loud and climb up to sit on the back of a street bench.

"Cure fan. Skinny black jeans, long black coat. Thinks he's David Blaine or something. He keeps doing these card tricks with fireballs and shit, but he made me see things that weren't there. And I think he's mind-controlling my cousins. He says his name is Simon Magus."

Devil takes a long breath. "Jim. Be careful. Don't fuck with the magic man."

"He does card tricks."

"Watch your back. Sure, sometimes it's just silly card tricks—sleight-of-hand and rigged-up bullshit—but sometimes it's terrible ancient power and the kind of evil you can't imagine in your worst nightmares. Secret shit that should stay secret. I'll check out the name."

"He puts them in a trance or something. Maybe he's putting something in the food? He says he's Emma's husband, but there's something strange about it . . . and Jules, he put her in some kind of coma-state."

"Jules?"

"My other cousin. You'd love her, she's a dancer."

"Dancer? Like, a stripper? A werewolf stripper?"

"And she has some kind of powers too. She was dancing, and these guys were just wandering in off of the street and dumping money in front of her, like they were hypnotized. *I* was hypnotized. She tried to attack me, like, *sexually*."

"*Like, sexually*? Are you for real, Jimmy Finn? She must be one hell of a stripper."

As if on cue, a familiar voice cuts the quiet of the street. I turn to see Jules pushing her brothers out of the diner, stepping back into the street, the Troll Doll waitress stabbing stubby fingers out toward Jules, her posse crowding in behind her.

"We don't want *your kind* down here, harlot! Witch!"

"You can go ahead and fuck yourself, you and your Lord and Saviour!" Jules screams at her.

I'm off the bench and running toward them, forgetting Devil on the other end of the phone.

"Jim? Jim!"

"Hang on, Devil. I'll call you back."

"What the hell is going on?"

"My cousin."

"Dream girl, or the stripper?"

"I'll call you back, Devil."

I hit the disconnect button and shove the phone in my pocket as I skid to a stop beside my cousins.

"You see?" Troll Doll shouts, "This new one is even on the phone with the Devil himself."

I blink and shake my head.

"Seriously, lady? Do you think I was on the phone with Satan? Like Beelzebub has a cell plan?"

I turn to Jules and the boys.

"What's going on?"

Kevin and Jamie, as usual, seem totally nonplussed and stare ahead at the women in the doorway of the restaurant, no more emotion than a couple of statues. Jules, on the other hand, looks ready to fight.

"You lousy cunt!" She screams, "You can't give these kids a

fucking hamburger?"

Troll Doll squints her beady eyes and makes the sign of the cross.

"You just take your filthy mouth and your demon-spawn back up the mountain and stay out of our town!"

"*Your* town?" Jules is practically foaming at the mouth. "My family built this fucking town!"

I jump in front of her before she takes a swipe at the woman. She clips my ear with one swing.

"Ladies, ladies!"

Troll Doll shoves a pudgy finger into my chest.

"Don't think we don't know who you are. You're the grandson of the beast himself. Your father was the worst one of all of you. Don't think we don't know who you are, Mac*Tyre*."

"Look, lady. They're just kids. They just want a burger for Chrissakes."

I realize the error of my statement before it's even fully out of my mouth.

The full assemblage of five or six of Troll Doll's army starts swinging—purses, umbrellas, keys—and I'm suddenly crushed under a hail of blows.

"Jesus Christ!" I holler, and they redouble their efforts.

I hear Jules growl, and the old ladies scream, the barrage stops, and I look up to the slamming of the door. Troll Doll calls out to us from the safety of the storefront window.

"You'll get yours, you shameless whore! You and your whole family are damned! Cursed! Demons! Monsters!"

She backs away from the window, and Kevin and Jamie are at either side, helping me up out of the mud.

"What the fuck was that?"

"Bitches," Jules grumbles, grabbing her brothers by the arms and dragging them behind her as she stomps off across the street.

I jog to catch up, still rubbing the back of my head, where some stray piece of metal seems to have taken a chunk.

"Hey! Wait up!"

Jules keeps walking. Kevin and Jamie keep stride beside her, despite their shorter legs.

"Where in the hell are you going?"

"To the fucking McDonald's, I guess. I promised these two milkshakes. What do you care?"

I keep walking behind them, trying to think of the right thing to break the impasse, the thing to set things right. This is my family. Family I've never known, family that I don't understand, but it's *my* family.

"I remember the milkshakes here. It's like they mix them with ice or something."

She keeps walking. One of the boys, I don't know which, turns an eye toward me as he's dragged off.

"What happened to you last night?" I call after her.

Jules stops dead in her tracks; the boys move ahead and gravitate to each other, wary of the situation. I should probably take my cue from them. From the identical look on their identical faces, I should run.

"What happened to me? What the fuck do you think happened to me, asshole?"

I don't recall telling my feet to move, but I'm backing away as her face contorts and her voice rises—a coming storm on the wind, ready to level the town around us.

"Look . . . I don't understand any of this . . ."

"Poor fucking baby."

"I just want to help."

Her eyes blaze like green fire.

"Well, you sure helped last night. Thanks for that. Do you know what it's like to have that stinking fucking ape climbing all over you? Fully conscious of what's going on and totally unable to disagree, fight, ask him to at least brush his nasty fucking teeth, put on a condom maybe?"

She jabs one of her long, red-clawed fingers into my chest and pushes me back three feet into the dirt road.

"Maybe you should try it some time. You've got the same parts he likes to ravage on me. Usually he's so drunk he wouldn't know the difference. Ever been to prison, Finn? Ever had your black cherry popped?"

"I . . . I didn't know."

"You didn't know." She turns to her little brothers, arm-in-arm and wide-eyed on the sidewalk. "He didn't know." She leans in close and growls into my ear. "Fuck. You."

"Jules—"

"You were supposed to be our almighty saviour. A whole family of fuck-ups and never-weres. Your dad was a fucking waste, and now you are too. He couldn't save Emma's parents, or mine, or anybody else. How are you gonna help, huh? Big bad wolf, fucking Alpha dog. You look like a lousy beat-up piece of cat shit to me, *cousin.*"

Her rage stinks, toxic and hot, and it leaks into the back of my mouth, a bitter taste of vinegar and bile and old coffee.

"Jules, I'm sorry," I offer. Even I can tell how pathetic it sounds. "Those women back there . . ."

"What? The Jesus-bitches? I can handle them. I can handle all of it. I don't need any help from you, little man. Simon's gonna get what he wants out of you, and out of that stuck-up bitch, and then he's going to see that I'm the one with power. *I* am the Alpha around here. Not you, and not fucking *Emma.*"

She shoves me, hard, and I tumble back into the mud, which makes Kevin and Jamie snicker in concert. She grabs them roughly by the arms and stomps off, and this time, I just watch her leave.

26

I SPEND THE next two hours wandering the streets of Pitamont, mulling over all of this bad craziness in my head. For the first time, in as long as I can remember, my head is clear and my thoughts make sense. I'm not sideswiped by thoughts of blood and haunted by nightmares about gnashing teeth tearing me apart. I haven't even thought about a drink today. Things are coming to me faster, clearer, stronger than they ever have before. Maybe it's because I'm off of the pills? Or off the booze? Maybe it's the fresh mountain air? Maybe it's because I'm finally where I'm supposed to be. Whatever it is, I know I'm thinking straight, but I'm still mired in confusion, this time from all around me instead of inside my own goddamn head.

As the sun starts to disappear out past the lake, and the trees start casting long shadows across my feet, I head down Main Street and across town to the garage. Maybe Bob can shed some light on this horror-show soap opera I've wandered into.

I come to the front of the Vargas Brothers Garage to find all three Vargas brothers sitting in a line, looking nearly identical, all in their blue coveralls, all staring straight ahead, all with a beer in their left hand and an oily rag in the right. They turn, nod, and lift their beverages in my direction. I salute back with a wave, and all three bob their heads in unison.

"Bob's out back," Jerry says.

"Thanks," I mumble as I dodge around the side of the building, past the old tow-truck and into the garage bay.

"Bob?"

It's dark as hell in here, creepy-calm like in a bad horror movie.

I step further into the dark garage, straining to see two feet in front of me, hoping not to walk into anything sharp. Hoping not to slip in a puddle, trip on a . . .

"What are you doing in there?"

I jump three feet higher than I would have thought possible. "Jesus!"

Bob is outside, shaking his head at me.

"Come on, kid. No time to screw around. We gotta go see your aunt."

I'm choking on my own heart.

"Aunt?"

"What I said, isn't it?"

"I thought my aunt was dead."

"Different aunt. Great-aunt."

I'm still asking questions and still getting very few answers as we rumble up the mountain road.

"Arthur's wife?"

"Sister."

"What's her name?"

"Raigan."

"Like the kid in *The Exorcist*?"

"I don't know, Finn. *Ray-ginn*. Raigan."

He pulls in at the first cabin where the boys live.

"Does she live with Kevin and Jamie?"

Bob shushes me, waves me out of the truck and behind the cabin, into the trees. He hands me a map drawn on a piece of paper towel, gives me hushed instructions to hike in through the trees, find the waterfall, the little cabin on the far side of what he calls "the spout".

"Aren't you coming with me?"

"Can't let them know you're back, or how to get to Raigan's. You burn that map once you get there, hear? Magus has been looking for it for a long time, but old Raigan, she has powers too."

"Again with the fucking powers? Is everybody up here a witch, or a fucking magician? Werewolves and powers? Next thing, you'll tell me to watch out for vampires."

"No, but there might be some angry bucks in there, your cousins have been picking them off in this part of the woods, but there's a couple of mean bastards yet. And *beware the frumious bandersnatch*, eh?"

"What does that even mean?" I ask, hopeless for a real answer as I watch Bob slink off, out of the trees, look around, and then bop on back to his tow-truck as if he hasn't a care in the world.

He looks through the trees and gives me a wink and a finger to his lips as he passes.

I hear rustling in the trees behind me and turn to find the two young wolves watching me again.

They turn their heads, as they did the night before, signalling me to follow. This time I go.

I tromp through the woods behind them, watching in wonder and envy as they hop and bounce over the brambles and scrub and dips in the ground that trip me up every second step. They stop every few minutes and wait for me to catch up. I'm out of breath, covered with a thousand scrapes and cuts from every stray branch and sticky burr that I pass, but every step further into the woods makes me stronger, more sure, and more committed to follow them.

We come to a steep incline that turns into a rocky outcrop. I watch them bound carefully up the rocks, pausing to make sure I'm still behind them. They both cast green eyes out over the forest, down onto the clearing and the big house. I get the feeling that they're checking to make sure that we're not seen. We circle the outcrop until we're shielded again, then continue the climb up, clinging to a narrow path around what's little more than a cliff. I'm terrified to look down, but I'm also increasingly confident, almost amazed at how sure-footed I am as we pick our way up the mountainside. We finally reach the top of the cliff, standing far above the forest, and they lead me on, until we come to a crack in the mountain, where the stream flows down from above, rushing into the crevice and cascading down to the forest floor below. Just past the falls, on the opposite side of the stream, is a cabin. A single tiny cabin, almost invisible in the trees, a willow-wisp of smoke rising from its chimney. As we come to the stream, the young wolves jump and splash, cavorting and leaping over each other in the cool water. I look for stones big enough to hop across and, finding none, resolve myself to wet socks, and wade in and across.

The cabin, when we reach it, smells of spices and burning pine, rich smells like cinnamon and apples. There are dozens upon dozens of little carved things hanging from the trees, totems and charms, swaying in the wind, rattling together like an orchestra of bones. The little wolves take up spots on either side of the cabin door—lookouts, or little furry gargoyles. They snuff at me, nod toward the door. Telling me where to go.

I kick off wet boots and wring out the water from my pant legs, feeling the cold numbing my toes and running up the bones of my shins. I knock lightly.

"Aunt Raigan?" I whisper.

The door opens, seemingly of its own accord, and the old woman is sitting across the gleaming gold of the cottage, swaddled up in a blanket in a rickety-looking rocking chair, a shotgun across her lap.

She sniffs at the air, wrinkled old face puckering up at the smell of me.

"Finn Bar MacTyre," she says, her voice thick with the Irish brogue that used to slip into my mother's voice.

"Aunt Raigan?" I venture a few steps into the room, wondering at the flickering candle and fire-light that seemed to glow from every corner, wondering at so much fire in a house of sticks, especially one inhabited by a blind old woman. And she was most certainly that. I watch her rise from her chair, head pointed in my direction by the nose, eyes milky white and wandering in no particular direction. I jump across the room to help her out of the chair.

"Let me help you."

She swats me away with a clawed hand that shoots out from the blanket faster than I would have thought possible, and with far more strength.

"You just watch yourself, child. Think just because I'm a hundred-and-fifty-seven I can't take care of myself? I've lived up here on the mountain by myself for damn near a century, boy!"

She lets me take her arm anyway, and I walk with her to a high wooden bench that runs the length of one side of her hovel. It's covered with tools and bits of wood, hunks of half-worked metal, rough-hewn figurines and charms. She takes my hand, feeling around my palm as if she's looking for something in the lines.

"Hmm. How can you be that old, yet have not had a full change? You poor soul. How mad you must be. Every seven. That's the rule, boy. Did that mother of yours not teach you? Damn fool girl, never was one for heritage or knowledge. Starting with that damned idiot you were named for. He brought ruination on us all. Fionn Bharr the Great, he thought himself. Ruined two families he did, and opened the door for our destruction at the hands of those pretenders down there. The magician and his mad dog."

She picks up what looks like a coin, a large silver coin, and presses it into my palm.

"This is for you, Finn. Keep it against you, always, yes? It'll ward off the machinations of the dark magic that poisons our home now."

I look closer at the medallion. One side is hammered and pocked like the moon, same as the one I saw on Emma's neck, the other has three roughly carved wolves, baying into the night.

"The maidens of the moon," Aunt Raigan says from behind me, as she settles herself back in her chair and under her blanket.

"*From the south, three sisters fair*
Ran athwart the gloom
Dressed of fur and fierce of tooth
The maidens of the moon."

The words tumble from my mouth as I think it, not meaning to recite the poem, but unable to stop myself.

The old woman giggles from her spot by the fire.

"Very good, young Finn. Very good. You know the story then?"

"My mother, I think she used to tell that poem to me when I was very young."

"Bah!" she says, waving an arm across the air in front of her. "Your mother never paid attention to a damn word I told her. I used to sing that song to you, when you were a boy. In the big house, on a summer's day, you and Emma were just wee. Still, even then, the family was wasting. Your grandfather broke the rules, then your father. Then Sean and Oonagh. Cursed they were, by the arrogance of Fionn Bharr."

"I don't . . . Arthur told me something about my grandfather. He killed someone?"

Aunt Raigan rocks back in her chair and looks at me with her cloudy eyes, seeing me without sight.

"Your grandfather thought a great deal of himself. He married our cousin, Bradach, even though he never loved her. She gave him four pups—your father and Oonagh, Emma's mother, among them. But he was never happy, your grandfather. Never complete. He wandered, he fell into the wilds of his lust and his appetites. He was always eating, and drinking. Loved the whiskey he did. Loved the girls, too. Village girls. Never get enough, that one. And then he had the damn fool idea that he could ignore his nature, that he could leave the Gift behind and live whatever life he wanted. He ignored the change, he fought his nature, and that poor girl paid for it, when the madness took him."

"The madness?"

"We're ancient, boy. And the true nature of a Strong Wolf must be respected. If ye don't let that wolf out to run, it seeps into your dreams. Eventually it feeds your nightmares, gnashing at the teeth to get out. Hold it prisoner long enough and it'll escape, come what may. I'm surprised you've not suffered it into total madness by now, boy. Seven years, that's the rule. Every seven, the madness peaks and there is no denying it, lest it devour you whole."

"Seven years from when?"

"From the first change. It's like the human changes. When you become grown full and your body changes, blossoms into womanhood, or manliness."

"Puberty." Say, around fourteen. Mad with lust and rage, lonely and terrified. Then seven years later when a full nervous breakdown puts you in the mental ward. Then back in the nuthouse before thirty, and yet again, another seven years later, attacking women in the street, puking up fingers, nightmares full of blood.

"She never told you, did she?"

"No," I say, feeling sick in the pit of my stomach. A roiling ocean of bile threatening to bubble to the surface. How did my own goddamn mother let me go through that four times over and not say a goddamn word?

"What happened to the rest? My father, Emma's parents?"

"Much the same, but they didn't have doctors filling them with filthy drugs to keep them calm." It seems like she winks at me, but I can't tell if it's a twitch or a dig. "Your father, he meant well, but he was confused. He thought Fionn Bharr had given in too much to his nature, and tried to subdue it in himself, not seeing that he was following the same path to destruction. He was lucky, and wasn't consumed by the madness, only changed."

"Is that why my mother took me away? He went mad?"

She shoots forward in her seat, claws swiping at the air.

"Your mother was the biggest fool of all! She left because she was selfish and vain. She was a princess in her own little imagined kingdom. She wasn't special enough here, and she wanted to be beautiful and desired and worshiped by men. Rose, she was named, but she could never live up to the beauty of Oonagh, or Siobhan for that matter. She was too damnably stupid to realize it was because she was all twisted up with envy and foolishness. Your father's madness was only an excuse to escape."

"Yes." It's all I can manage.

"The others tried to emulate your father, as he was the Alpha once Fionn Bharr was gone. Once your mother left, the rest all tried to hold back the nature. Sean and Oonagh, poor Emma's mother and father, they went the worst. Tore each other to pieces."

"After my mother left? But I was there, hiding in the room. I saw it. I've been having nightmares about it my whole life."

"The third eye, boy. You and Emma, you were paired. Had you stayed, you two would have been the next generation to lead the families. Should have been mated and raising your own family a long time ago. That's what keeps us strong."

"But I was *there*!"

"You saw it through her eyes. Felt her pain. No doubt she called out to you. You were her mate. Probably still lingers, despite the years and confusions, eh? Despite the intruder, and his dark curses."

I think about Emma, imagine her pressed against me, her warmth on my skin, a deep smile on her face, and in her eyes. The eyes of the girl from my dreams, but in the face of the woman.

"Mated? Jules said something about being mated with me."

Raigan huffs and crosses her arms.

"Julia? That girl is the most troubled yet. Broken and filthy with anger. I taught her the secrets. Taught her the ancient magic, and what does she do? Goes running to that foul conjurer, the very one that killed her parents, and begs for favour, she does."

"Magus killed their parents?"

She leans forward, the shrouds on her eyes floating like dark clouds over the moon.

"Of course he did. And your father. Magus, and that rabid dog of his."

I'm standing, muscles tensed with new energy, rage boiling up inside me, rising up into my ears, roaring like a furnace.

"Sit down, boy. There's no vengeance to be had . . . yet."

I grip the medallion tight in my hand and, much like Arthur's cane, it soothes me, cooling my veins and bringing me back to my senses. I sit and open my hand to look at the trinket.

"How? How does this work? Arthur's cane? It's the same thing? What? Magic?"

"Yes. The oldest magic. I told you, boy. We are ancient. That's the secret that Magus is seeking. He wants to find our power and take it for himself. There are few magical things as powerful as real, natural transformation. He could take that power and raise him an army like no other. He could live for another hundred years on what he might steal from just one of us. Once he figures out how. He thinks he can twist it and turn it into something that will make him invincible. There are other ways to become a wolf, some of which he used himself to worm his way into this family. Then he enchanted your Emma, and Julia. Magus, he's strong, but he's not ancient."

"And Arthur?"

"My brother has my protection. As do you now, long as you keep that trinket on your skin."

She produces a leather strap and runs it through a small hole in the medallion, hanging it loose around my neck. Confidence and calm spread through me. My head clears, and my focus becomes sharp.

"I tried to protect the girls as best I could," Raigan continues. "Magus was able to counteract it. You're all more vulnerable without the pairing of a mate, and without a proper leader. Mostly he's used the folly of youth—the hunger of the young—pretty things and vainglory, drink and drugs and the promise of *more*. You've seen that hunger. The very same that took your mother. I see it in the age of your eyes, boy. Long years lost, eh?"

"Yes," I reply.

Her eyes reach in and pull at that ache deep inside of me.

"It's like a hollow scream deep inside, always begging, pleading, dying for . . . something. And you can never find that thing, can you?

"You made it through the other side, Finn. You're here, and wiser than you think. And now that you've seen those demons, you've fought and lost, and drowned those hungers—and survived—you are the best chance we have to survive. Let you be the last of the circle of madness. Let you bring the strength back to Binn Connall. Maybe now that you're back, maybe Emma . . ."

She drifts off into her thoughts, finally seeming as old as she looks.

"What about the boys?" I ask. "Kevin and Jamie."

"Good boys. Such very good boys. I fear for them the most," she says. "Magus has no need of them—they're too young to mate, too smart and too strong to be turned to his own uses. If he leaves them to grow, they become a threat. If he kills them now, he would surely lose his pet. Julia would be overcome with rage. But soon, Finn. Soon, I fear. The dog would surely love another trophy or two."

"They're just kids!"

"And the smartest of us in a thousand years, but I fear they won't survive the coming storm. Whatever happens, you protect those boys."

"How do I . . . I mean, what can I do?"

"First thing you need to do is take the change, the full change, and let the Strong Wolf come home. Then you find your mate, and bring that strength back to Bensonhall. Maybe then, if Emma is freed, and Julia can see the error of her ways . . . Then, perhaps, the strength of all three could stand against Simon Magus and his killer."

"Airitech . . ."

"Yes, boy."

"But *sisters* fair, *maidens* of the moon . . . they were slaughtered, speared through."

"It's a bloody poem, boy. Just a story, and two-thousand years old. But so are the Strong Wolves. That damnable magician, he'll underestimate you. He came into a broken house and hid in the rubble, picking away at ruins. He's a thieving coyote in wolf's clothing."

"*Skinkuk*."

A strange expression takes her face, twisting and crawling over her yellowed and broken teeth.

"Yes!" she shouts, throwing her fists in the air. "You listen to old Bob Dylan. He'll show you the way. We wouldn't be nowhere without the Ktunaxa."

She pops out of her chair, again, far faster than I would have thought possible, and she's at my ear, whispering, telling me the secret of the Strong Wolves, the secret of our clan.

"Now go, the boys will tell you what you need to know, young Finn."

She pulls me down to kiss my face, then shoves me toward the door.

"Fare thee well, Finn Bar. And give 'em hell, my boy."

Kevin and Jamie are waiting outside, green eyes gleaming in the darkness.

27

THE LITTLE WOLVES lead me further into the woods, away from the cabin, away from Bensonhall, until we come to a tiny clearing, no more than twenty feet of a circle. The moon is bright and full overhead, cascading down into the grass around us and lighting up the night with silver.

They circle me a few times, walking me into the middle of the clearing, then they jog around to face me.

I watch as they hunch forward, muscles tensing under the fur, a grey smoke rising from them like steam. They twitch and groan, snarling in pain as their skin comes away in ribbons, spinning out and whipping around them in tendrils, mixing and dissolving into the grey smoke that covers them. I can see their bones reform, their muscles reshape around them. They both lurch backwards, up onto their knees, and then they're standing, the smoke recedes and pales, resolving itself into white skin and blonde hair.

The two boys stand proud and smiling in front of me. They look smaller in this form, and cold.

"Your turn, Uncle Finn."

"I'm your cousin, not your uncle," I say to whichever one has addressed me.

"Yeah, but you're old," says the other one. "Like an uncle."

They both laugh, the tittering giggles of twelve-year-olds.

"Very funny," I groan. "Show me how to do that."

"We wouldn't want you to have a heart attack or something."

"Yeah, you are pretty old to be starting now."

They walk around me like a couple of drill sergeants out of a movie, circling me in opposite directions, hands clasped behind their backs, eyeing me up and down, appraising my suitability as a cadet.

"You haven't changed at all? Like, *ever*?"

"No," I stammer. "I don't know. Maybe?" They give me a pair of sideways glances. "I messed up some dudes in the park, and I maybe ate somebody's fingers?"

They chuckle in concert.

"You're supposed to do it when you're a teenager. When you're like eighteen. Like drinking."

"Or voting."

I swing my head from side to side, trying to catch both of them in my field of vision at once. They're making me dizzy. I decide to focus on the one moving clockwise.

"You guys can do it, and you're not eighteen yet," I shrewdly point out.

They switch places in my eye line, and I find myself moving counter-clockwise, despite my best efforts.

"We're very smart."

"Auntie Raigan says we're *prodigies*."

"Because we're twins," they say together. "Take off your clothes, dummy."

I stare at the ground in front of me and reach for my boots, feeling the world continue to swirl around me as if I was circling the drain. I barely feel the backward momentum compared to the side-to-side, and the ground hits my ass hard, without me even realizing that I'm falling.

"Fuck."

The boys laugh and crouch on either side of me.

"You're never going to handle the change."

"Poor, dumb old Uncle Finn."

My boot is in my hand, and I let it fly toward whichever one is spinning closest to me.

"Get up." They laugh.

I waver and wobble, but I manage to take one knee, and then the other, slowly hauling myself up to standing.

I drop my pants, shrug off my jacket, and pull my shirt over my head. I hesitate with my hands on the waistband of my boxers.

"If you leave them on, you'll get tangled up."

"Or you'll be a wolf in underpants. That sounds scary."

I drop the shorts and pull my socks off. No sense in being a wolf in socks either. We're trying for fierce hero-animal, not Dr. Seuss.

"Good. Now, close your eyes . . ."

"And think of England."

They laugh hysterically, in that way that only smartass kids, pleased with their own daring and insight, can cackle and twitter.

"Very funny, guys. Come on, show me."

Goosebumps are rising on every part of me in this cold. I shiver and feel my balls pull up close, hoping for some warmth. My thighs are stinging, and I can see my breath.

"Come on, man. It's fucking freezing out here!"

They stand in front of me, red-faced and shivering, yet still smirking despite the cold.

"You just need to know who you are, Finn," the first one says. I still can't tell which is which.

"You need to let go of everything else, and know that your true self is the one underneath the skin. All the way under the fur."

"Does it hurt?" I ask, shaking.

"It . . . *tingles*."

"How do I turn back? Obviously it's not the moon, right? It's not like in the movies?"

They snicker and shake their heads at me. "You just have to want to be *this* Finn again."

"If you really want to. You might just want to stay changed. This you is sad."

"And old."

"Very old."

The little bastards laugh again, but the laughter changes into something else, something wild and free, as the smoke overtakes them again, and both of them twist and swirl and are torn apart and remade. Ten times faster than they changed before, the smoke roils and clears and the two wolves are standing before me. They dance and hop, impatient for me to join them, or maybe just still mocking me in their wolf language.

I brace myself against the cold, close my eyes, and wish to be free. I take a deep breath and try to release myself, everything that I've ever felt was wrong, and terrible, and human. I focus on the cool, fresh air in my snout, the wind in my fur, the smell of the pines, the rush of the river in the distance.

The tingling starts at my feet, as if all ten of my toes had suddenly gone to sleep and then lit up with pins and needles. The sensation moves quickly from there, rushing over the bottom half of my body like an electric pulse. Am I imagining it? Is it happening? I don't dare open my eyes. I'm terrified to look down and see my body twisting into ribbons of smoke and bone. What if I look and it stops, and I'm caught halfway? Some terrible half-life beast made of parts with no whole? A mud puddle of wasted humanity and partially chewed dog. Despite my paranoia and my terror, the tingling takes me over. It runs through my veins, winding through the air like streamers now, warm and soothing.

My body buckles, and the smell of the wet grass and scrub comes into my snout. Is it a snout now? I still can't will my eyes to open, even though it seems like an eternity has passed. Something changes, and the night opens to me. Even without my eyes, the world becomes brighter, thicker, more alive than ever before. Sounds, smells, I can feel the wind prickling against my skin like soft fingers, rubbing against me in a thousand different places. I feel like I'm drowning, like I'm overloading, like I'm lost in an endless miasma of colour and noise inside my head.

Just as my panic reaches fever pitch, there's a thought, soft, warm, quiet. Not a word, not an image, exactly. A thought, pure and simple and uncluttered. Like putting your hand near a flame and knowing *hot* by instinct.

Look, it says.

I open new eyes onto the night. A night brighter and louder than anything I've ever seen. My thoughts are simpler, quieter, more assured. My senses are alive, my body is electric. I feel everything. I sense everything.

Run, it says. *Follow.*

And I do.

I BOUND AND hop behind the little wolves, my head low to the ground, shoulders up and new legs propelling me faster, stronger than I have ever moved before. It's as if my feet know where to land, my body knows where to fit, and twist, and maneuver, before I even get there. I'm strong and free and ready. More than anything, I feel *right*. Like this is the real me. The me I've never met. I overtake the two smaller wolves and run through the forest, King of my new lands.

We come to another small clearing in the trees, and I sense it. I catch myself on the edge of the treeline and come to a silent stop, down-shifting without a thought, my heart dropping to a rumble from a scream. There, twenty feet away, are three deer—skittering, dumb, and innocent. Their ears perk up, their heads bobbing up from the grass, eyes darting left and right at the sound of our approach. We're so quiet, so strong. They sense us too late, and I know it. I leap from my place, secret in the trees, as the deer spring forward, and I catch one on the back legs, my claws sinking deep into the meat of its hindquarters. It pulls away, tries to kick free, but I'm on top of it already, over its back, turning it, teeth to throat, ripping, snapping. It kicks, and twists, and spasms, pumping more of its life into my mouth, the red gushing forth, filling me. It quivers, one last convulsion of Life, and falls quiet. My teeth are tearing the meat away from the bone even as I feel the spirit leaving it.

The small wolves join me, ripping away chunks of fur, yanking the carcass back and forth between us, rending the thing limb from limb. We savage its innards, warm, bloody, and delicious. We lap the blood from the ground. The black birds are in between us, underneath us, dropping in and flying away.

I understand it now, all of it. Stretched out in the long grass, a sky full of stars above, the smell of fresh blood and the squalling of those black birds, picking the remains of my kill, my feast.

Nature. You are what you're born to be.

Me?

I'm a Strong Wolf. There's another word, but it won't come to my wolf brain the same way it does to human lips. I picture the little jade statue. I feel a wide, sure strength swelling in my chest.

THE BOYS LEAD me through the woods, past Raigan's little cottage, down the winding mountain path—much easier in my new form—and back into Bensonhall, where we creep to the furthest edge of the little stream and drink deep one last time. We skirt the cabins in the edges of the wood, slowing and moving deeper in as we pass McQueen's place, until we come out more or less where we started, where Bob had left me in the twilight.

There, I watch with hesitant curiosity as the smoke swirls and the boys take their shape again, seeming taller and paler than I remember. They stand, naked and shivering, expectant eyes waiting for me to follow their example. I don't want to give this up. I feel like I could stay like this forever, strong and free. I know I can't, but I cling to it anyways. I nuzzle my snout into my own white fur, thick and soft and full. The scents of blood and meat still thick on me. I rest on my haunches, tongue wagging like a happy Pomeranian. The thought of my human self, the one I've lived inside for more than thirty years, is a half-forgotten dream. The change won't come.

One of them goes to the door of the house, turning the handle and opening the door ever-so-carefully, and ushers us inside. In the dark of the cabin, surrounded by people smells, plastic and metal, pent in with dust and dead skin floating in the air, I find myself, and I feel the room swirl as my body changes.

I come back to myself, lying on the floor, freezing and nude as the day I was born.

One of the boys—Jamie, I think—throws a blanket over me, and Kevin emerges from another room, still naked, with a pile of clothes in his arms.

Their father's clothes, an uncle I'll never meet.

Jamie brings me tea, and they tell me to practice changing in secret, for a few days longer.

"That was good, though," Kevin says.

"Yeah. We've never heard of somebody making a kill first time out."

"Usually takes a few months to get used to it."

"The first time, I just curled up on the ground for an hour."

"I threw up."

"Yeah. All over me," Jamie says.

The clothes fit me perfectly, but I wave off the offer of their father's boots. There's something about another man's shoes. A dead man's shoes. They still haven't dressed as I'm ready to leave.

"Don't you wish you could stay that way?" I ask. "Stay wolves?"

"It's better," they say in chorus.

"But it's not *us*," Jamie says.

"In the middle of all things. Always," Kevin adds. "That's what

Auntie says."

I think about myself at their age, angry, terrified, and mostly alone.

I look back on a thousand drunken nights, a hundred drugs I used to try to curb the pain. I can see what she sees in them. These boys—parents murdered, sister insane, living alone on the edge of the forest, wolf-boys in a world of hunters, three hundred yards from a man who could kill and skin them in his sleep, the same man who killed their parents—yet these boys are the sanest, most together people I've ever met.

"She's absolutely right. You guys just be you."

They smile at me, unified, as they always are. They're going to be just fine, so long as I can protect them from whatever is about to come our way.

"Thank you," I say, turning back at the door.

"We're glad you came back," Jamie says.

"You're going to be a good uncle," Kev adds.

They leap out and wrap their arms around me. It feels good to have someone that wants me here, to have someone connect.

They release their bear hug and both look down at my bare feet.

"I'll be fine. You boys go get some sleep."

And I leave them there, to make my way through the pre-morning dew, cold and wet on my feet.

28

I SNEAK IN the front door. There are no locks here. Not anywhere I've been yet, anyways.

I creep up the stairs past the bedrooms, the parlour, the giant bear looming claws-out in the hallway.

I stop, step up into his terrible, tooth-filled maw and his dead glass eyes.

I bare my teeth, and I dare him to move.

"Boo."

THE ROOM IS dark, save the moonlight streaming through the open window. Instead of turning on the light, I duck into the bathroom, strip the borrowed clothes off of me, and start the shower in the dark.

I come out and stare at the long table full of exotic bottles, tasting the memory of those thousand whiskey burns on my tongue. I'm almost surprised, and certainly pleased, that it offers me no further urge. They're just bottles. Just things piled up on a table. No saviour, no friend, nothing more than bottles.

"Are you going to have one, or just stare at them all night?"

There's a clink in the corner. Ice on crystal. My distraction at the events of the night has betrayed me.

She leans out of the shadows in the corner and shakes her glass at me.

"What are you doing, Emma?"

She's out of the chair and slinking toward me through the moonlight that casts down in sparkling slivers through the half-drawn blinds. She turns to set down her glass and I see the amulet catch the light, the moon bouncing like a mirror, dangling from her neck, but there's something strange about the light. It seems diffused, muted, as if there were a fine mist of grey fog surrounding it.

Emma moves closer, barely dressed in a short piece of lingerie, what I think they call a teddy. Black silk against her milk-white skin, hard nipples poking against the fabric.

"Finn," she purrs. I feel the accumulated energy of a lifetime climb up into my throat. My whole body feels electric and jittery, like too much coffee on top of too much speed.

"What are you doing here?" I repeat. "Did Simon send you here?"

"Simon?" she says softly, close enough for me to feel her breath. "Forget Simon."

Her hands are on me, light touches, running up my naked thighs, over my side, and up to my chest as she moves in front of me, pressing her soft, silken body against me. The vanilla and chocolate smell is gone, replaced with something lighter, softer. It smells fresh, like rain. She reaches fingers around the medallion at my neck.

"What's this?" she asks in a whisper. "You've been up to see the witch. I suppose you've made the change?"

Her voice is all wrong, it carries an echo of somewhere, as if she's throwing her voice, or there's a speaker in her throat. It's her voice, but not her words.

Her fingers curl around my neck, up into my hair, pulling me close. Her lips, pink and full and so perfect, brushing against mine. As they separate, the tiny tip of her tongue drags across my upper lip, teasing, welcoming. Her other hand slides down the front of me, over ribs and past my hip, down to my balls before sliding up and around the shaft of my hard and ready manhood. I tremble and draw a stuttering sigh.

"Emma," I groan, wrapping an arm around the small of her back and pulling her into me. Her back arches, and her neck falls open to me. I wrap my lips around the skin there, kissing, licking, tasting her up to her little ears, burying my face in her hair and breathing deep of the smell of her. I pull her hair back, hard, to look down into her face, those delicate cheekbones, those luscious lips, those dark eyes, olive green and deep as the ocean.

Except they're not.

There's a smoky haze over her eyes. The same haze I'd caught in the moonlight, seeping from that thing around her neck. I shove her onto the bed, the spell broken. The energy falters, fades, but it's replaced by the fury of knowing that I'm being played for a fool, and that Emma is being used like a marionette.

"What the fuck are you doing here?"

She crawls forward, lust dripping from every movement. She twists and poses and opens herself up to me.

I grab her shoulders with rough hands, shaking, part of me wanting to throw myself on top of her and devour her whole. The other part of me wants answers, wants the real Emma. Not this puppet in silk.

She smiles, wan and confused. Something slipping in the fog that's covering her. I grip the moon medallion in my hand and a tremor of filthy energy crawls up my arm. I yank, I pull, I tear at the frail-looking chain, but it won't give. Emma slumps, as if she's drunk and exhausted, falling limp as I pull at the foul thing around her neck.

I step away, frustration and anger boiling up under the skin. Slapping my hand against the silver at my own neck, I take a breath, close my eyes, and feel the world spin again. I beg for more power, and I feel it course through me.

The smoke whirls around me, and I crumple and change, reborn into the beast inside.

The chain is hot and evil between my teeth. I can taste the darkness of it, death and unnatural power.

I twist, and growl, and grind my teeth against it, until I feel it disintegrate and give, and the momentum leaves me scrambling backwards.

Emma lurches and sucks in a huge breath, falling back against the bed as the mist flows out of her and dissolves into the air. She sits bolt upright on the edge of the bed, panicked and confused until her gaze falls on me, crouching in the shadows.

I sniff at the amulet lying in front of me, draw back, bare my teeth at it. I snatch it up by the chain and whip it with my head, growling as it spins through the air and lands near the door.

"Finn?" she whispers. There are tears in her eyes. "You're beautiful."

She sits, hand outstretched, until I creep closer, sniffing at the fingers, unsure of whether the evil has left her entirely. All I can smell, even in this form, is that light, airy perfume, like fresh rain on the wind.

Emma ruffles my white fur, hands digging deep, fingers pushing hard into my skin, sending waves of pleasure rifling up through my spine and into my head. My eyes roll, and my legs buckle at her touch.

"Come back?" she says. "Please?"

I step into the shadows and will Finn back into reality. This time it's easy. The smoke swirls, and I spin out into the ether, reforming and standing stronger and more powerful than I've ever felt in my life.

The medallion is still lying by the door, still oozing its black evil. I pick it up by the chain and take it to a drawer in the bathroom, drop it in and close it, as far away from us as possible, leaving it in the dark.

"I don't understand," Emma says, holding her drink in her hand. "Aunt Raigan gave me that."

"Did you ever take it off? Lose it?"

"No. I wear it all the time, just like she told me to. Except . . ."

"Except, what?" I ask, taking the glass from her hand and dumping it into the sink.

"Hey!"

"No more of that. For either of us. That's how he got in, got control of this place."

"He's my husband," she says, crossing her arms tight against her chest, the same way she'd done when we met.

I sit next to her on the bed. The fresh boxers I've put on feel weird and unnatural now. I understand why Kev and Jamie walk around their house naked.

"Do you even remember meeting him?" I ask. "He said you met in Seattle, but you didn't seem to know for sure."

"He . . . He . . . The amulet. Aunty Raigan's amulet. The chain broke. I woke up and the chain was broken. Simon offered to get it fixed in town."

Her hand is soft in mine, comfortable, fingers fitting together effortless and true. As if they were made to interlock that way.

"He's not who you think he is," I say. "He's lied to you. He killed my father, our aunts and uncles."

"No. He's my husband. He wouldn't . . ."

My voice is calm and reassuring. Decades of sitting in support groups and listening to Doctor Rhodes trying to keep me calm and talking. I guess it was worth something.

"When did he come here? He and McQueen."

"I don't . . ."

"Was that when everyone started dying? My father? The others?"

She pulls her hand away, puts it to her mouth. I can feel her quivering beside me, the reality of it all sinking in like a ship taking water.

"Oh God! I brought him here." She weeps into her hand.

"No. He sought you out. He's a magician, a con-man. This is a long con, coming here, taking over, and killing off anyone who poses a threat. Who's left? With you and Jules under his spell, it's just an old man and a couple of kids. He needs something. What is it? Why did he bring me back here?"

"I don't know."

"Why did he send you up here tonight? To seduce me? So he can take control of me too? For what?"

"He couldn't have sent me. For that? Did we? He's my husband, for Chrissakes!"

"Emma," I turn her face toward mine. "He's controlling you, using you."

She pulls away and turns to stare at the side-counter full of booze.

"Where were you, Finn? It was supposed to be you. They've been telling me that as long as I can remember. Finn will come back. Finn will be your one and only. Finn will make you whole. Do you know how fucked up that is? To have the memory of some little boy as your one and only hope for happiness? To have everyone around you feeding that insanity?"

My heart sinks.

"I know. I'm sorry. I didn't know." It's a different misery than I've ever felt. Guilt and failure, but tempered with reality. No melodrama, no blame, just honest regret.

She lets go of my hand. "They've told me my whole life, you know? It was supposed to be you and me. Like an arranged marriage. Do you know what that's like? That kind of expectation from everyone in your life? I went off to college, I was afraid to even talk to anybody, to ever have a relationship. Nobody else would be you, nobody else would be enough for them."

"I didn't know. Any of it. I've been floundering. I've wasted a whole lifetime thinking I was someone I'm not. My mother took me away from here, lied to me my whole life. I was a completely different person until a few days ago. Jimmy Finn. Fuck-up. Maniac. Loser. Drunk and angry for thirty years. Until Simon brought me here. McQueen helped me escape from the police, and *told me* to come here. McQueen *told me* my father was looking for me. Then I come here and he's been dead for a year. You want to talk about mind-fucks."

She sniffs back tears, rests her head on my shoulder, slides an arm around the small of my back.

"Finn, I'm so sorry."

It feels good to be next to her. Like a missing piece of myself. She's been a phantom limb my whole life, and now the missing piece is regrown and whole.

"I dream about you. About us. When we were kids. I've felt my entire life like we were meant to be together, and I didn't even know who the hell you were. If you were even real. I'd ask my mother, and she'd tell me you weren't real!

"What the hell does that mean?" I wonder out loud. "How much does that mess somebody up? I've dreamt of you every night of my life, and never even knew who you were until yesterday. I couldn't remember. What the fuck does that mean?"

"I always hated them, hated being told that some little boy I barely remembered was my destiny. I hated you."

I wince, but I understand.

"I've hated my mother every minute of my life for taking me away from this place, even though I had no idea what it was, what we are."

"I remember your mother." Emma tells me, a soft hand on mine, "She was beautiful, but sad. Always so sad. I dream about you too, and her—telling us to run away. I don't hate you, Finn." She smiles and puts her hands to my face. Her kiss is light, tender.

"I think it all means that they were right." The words start coming more easily, more confidently. "Not that we were destined to be here, but that we have always *been* together. Raigan said we were joined. That I could see through your eyes. That we're connected beyond anything my mother, or Simon, or anybody else could understand."

I put my arms around her, feeling closer to this woman than I have to anyone in my life.

And we fall into it.

Savage and natural, fierce and passionate, the room swirling as we melt into each other. As we merge our bodies and our minds and our fates. Her body gives way to mine, and mine to her, and we come together, in the cascade of moonlight, howling together with the fury of our family exploding in our blood.

The king and queen of the moonlight. Lovers of the night. Warriors of the moon.

29

EMMA IS PACING in the red light of dawn that's breaking through the window.

She has a pair of jeans from the drawer cinched up around her waist, and she's swimming inside of a flannel shirt rolled up to her elbows. She's still the most beautiful thing I've ever seen.

"What if he knows?" she says, chewing at nails that were gnawed away a half-hour earlier.

I pull on boots and lace them loose enough to kick off, just in case I need to make a quick getaway.

I've thrown on a pair of jeans and a worn t-shirt of my own, no underwear, no socks. I'm trying to think of all the angles. If I need to make a fast turn, the less clothes to lose the better. What I wouldn't give for a pair of tear-away hockey pants. Not a thought I could have ever anticipated.

I lift the leather strap from around my neck and go to her, placing it carefully over her head and around her neck, before I take her face in my hands and press my lips against hers.

"I want you to wear this."

"But, what about you? You're the one he wants!"

"I don't really think so. And I have you. Raigan told me we would be far more powerful as a pair. That once we were mated, we'd be unbeatable, especially if we can get Jules back. Family. That's what all of this is about."

"But, Simon. He's going to know that we . . ."

"He's counting on it. He sent you here in the first place. Why would he do that?"

She stares at me, those olive green eyes searching for something.

"Mated?"

"Exactly. Why would he do that?"

Emma turns to look out the window, wrapping her arms around her chest again, the shy little girl locking herself away.

"He had Jules attack me when I got here."

"Attack you? Attack you how?"

"You know, like *sexually*." Now I hear it. Devil was right. I sound like an idiot.

Emma turns back to face me, but cinches her arms even tighter.

"And what happened?" she asks, no effort at all in covering the subtext of that question.

"Nothing. I didn't even know what the hell was going on. I hadn't even come up the hill yet. I got the hell out of there in a hurry. What do you think she was up here screaming about the other day?"

"And you think Simon told her to do that?"

"I know he did," I answer, putting my hands on her shoulders, gentle and reassuring.

"Why else would he bring me here? He had this place locked down. Nobody to oppose him. If all he wanted was Arthur's money, or this place, or *you* . . . why bring in another person he'd have to control? There has to be a reason he wants us together."

"So, what? My own husband brought you here to fuck me? To *mate* me?"

She stiffens in my arms, eyes wide and locked on the door behind me.

"Very good, Finn. Very good, indeed. Though she was supposed to kill you, once you'd served your purpose. So why are you still alive, hmm? And why is *my* wife in *your* arms?"

Magus steps into the room, silent as a ghost, floating past us in his long black coat.

He turns and stands in the window, back-lighting himself for effect, no doubt.

A terrible animal funk permeates the air.

"Sounds like you two had a helluva night, mate. Good on ya. Wouldn't mind a crack at that ass myself!"

McQueen is in the doorway, leaning casually with his crossbow cradled like a baby in his arms.

Hot fury wells up from the bottoms of my feet and boils up like a thermometer in the red.

"McQueen, please," Magus groans. "That *is* my wife you're talking about."

Magus steps forward and reaches for the strap around her neck. Pausing and drawing his long fingers back as he gets close enough to graze it with his long nails.

"Hmm. Curious. That's not your necklace. Where is that lovely bauble your aunt gave you, darling? You were not to take that off," he says, straightening his back to regain his composure. He can't touch it. She's safe from his machinations.

"Mister McQueen," he says, softly, "would you be so kind as to take my wife downstairs and remove that thing from her neck?"

I feel a poke at the back of my head as McQueen slides up behind me, the hard metal point of the crossbow bolt digging behind my ear.

"You just stay right there, boyo," he says, grinning at me through the scrub of his face. My nostrils are full of his monkey stink, and it makes me want to rip his arms out of the sockets.

He reaches with his free hand to grip Emma around the arm.

"You touch her and you fucking die, kiwi."

"Kiwis are from New Zealand. I'm a fucking Aussie, you cunt!" He spits at my feet, and I take the split-second distraction to spin underneath his weapon and wrap an arm around his, putting all my weight on his shoulder and forcing him down to his knees. He squeezes the trigger, and the bolt fires, grazing my leg as I come down on top of him.

"Emma! Run!"

She steps over top of us, keeping her eyes on Magus as she backs out of the room.

The magician waves his hand, the same as he did to Jules, muttering something under his breath.

Emma's eyes are wide with terror, but she's still moving. Magus unleashes a hellish banshee scream and leaps for her. My fingers catch him mid-flight, yanking on that ridiculous coat as I force him down on the floor.

"Run, goddammit!"

Emma turns and bolts from the room. I hear her feet hit the stairs, land hard at the bottom. I hear the door open and slam shut.

McQueen twists underneath me, and there's a sound of ripping cloth, a familiar cold sting and a rush of warmth. The knife flails up past my face, and my strength falters. I grab for my side, where he's sliced a gash along my ribs. A few inches more give in my hold on his arm and he would have gutted me. I slam my elbow down on top of his head, ramming it into the floorboards with a satisfying thud, and I feel him go limp just long enough for me to make a break for the door. I chance a glance at Magus, who is only just pulling himself up off of the floor, still winded. He whispers something dark in some strange language and burns, a blue flame consuming him, twisting into smoke and fire. The glass of the window shatters, and a huge hawk emerges from the maelstrom, winging out the window to freedom.

I hammer down on McQueen's head again, using the momentum to push myself up and stumble toward the door, a gout of blood falling from my side as I rise. I hear him, cursing me as I make the corner of the upper hall. I hear the click of the crossbow bolt. That bloody stuffed bear is looming over me, and I tackle it, bringing it to the floor in a crash of fur and bone. It smashes the bannister, and I tumble with it down into the air, rolling as I fall to land on my feet in a hard crouch, the pain in my ribs screaming, another rush of fresh blood filling my nose as lightning cracks through my brain and in front of my eyes. The arrow whistles past my head and lodges in the door frame, just as I crash, shoulder-first, through the screen and out into the morning.

I head straight for the treeline. I know if McQueen makes the field before I'm out of sight, I'm a dead man.

I collapse into the trees, scrabbling backwards on my back, kicking the boots away as I drag myself further into the brush. I'm praying that Kevin and Jamie are safe, that Emma made it to her car, or one of the cabins. I know I'm bleeding to death. My only chance is to change and heal. To run. Regroup and form a plan. I shrug out of the pants and crawl onto my knees, feeling the blood pouring through my fingers, sticky and warm. I take my hand away to pull the shirt over my neck, and my legs buckle. I'm on the ground, everything growing dim. I hear a scream in the distance. Emma. Then black.

30

RUN.

That's the only thought going through my head, and I listen, legs pulling and stretching, galloping harder and harder, springing over rocks and roots, through trees and over the earth, the dirt road just in sight beyond the trees. I run hard until I come to the edge of the woods, the edge of town. I can smell people and food, chemicals and gasoline, coffee and asphalt.

I creep out between stores, out onto Main Street. I know I shouldn't be here, but I need to find Bob, Arthur, the boys. Anybody.

I creep low and long, from building to building, ducking away beside stairways and under parked cars as feet approach and pass me by. I smell the diner, with its rare burgers and chocolate ice cream, and I finally have my bearings. A straight shot down the road to the Vargas Brothers garage. I have a reassuring feeling when I think of that place. Safety. Friends.

Run.

As I come out from under the tires of the truck I'd been hiding under, I hear a wild scream. I catch a whiff of blueberries and sickly-sweet raisin pie. The Troll Doll stands frozen in the sidewalk, screaming and pointing with one pink-nailed hand. Her entourage of fat, make-up caked women all take up the siren call and wail as if the world is coming to an end. Everyone in the street. People are running out from shops and leaning out of windows.

I bolt, trying to outrun the sound, sailing down the middle of Main Street as fast as I can, car horns sounding behind me, adding to the cacophony. My legs are burning, but I'm close. So close. I can see the curve in the road. Two blocks and I'll be there, safe and silent. Somewhere to breathe.

As I round the curve, a jeep screeches to a halt, and the firecracker sound of a hundred bullets take the air, whistling past. One clips my ear. And I stumble and roll, crumpling to a stop in the shade of the yellow tow truck.

I can smell Bob just past the bay door of the garage. I hear his voice, hollering something. My ears are ringing, and the world is so loud and distorted, like my head is underwater.

Little bits of the ground around me keep jumping out as if they were alive. Bullets still seeking me out, even as I crawl under the truck for cover. Then three sets of blue legs appear on the other side of the truck, and I feel vibrations above me. Bob comes rushing toward me, crouching down, reaching under the truck. I let the thought of me take hold, feel the world spinning, the water clearing from my ears, the pain fading as the smoke swirls and becomes skin.

"Run, Finn. Come on. Run with me," Bob says, pulling me out from under the truck. The Vargas brothers are behind us as we run, sending their own hail of gunfire at the jeep in the road. As Bob and I fall into the safety of the dark garage, I hear tires squeal, and the explosions of gunfire finally stop.

The oldest brother, Jerry, backs into the open door.

"Everybody okay? Bob?"

Bob pats me on the back. Then he steps away.

"Jesus, Finn! Did he get you?"

I look down at the blood pooling at my feet. The drip is slow, and the puddle is tiny. My fingers go to my side, where McQueen had opened me up, the ten-inch gash now barely an inch.

"I think I'm okay. It's almost healed."

I feel at my ear, and my fingers come away sticky. "Fuck."

"What happened, Finn?" Bob asks.

The youngest Vargas brother, Jonah, rushes in with some kind of white case, popping a latch and throwing it open to reveal a loose pile of bandages and gauze, tape, and sealed plastic packages of white pads. He clamps a hand to my side, slapping one of the bandages in place.

"Hold this," he says, pulling tape away from the roll and tearing it with his teeth.

"Really, I'm oka . . ." All of a sudden, the room spins, and all the energy leaves me. I flop down on the floor.

"Okay," I finish. "Maybe I need a minute."

Bob runs out to his truck, head darting in all directions before he ventures out, hustling back with a blanket from the back seat, which he throws around my shoulders.

"You look like shit, Finn."

"Thanks?" I mumble. "I feel like twelve bucks."

Jonah Vargas hands me a cup of something dark and warm.

"Here," he says. "Drink this."

I sip at the liquid, thick and rich. I know what it is, and I don't care. I guzzle it down.

"You lost a lot of blood, dude," he says. "You need to feed."

I cough, bringing a swell of it up into the back of my throat.

Jonah helps me to the front office and brings me another cup of warm, velvet blood before he disappears without a word.

I wait for Bob, looking around the office until my eyes fall on a photo on the wall. The same garage, thirty years ago, with a different sign. *MacTyre Tire and Tow*. There's a man in the picture, tall and blonde, a thick sandy beard and moustache, dazzling green eyes. One arm is around Bob Dylan, but Bob Dylan a lifetime ago. Long black hair, thick and straight, that same lopsided grin. In the man's other arm is a tiny boy with a shock of white hair. Beside them is a dark haired man in blue coveralls, undoubtedly a Vargas, but with dark circles under his eyes, sneering at three boys of varying size at his feet.

"You were about four years old there. We used to play with you when we were little," Jed, the middle brother, says from behind me. "This was your dad's place. A long time ago. Gave it to me and my brothers when things got bad for him."

He hands me a folded pair of the same blue coveralls he's wearing.

"Sometimes, when he was in a bad way, he'd get lost and end up here, sick as a dog . . ."

I feel the eyebrow raise all on its own.

"Sorry. Bad joke." Jed says, "Bob used to bring medical

supplies out to the clinic on the reservation, and he'd sneak a bag or two for your dad once in a while. We kept them in a little beer fridge in the back. Good thing."

"Thank you. You saved me."

"Payback. Your dad saved us. Our old man, he was a drunk too, but a real sonofabitch. Used to beat us, beat our mom. Jonah doesn't remember it so much, he was pretty young. Jerry got it the worst. Until your dad put a stop to it. Mom had kind of lost it by then. Barry MacTyre took us in, gave us this place, something of our own. This is our town, and you don't shoot wolves in our town."

Bob appears in the doorway, a quiet look of concern on his face. He comes in and pats Jed on the back.

"You see, Finn, we're all family."

Jed nods and disappears behind him.

Bob sits in front of me, stares deep into my eyes, as if he's looking for something very small hidden in the black holes that lead inside. I get it. I'm not the only one who has suffered.

"Magus," I stammer. "He's after me. He might have Emma. I don't know what happened. I thought she got away."

I take another deep swallow from the cup, feeling stronger with each drop. Bob still gazing deep inside of me.

"McQueen nearly cut me in two. Magus turned into a fucking bird, man!"

"You turn into a wolf," he says, finally satisfied by whatever he was looking for.

"They're all in danger. I have to get back there."

"Whoa there, cowboy," Bob says, holding me into the office chair. "Arthur's in town. You rest for a minute, and we'll go find him. I need to get a couple of things."

The coveralls are roomy, and surprisingly comfortable. When Bob comes back he's decked out in buckskin with a pile of necklaces and charms around his neck, black feathers in his hair. He's straight out of a Hollywood western, except for the heavy workboots still on his feet. He's got a rifle in one hand, and a hatchet in the other.

"What are you going to do with that?" I ask, nodding at the hatchet with the black plastic grip.

"Gonna cut me down a sorcerer."

"Is that what we're going to call him? *Sorcerer*?"

"What do you want me to call him? A *wizard*? This ain't *Harry Potter*, man."

"You got one of those for me, then?"

He gives a little huff through his nose and tucks the handle of the hatchet into his belt

"You're a Strong Wolf, Finn. You got more magic, and more power, than any damn sorcerer."

I reach a hand inside the coveralls and feel under the bandage at my ribs. Dry as a bone, and no more than a ridge of scar left to remember McQueen's knife by.

"Can I take one of those rifles until we get out of town? I already freaked out a bunch of people running down Main Street. I thought that old Troll Doll woman from the pie place was going to steal a car just to run me down."

"Mary-Ellen? She's harmless. They talk a lot of bullshit."

"Maybe armed men in the street will keep her mouth shut?" I ask, peering out the office window into the empty street in front of us. "Aren't there any cops around here? I would have expected sirens by now."

"RCMP is about ninety kilometres away." Bob moves the tangle of beads and charms around his neck aside. There's a metal badge pinned to his buckskin shirt. "I'm the auxiliary constable until they get here."

Bob Dylan giggles—an honest-to-God, schoolgirl giggle—and hands me the rifle.

"Now you're my duly appointed deputy."

THE STREET IS a wasteland of absolute silence. Not so much as a bird squawking, or a chipmunk's twitter.

I can feel the eyes on us, every single person in town barricaded inside and terrified to breathe. This is Canada. People don't barrel through the streets firing off machine guns at stray animals. Indian braves and dirty mechanics don't walk the avenue with hunting rifles. The tension is electric and alive, like a blanket of crackling voltage between the buildings. We pass the jeep, a handful of guns and bags of ammo drenched in monkey sweat are just lying there, like cast off food wrappers. I sniff the air, and under the still-strong stench of cordite and gunpowder, I smell blood. I search the ground and find it, a small spatter on the sidewall, a smear on the seat. McQueen is bleeding and hiding somewhere nearby. I try to play bloodhound and follow the stink of him, the smell of the blood, but it's lost a few feet from the car, cut off by the impermeable concrete and the smells wafting down from the diner, the bakery, and the little corner store that sells nachos with processed cheese and some kind of pork-grease chili.

I show Bob the blood, silently pointing to the dribble leading away from the car. He gives me some kind of hand signals, two fingers to his eyes, then pointing off down the street.

"What? What is that? You want me to look over there? Or are you going to search that side?"

"Navy SEAL signs. It's what they always do in the movies. Keep your eyes on that side. I'll go over here," he whispers, shaking his head. "Come on, man."

I shrug and follow his signal, taking the south side of the street, while Bob creeps up on the north sidewalk.

I can hear people whispering inside the stores, huddling down against the baseboards. I see the tops of heads popping up in windows ahead of me, only to disappear as I get closer, with gasps and creaking floors. Bob peers into the wide window of the hardware store, waves to somebody inside, then puts a finger to his lips and moves along.

As we reach the middle of the main street drag, a strange scent fills the air. Sulfur and rotten flesh. Like somebody burned down a fish market with a truck full of matches. Bob stumbles out into the middle of the road.

"Finn!" he calls, spinning on his feet, eyes up to the sky.

The clouds are swirling black above us, a vortex of darkness and ice-cold wind.

"What the hell is that?" I'm screaming it, and Bob still doesn't seem to hear me over the din. A cyclone is coming, picking up the dirt and the garbage off of the street, turning it into a wild funnel of filth, a dust devil trying to devour us. We huddle in the centre of the street, rifles up at the eye of the storm, looking for some sign of the man we know is causing the chaos.

A hawk flies over us, seemingly unaffected by the winds tearing at the buildings around us. It swoops down as if coming in for a landing, but instead spins and twists into a fist of blue flame, growing larger and brighter and hotter, until it sputters and reforms and stretches itself into a new shape. The tall, thin figure of a man in a long black coat.

"Come, Finn." His voice booms out at me, bouncing from the buildings, pent in by the black sky above us. We're in a cave of his making, and his voice echoes like thunder. "We have unfinished business, you and I."

31

SIMON MAGUS IS floating in front of me, looming ten feet tall, the same grey mist that I had seen coming from Emma and the medallion seeping from his skin like steam.

I shoot from the hip, on instinct, the rifle kicking back against me, but it's nothing but noise and motion. The bullet freezes mid-trajectory and falls, as if it were no more than a fly, swatted out of the air. The cold terror of mortal doubt takes hold and climbs through my veins, frozen spiderwebs creeping across every muscle. The rifle clatters to the ground, useless.

"Child's toys," he calls, his voice coming from all around us.

Bob is behind me, panicked, swinging left and right, trying to make sense of the whirling chaos that surrounds us.

Rage and rebellion begin to boil through the terror in my veins.

"What do you want, Simon? If you're so goddamn powerful, what is it that we have that you can't just take?"

"First? You on your knees, *mongrel.*"

As he says it, the sky explodes with light, and blue tendrils of electricity crackle through the air, stabbing into my shoulders, knocking me to my knees, coursing through my muscles and bleeding out through my hands and feet into the earth, pinning me to the ground, like an insect on display.

I scream out, despite myself, and twist my muscles against the steel girders that have replaced my bones.

"That's right, good dog." He laughs. My muscles are bleeding away, I can feel them coming apart under the strain. I can't fight it. I fall limp under his spell.

"Secondly, *James*," he taunts, his proper English accent lost as he bellows over the din. "You were only brought here to stud, and you've only impregnated one of my pets. Jules is so anxiously awaiting her turn."

The girders twist and bend and take me with them, up off of my knees, straight as an arrow, sliding toward the sorcerer, my feet dragging behind me in the dirt. I'm like a bendy toy with hard-wired limbs. I stay right where he wants me to be.

He's looking down on me, breathing his hot stench of sulfur and dead fish.

"Now you will come with me and finish the job." Close enough that I can taste it. "Then I believe I shall let Mister McQueen mount your head for my wall."

Something flies past my ear, spinning, something flat and cold, and it glances off of the sorcerer's head, taking a sliver of red with it as it goes. Magus stumbles back with a screech, and his spell is broken. My arms and legs are my own again.

"Run, Finn!" Bob hollers, rifle at his shoulder.

I drop and roll as the bullets sing over my head. I hear them land—*thud thud thud*—and I look up to see Magus stagger into his own fog. I don't wait to see him come back up. I'm already running for Bob, on one knee in the centre of the street, when I see Arthur emerge in a crouch from the cedar door of the diner.

"Finn, my boy!" He waves, hobbling out to join us, as if we were just ducking from a little rain.

"Arthur! Get down!" I scream, diving toward him as the rat-a-tat of McQueen's machine gun sounds in my ears for the second time in as many hours. I feel the hot sear of one passing through my shoulder and catch it in the corner of my eye as it lands in the cedar of the door jamb. I roll over Arthur and pull him with me, into the dark of the small space between the diner and the hardware store.

"My word!" He says, clutching at his cane, "What in hell's bells is going on here?"

"Emma." I groan, clutching at my shoulder, blood already oozing through my fingers and darkening the blue of the coveralls by three shades. “He’s got Emma, and Jules, maybe the boys . . .”

“Got them?” He repeats, “What do you mean *he’s got them*? You’ve been shot, boy!”

“Arthur, we need to get out of here. Right now. We need to get back to Bensonhall before Magus and McQueen.”

Bob is calling from the cloud of dust that used to be Main Street.

“Let’s go! Finn! Now!”

I grip Arthur by his coat sleeve and pull him along behind me.

“Stay low, and don’t make a sound.”

We’re halfway to Bob when the bullets rain down again. I drop to the ground with my hands over my head. I hear Arthur shout.

“Bloody hell!”

His coat tears away from my grip. I turn, and he’s already lost to the swirling cloud of grit and earth flying around us.

McQueen’s voice comes close and clear.

“Up and at ’em, you filthy cunt.”

I feel the muzzle of his gun pressed into the small of my back, the heat singeing my skin, even through the thick cloth of the coveralls. I stretch my arms above my head, wincing and pulling back with the right as the new hole in me tears and bleeds again.

“Gotcha, eh? That’s what you get, you bloody bastard.” He jabs at me with the barrel. “Get up!”

Arthur’s cane is lying in the dirt, just out of reach.

“Pretty good shot for a kiwi.” I laugh, tensing my muscles for the blow I know is coming. It lands just to the left of my spine, and I use the momentum of it to slide the two inches I need.

“I told you I’m a fucking Auss—”

The thick silver head of the cane connects with the side of his face with a sickening crunch. He drops, clenching his fists and spattering the ground around us with fire. I roll the opposite direction and am up on the sidewalk before he can swing toward me, and I lay a boot directly into the same side of his head that the cane has left its mark. McQueen drops to the ground, groaning and nearly still. I step over him to kick the machine gun away, calling out to Arthur. There’s only silence.

“Bob?” I holler into the cloud. “Arthur?”

“Finn! Get the hell out of here,” Bob is yelling from somewhere in the dark. I hear the vague patter of feet on the sidewalks through the maelstrom. A lot of feet.

McQueen is still lying in front of me, but I sense someone at my shoulder.

"Arthur!" I spin, and come face to pink lacquered talons with Mary-Ellen, the pie troll.

Mary-Ellen's chubby face is twisted into a hellish grimace. Strange, guttural mixtures of vowels pour out of her throat in a squeal of anguish as she swings wildly at me, tearing and lurching like some kind of rabid pink wolverine.

She swipes at my face and catches me just above the eyebrow, opening me up, red filling my vision as the blood streams down into my eye.

I hear Bob in the street, telling someone to stay back, a bunch of someones.

"Don't worry, Finn. They won't kill *you*." Magus laughs from somewhere above me, cackling and booming through the streets, as more shadows move toward me through the dust. "But they will kill your friends and leave you short everything but your one useful appendage."

"People. Please!" I shout. "He's controlling you!"

I shove Mary-Ellen back with the head of Arthur's cane, and her eyes clear, just for a second, before the grey mist seeps over them again, and her teeth begin gnashing as she throws wild arcs with her clawed hands.

I back into the street, holding the cane out in front of me, a makeshift shillelagh ready to swing for the fences. The troll doll and her friends and neighbours don't want to touch it, so as long as I keep them in front of me, I might have a chance.

I press up against someone, back to back. Bob turns, blind, and swings the rifle toward my head. I duck just in time for it to crack, shoulder-stock first, into the broad side of Mary-Ellen's cotton candy head. She crumples to the ground in front of me, but five shadows lunge forward to take her place.

"Aw shit, Mary-Ellen!" Bob yells, spinning his own makeshift bat toward his side of the street. "We gotta get out of here. What the hell is this?"

"Like you said, buddy. Goddamn sorcerer."

I swing the cane in a wide arc in front of me. "Get back!"

Magus cackles from the clouds again.

"There's no escape, you fool. I own you. Just as I own your whole accursed family. *The heeled mongrels of Binn Connall.*"

He laughs again, and the air around us crackles and burns.

The cyclone spins faster, thicker, and the bodies press in on top of us. We're about ten seconds from doom. Bob presses closer, and we turn in a slow circle, holding the mindless horde out in front of us.

Then we hear it. It sounds a mile away, a high whistle, the fingers-under-the-tongue whistle perfected by untold numbers of boys to call their friends across the ballpark, or down the street at sundown.

It's followed by the roar of an engine and the squeal of tires as the jeep skids to a stop a dozen feet away. Bob grips me by the arm and shoves. I'm tumbling across the ground, through the collected townspeople like a cannonball. They split like bowling pins, and I'm scrambling toward the sound of the jeep, praying that we can make the few feet before we're crushed by the entire town of Pitamont.

"Not on my watch, you bastards!" McQueen's voice rises from behind me, and I can hear the click of the first bullet hitting the chamber before it fires. I'm leaping through the air, diving for the car, and I hear it again, the pop-pop-pop in slow motion. This time they're muffled mid-air and accompanied by a bloodcurdling howl.

I turn in time to see the last rounds hit, just barely able to make out the shape of the old grey wolf spinning in the air, ragged pieces of fur and bone flying away from its side.

The animal hits the ground with a yelp, at the very same second that Bob yanks my collar against my throat and heaves me into the back of the jeep. The two younger Vargas brothers are reeling me in, holding me down into the seat as Bob clambers for a hold on the car. Jed is half-out of the car, reaching for him. I throw my own hand out and catch Bob's fingers just as the mass of villagers presses down on top of him. They're climbing over him, grabbing at the three of us in the back.

Jed is out of the jeep and swinging. "Bob!"

Fists flying left and right at his friends and neighbours. "Goddammmit, you let go of him!"

Bob is being pulled under. I can't hold him. I'm losing my grip.

Jed stomps a boot down on the mindless zombies clinging to Bob's back, and his fingers are gone.

I hop out, kicking and screaming, Jed and I both pulling

bodies off from the pile, while shrugging off clawing hands and grappling arms. A huge arm flies past my head. I turn and come face to mangled face with the bartender from the Victory. He's wearing the same torn Dead Kennedys shirt and is still seven feet of bad news. His eyes are misted with grey, and the snarl that contorts his face makes the scarred and paralyzed half of his head even more terrifying. His giant hands find my throat and heave me into the air, my feet dangling and kicking at nothing.

I feel the blood trapped in my head. He's going to pop me like an overgrown zit. My vision is swimming, and I'm struggling to stay awake, let alone alive. My feeble swats at his tree-trunk arms accomplish nothing. I catch something moving far off in my periphery, something that's not moving like a shambling meat-puppet. I put all of my strength into one hard twist, and I swing my legs out, catching the momentum at the top of the swing and reversing, heaving just far enough to pull the big biker off balance and move him two steps to the right, just as the bullet that was meant for my head explodes in a cascade of hot blood, bone, and soft, pink meat. His vice grip releases and we crumple together. I can hear McQueen cursing in the gloom, trying to reload his empty gun.

Jonah is screaming, "Go! Go! Go!", and I struggle to my feet. We each grab handfuls of buckskin and pull. I collapse into the jeep, still hanging on to Bob's shirt as I hack and cough, my throat raw and ragged and struggling to reopen itself. The jeep spits gravel as the tires find purchase, and Bob's feet drag behind us for the five seconds it takes us to haul him in like a big leather-clad tuna.

Jed and Jonah watch in disbelief as Main Street disappears into the wall of dust behind us.

Bob slumps beside me. "Holy shit." He pats me down, puts a finger to the blood on my face where Mary-Ellen Troll Doll had gouged and carved me. "You all right, kid?"

"Arthur," I say in disbelief. "He shot Arthur."

Bob looks at me with wet eyes and says nothing. He just pats a hand on my leg, but I can feel the hitch in his chest as he fights back his own tears.

I hang my head and stare in disbelief at the silver-headed cane lying at my feet.

32

EACH OF THE brothers grabs a bag from the back, as we all pile out of the jeep and stumble into the garage. Bob tells them to hole up and wait out the storm. He's limping on his left leg, and one side of his face is swollen and purple. I ask him if he's okay.

"Blood's on the inside, right?" he says. "Most of it."

I'm guessing that Magus will only have control as long as he stays in town. "He'll assume we're already headed for Bensonhall, and he'll want to cut us off at the pass."

"You're going to need help," Jonah says, stuffing bullets into rifles as his brothers pull the tow trucks up in front of the bay doors, locking the place down.

"So will everybody in town, your mom is out there. She might be hurt," Bob says. "I'll go with Finn. This ain't your fight."

"Bob is right," Jerry says, rushing in from the side door. "Whatever that guy did out there, it's almost cleared. If what Bob and Finn says is true, there's going to be a lot of confused, hurt, and pissed-off people over on Main Street."

I shake each of their hands as we leave, Jerry pulling me in close, strong arms around me, and his brothers follow suit, all three of them huddling in on me.

"You go kick that wizard's ass," Jed says, handing me a thermos. "All that was left."

MAYBE FIVE MINUTES have passed since we escaped Main Street. I'm behind the wheel, and Bob is in the back of the jeep, digging through duffel bags of ammo and guns, matching up what he can, loading and checking weapons as if he'd been doing it all his life.

"You said the Vargas boys' mother was back there?"

"Mary-Ellen. Runs the diner. I think I hit her with the rifle . . . by accident. Wasn't gonna tell them that."

A momentary whiff of raisin pie hits me. Jesus.

Bob lifts a complicated-looking death machine in his hands, twists some knobs and cranks that part underneath like he's Steven fucking Seagal.

"Did you learn that watching movies too?" I holler back to him.

He gives me a sly smile from the side of his face that doesn't look like he went three rounds with a Mack truck.

"I told you. Navy SEALs."

I watch him in the rear-view as we kick and bounce up the dirt road through the trees.

"There's no Navy SEALs in Canada. Is there?"

He winks at me.

"Shoot to kill, shoot to thrill, baby."

BOB TAPS MY shoulder and points where he wants me to go.

I pull the jeep in at the house in the woods. My father's house. My house. I rumble the thing around the back where the clothesline is still rusting in the yard. Bob hops out on his good leg and hobbles around the house, swinging his rifle in wide, slow arcs as he goes. Seeing the calm intensity, the eagle-eyed calculation, and the way he holds the gun, it's obvious that he wasn't kidding. Bob Dylan was a goddamn Navy SEAL, or whatever the Canadian equivalent is.

He makes with the hand signals again, two fingers to the eyes, then sweeps them across the perimeter. The fingers go to his chest, then point at the house. He does all this as his eyes are elsewhere, scanning every possible hiding place in the surrounding brush and forest. Bob climbs the back steps, lifts the gun in one hand, pointing to the sky, and tests the knob. As it turns, Bob freezes, stiffens, then catapults himself over the railing into the grass as the top half of the door explodes in a hail of splintering wood.

"Run, Finn!" he shouts and dives for the treeline.

McQueen is standing on the other side of the ruined door, a wide, wild-eyed grin on his face.

"Welcome home, little Finn!" he calls, levelling the shotgun from his hip and racking another load into the chamber.

I dive left as the ground explodes on my right. McQueen steps out into the light, racking the gun again.

"You stole my jeep, you mutt-dingo bastard. Putting up a good fight though. I do love me a challenge."

He steps out into the grass, his foul reek mixing with the smell of gunpowder to overpower the smell of the mouldering autumn forest.

"Your old man never had this kind of spirit, Finn. You know how he died?"

I'm scrabbling backwards in the grass, kicking the work boots off of my feet. I'm almost to the trees, wondering at the chances that I have enough time to change and make the leap to safe cover. Maybe I jump the other way. Rip this bastard's throat out and shut his mouth for good.

"You know that old joke about the bear taking a shit in the woods?" he says, creeping up. "I caught your daddy all alone with his pants down. I put a bullet right between his fuckin' eyes."

He lifts the shotgun and takes aim. I'm pulling at the buttons on the coveralls. The smoke is swirling, and my bones are twisting. The sky swims in circles. My feet are under me and my senses keened, just as the blast crashes through the air. It shatters a tree far to the left of me.

I turn with wolf eyes and watch Bob grappling with McQueen in the long grass. Bob has the shotgun pressed against McQueen's throat, pinning him to the ground. McQueen struggles and squirms, fighting to keep the hot metal off of his neck

"Go, goddammit! Raigan's! Go to Raigan's!"

I lunge forward, ready to tear McQueen to pieces. There's a fury behind my bloodlust. Something I don't quite fathom in this form, but I understand Bob's words.

Go. Raigan.

Run.

I PICK MY way through the trees, through the underbrush, until I catch the scent of the trail I'd run with the two little wolves. I run, leaping and bounding, faster and faster, green and orange and brown blurring in my eyes. I smell the stream at the top of the cliff, I hear the water rushing down. The familiar tang of apples, cinnamon, rich spices.

I splash across the stream and heel at the edge of the woods. The charms are gone, the trees scorched as if some strange flame had licked just this spot. There's no fire burning. No smell of charcoal and ash.

The unmistakable scent of sulfur and ammonia. Dead fish. Rotting oceans. Nothing that should be here.

I step carefully into the black remains of the little yard in front of Raigan's cabin. There is a tiny sound of life, somewhere inside. Ragged breathing and almost inaudible moans. If I had human ears I'd never hear it.

I sniff at the air inside the cabin. The evil stops at the door. The inside of the cabin is untouched, aside from a chair lying across the floor, a smashed cup in a puddle of brown tea, and the old woman dying in the corner.

I can smell the death on her. It's coming soon. Raigan is scorched like the outside of her house, hair singed away, skin mottled and flayed, black at the edges of a dozen oozing red patches that cover the majority of her face. I nudge her with my snout, and she cries out, a garbled mess of sound, more anguish than pain. She reaches a blistered hand to touch me behind the ears, running broken, gnarled fingers through my fur. It seems to calm her. She takes a shuddering breath in through what's left of her nose and coughs.

"Finn? Thank the mother!" The words sputter and fade as they leave her lips. She has minutes, maybe less. I will myself back into being, the room spinning out of focus and then clearing, the ghost of transformation seeping out of me and then sucked inside as my skin swallows up the fur, and I'm Finn again.

"Raigan," I say softly. "You're going to be okay." The panicked words of someone with no idea what else to say. I know she's dying. She knows it too.

A curdled laugh chokes out of her throat, and she clasps her ruined hands on mine.

"We both know that's not to be."

"What happened? Magus?"

"Julia brought him here. Took the boys. I tried . . ."

"They took the boys? Jules let him take them?" A red fever swells up into my eyes, and my head is pounding with blood. Panic and doubt are eclipsed by absolute fury. My hands tighten around hers, and she winces.

"How do I stop him?"

She coughs again, a red foam of spittle catching at the edges of her mouth.

"I felt his power, Finn. He's not ancient, but he has stolen so much power that is. He is death for the Strong Wolves."

A sliver of despair lodges in my heart like a knife, cold and hard.

"No. There has to be something. Some way. We can't all die for nothing."

She coughs again, and the blood comes thick and black, filling her mouth and drooling out into a pool beneath her. She spasms, tightening the grip on my hands. Her milky eyes widen and bulge.

"The secret! He wants the secret!" she shouts, her words gurgling and spitting from deep in her throat.

I pull her up from the floor, hoping to stem the choking gouts of blood that seem to be drowning her.

"*Strong wolves*!" she screams. "Strong. Wolves. Dressed of fur."

She grips my arm so hard that the bare tendons pop.

"*Fierce of teeth*!"

Aunty Raigan coughs once more, the black blood pooling at her lips, stagnant.

One more maiden lost athwart the gloom.

33

I LIFT RAIGAN from the floor and lay her across the thin mattress in one corner of her cottage. I drape her with a long knit afghan.

I sit, exhausted, defeated. Raigan is dead. Arthur is dead. Kevin and Jamie on their way to their doom, if they're not already dead too. Jules lost to the enemy. Bob left behind to fight the hunter. Sacrificing himself, for what? So I could come here and watch another one of us die. Emma . . .

Emma.

What had Magus said? *She belongs to me.* But there was something else, something lost in the nightmare of that storm that swallowed them all whole.

I close my eyes, see him floating over me, tumbling the world around us like a snowglobe. The winds swirling dust in every direction. A cyclone of confusion and noise. *Brought here to stud.* That's what he'd said. *One of my pets. She belongs to me.*

Impregnated.

Mated.

I CLOSE MY eyes again, reach out into the ether and try to find the third eye Raigan spoke of, the thing that connects me to Emma, the thing we share in our dreams. A window opens in my mind, a room cascading with white, echoes all around. Music. Not the light, airy tinkling of Arthur's playing. Loud, angry chords, hammering down, with a manic tinkling. I've heard it before. Russian. Something scary from a marionette show when I was little. A girl who dances herself to death. *The Rites of Spring*.

I step out into the dusk, running to the edge of the cliff, pink fading to purple above me, and I train my ears on the valley below. I hear it still, now a rolling procession of notes with a steady thump-thump-thump behind it. They're in the big house. In Arthur's parlour. Emma is there, right now.

One breath as I turn, and the change is already upon me. My body changes as I move, the smoke of one body trailing after me as I bound down the trail in the other. My legs carry me fast, charging down the cliff face, across the woods, and to the edge of the clearing. The music growing louder and more terrible as I get closer. A madman's terrifying interpretation of something beautiful. It hurts my ears, and I want to yowl out against it, but I stay quiet and low to the ground, creeping around to the furthest cabin, the cabin where Kevin and Jamie live, sniffing at the air for some trace of them. There is nothing but the faded remnants of their presence. The next cabin yields the same results, the vague remembrance of Jules, but no sign of life.

I feel my hackles rise as I step carefully past McQueen's cabin, the stench of him filling my nostrils, but a stale version of it that tells me he's no longer there either. Which leaves only one place for me to go. The big house.

I steal in from behind the house, past the mechanical shed, the ammonia and machine-oil smell making me swing wide into the trees. I come to the back wall with my eyes up to the open window of the parlour, the strange and unpleasant hammering of piano keys still filling the night around me.

The side of the house is dark and quiet. I step carefully from the shadows, testing the air for the foul odours of either of my enemies. Soft-padded paws climb the steps onto the wide porch, but it's human hands that open the door, and I step into the dim expanse of the front foyer naked and unprotected. I catch the faintest whiff of McQueen, hidden under layers of chemical.

He hits me full force from behind, and I'm caught, breath forced out in a blast underneath the weight of him.

I struggle to free my arms enough to reach him, his knee in the middle of my back, strong arms twisting my own behind me. He pins them with his knees and twists his weight to dig his kneecap as far into my spine as possible.

"Didn't see that coming? Oldest trick in the book, mate. Give you my scent, let you get used to it, set it in your tiny little dog-brain, then I cover it up with something stronger, and you couldn't sniff me out if I was right on top of you." He laughs. "Which I fucking am!"

I groan and squirm, but he has me. I will myself to smoke and hope the change will let me slip out from under him. The pain in my shoulders comes in blasts of hot fear, the arms twisted away from the sockets, tendons and ligaments screaming. I can't focus. I close my eyes and pray for the smoke to swallow me up and set me free.

"Not this time!" He spits and shoves my face into the floor, his other hand deftly sliding under my throat. A hot band of thick leather closes around my neck with a snap, and my will to fight is gone.

McQueen is up on his feet. I see his legs in front of me and, deep inside, I want to attack. I want to turn and sink my teeth into them, twist and feel the bones snap, see the red burst forth as the jagged splinters tear through the skin. The thoughts are far off and fuzzy, like trying to remember a dream. The inside of my head is filled with grey mist. It clouds everything. I just want to close my eyes against it—not move, not think—just close my eyes and sleep.

"Get up, you fucking mutt," McQueen snarls. He swings his foot back and drives it straight into my belly. I feel the impact, feel myself lift up off of the floor and fall hard back against the wood of the floor. I feel my stomach lurch. I feel the bile burn up through my throat and explode out of my mouth. I can feel it, wet, on the side of my face. I can smell it, acid and old blood. I lay in it. Broken.

There's a tug at the back of my neck, the leather band pulls tight at my throat, and I obey. I climb to my feet, stand, and wait for McQueen to show me the way. Inside I'm screaming. Wailing. Thrashing my fists against the walls.

Kill him! Tear him to pieces!

What are you waiting for?

My feet, my legs, they move all on their own, against every impulse I'm sending from my own brain.

McQueen leads me outside and into the shed. The chemical stink is fierce and brings tears to my eyes as soon as he opens the door and shoves me in ahead of him.

He loops the end of the long chain around one of the dull metal pipes and fishes a padlock out of his pocket.

"You're a tough one, I'll give you that. I thought I'd cut ya in two this morning. Then I had you dead to rights twice again, and both times you managed to slip me."

He may have doused himself in pool chemicals to cover the zoo stink, but his breath is still a foul mixture of mould and stale whiskey.

The door opens behind us, and I hear the jangle of more chains.

"Chain them up together," Simon Magus says from behind me, his voice low and velvet smooth.

Jules passes in front of me, haggard and naked and cowering into the corner opposite me. Her hair is a straggled mess of filthy straw, and she keeps her face buried behind her hands, twitching as she walks, as if she's hurt, or has been hurt enough for a lifetime. McQueen ties her chain around the same pipe and locks us together.

Magus steps in front of me, hands behind his back, chest out, chin up. He stares down his long face at me, and deep in the fog I imagine the snap of cartilage as I bite through the ridge of that nose, feeling the blood burst into the back of my throat as he screams for mercy.

It's only a dream. A distant, hollow dream of revenge, playing on a loop somewhere in my memory. The only response my body has to him is a hard swallow of the lump of bile-and-blood infused phlegm that seems lodged in my windpipe.

Magus grips my face in his long fingers, the metal of his rings sending motes of grey mist swimming up to join with the ones already swirling in front of my vision. He leans in close, his own cherrywood-tinted irises alive with flame.

"Took you long enough, McQueen. This one should have hardly been so much trouble. Weak and foolish. Practically a virgin."

Magus slaps my face, almost playfully, and steps back, swirling the tails of his long black coat aside as he perches on the white pvc conduit facing me.

"You have no idea what you are, do you? The power that you lousy curs represent, and you act as if it's some familial *quirk*." His mysterious deck of playing cards appear in his hands, cutting and flipping as those long chicken-bone fingers twist and twirl.

"I began this road more than a century ago. I chased your great-great grandfather across the continent. Him and his *brood*. I was a boy, a *Mormon* son, if you can believe it, when the Strong Wolves killed my father. He went into the woods after the beasts that stole our cattle, and he came out crippled, faithless, and mad."

I see it in my head, shrouded in fog, as if it's playing on a drive-in screen. A boy, thin and frail, wide-eyed in terror at his father's bedside, the old man, beard crusted with blood and spittle, mumbling of the devil and the creatures of the night.

"The tales were fantastic and terrifying—men becoming wolves, running wild in the forest and devouring our herd.

"My father was despondent after witnessing what he called 'the Devil's spawn'. He was violent. Disturbed. He drowned my mother, my brother, and my baby sister in the river beside our homestead. I alone escaped his madness. I watched from the very woods where your family had destroyed him. I watched him douse himself in kerosene and set the house alight. I listened to him scream for nearly an hour before I put him out of his misery."

The cards keep flipping and flipping. My eyes combine the two worlds, the constant ebb and flow of the cards in his hand over the smell of burning flesh, and the little boy with the shotgun on the movie screen in my mind.

"I was lost, alone," he continues, "wandering in the mountains of Utah. I was taken by a band of savages—Apaches—I'll save you the list of indignities I suffered at their hands. Suffice it to say, the remainder of my childhood was spent in chains of one kind or another. Eventually, destiny put me in the hands of a pagan enchantress in New Orleans."

He reaches his free hand out toward Jules, still shivering under the pipe we've been chained to. Like an obedient pet, she crawls to his side, still hiding her face. Magus runs his long fingers into her hair, rubbing at her scalp and behind her ears absently as he tells his tale.

"She taught me many things, my lovely Gaelic witch, including the truth of the monsters that had been the ruination of my family. She gave me the rudimentary skills of my craft—sleight of hand, illusion—simple spells that allowed me to amass wealth and the meagre power that most men crave. I left the past behind me. I became a very successful prestidigitator in Victoria's England. I travelled the world, seeking more power, more knowledge, more *magic*.

"What I found, when I had discovered all that there was to be discovered, was that Life truly does move in the circles of destiny. The one true, great mystery of the ages."

Magus wraps his fingers around tufts of Jules' blonde hair, matted and dirty, and yanks her head back, pulling her face up toward him, showing the ruin they've made of her. He looks down at her, at the jagged wound that starts above her right eyebrow, white bone showing through the pink flesh, running halfway down her cheekbone. Her eyelid is peeled away, the dazzling emerald eye that had looked so much like my own is gone. All that remains is a bloody pit, empty and dark with blood and dirt. Her remaining eye is dull and grey, silently pleading for mercy from her master. She's wearing a thick leather collar, with a silver plate sewn in the front. It has some kind of symbols carved into it. I imagine my own collar is the same.

Magus raises his eyes to McQueen, still standing behind me at the door.

"Your technique leaves something to be desired, Mister McQueen. Still . . ." Magus releases his grip on Jules and impossibly crumples the deck of cards into his fist, opening it to reveal a white glob, red tendrils snaking away from the back, an emerald green circle, glassy and wet in the centre. "The end result is that I will have what I desire."

He holds the eyeball in front of him, up to my face, so that it stares deep into my own emerald eyes, past the fog, and Simon Magus speaks inside of my head, whispering in the deepest parts of me, seeping into every open space, letting me know that he controls every last cell in my body by trampling over them all at once.

Do you know what the secret is, Finn?

His voice is everywhere. Inside of me. Surrounding me. It *is* me.

The secret of how to live forever.

34

"You see, Finn," Magus says, closing his fist around the eyeball, taking his voice out of my head and into his own mouth, "Once I understand how you were made in the first place, who will be able to stop me from using that power? From enslaving whole countries, whole continents? From living on into eternity as the master of all creation?"

He opens the fist and shows me his empty palm.

"Saint Patrick himself, the greatest wizard of the first century, he was the one who cursed you. Two-thousand years ago. He went to Ireland to convert the pagan heathens. What he actually did was steal the secrets of the Druids." He stops his monologue and peers into the mist over my eyes again. He's enjoying himself now. Proving his superiority, his master intelligence. "While there, he encountered the resistance of a small tribe known as the *Laegnach Faelad*, whom the island was named for. History barely remembers them now, I'm afraid. Down the centuries they were maligned as cannibals, baby killers, wild fiends who would steal your children by night. Something akin to the Viking berserkers. Really, they were just another band of filthy Irish cavemen. Their real importance is in their rebellion against Patrick. He cursed them, you see, to become the monsters they were rumoured to be. He cursed them to change by night, by moon, to become wild dogs and ravage the countryside.

Werewolves."

Magus slaps my face, hard, and my head snaps against the pipe behind me with a clang. I feel almost nothing. "Do you understand? He changed them. Forever. Cursed not a single man, or a living group of people. He cursed a bloodline. *How?* How did he do it? The secret is lost to the ages."

My body may be useless, and my mind may be clouded in black, but I still hear him. I still see him. His little trick, forcing his way into my mind, has opened something up. He's taken some of the mist with him when he left. My senses are returning. I can feel his arrogance, and I'm rebelling against it, from the inside out.

He paces in front of me, unable or unwilling to leave off without explaining his brilliance. He is most certainly the smartest man in the room. He looks older. The more he talks and the more he turns in tiny circles, distracted by his own explanations, his true age begins to show. He no longer seems like a gangly thirty-year-old playing at being a moody goth teenager. The more he rambles and swaggers and explains, the more he reveals what he is. He's a ghost. Thin paper skin wrapped tight around a skeleton of dust. He's held together by his own magic, a terrible, decrepit mummy, wrapped in the strips of another man's skin.

I watch his jaw move and his bones dance around as he continues to pace the room. If I had control of my voice, I would scream.

"All of you fools, so far removed from your own history, your own creation, you can't possibly give me any insight into the magic that made you. I need to start fresh, with the newborn pup, as it were. None of you are half the killer that your predecessors were. Your instincts are lost to you, no more than mongrels born of mongrels, generations removed from anything that resembles your true nature. Your children, though . . ."

Magus turns to wrap his skeleton fingers around my face once more, turning my eyes to his as a terrible, wide grin splits his face, leaving me with the image of a fiery skull, burning its way into my soul.

"Your children will be those demon hounds of legend. I'll see to that. And when they've revealed Saint Patrick's curse to me, and they've served their purpose as servants, experiments, and playthings, I'll happily toast the death of your line as I watch the last of your progeny burn."

My feet and my fingers tingle and pulse, but I still can't will them to move. I watch, helpless, as Simon Magus turns his back on me, swirling his coat behind him as he exits the shed.

"Bring her to me when the deed is done. I need to make sure it takes. Who knows how much you've damaged her."

"I never once used the front door," McQueen says, "just like you told me."

"Just be sure they procreate. No more mistakes, Mister McQueen."

"I'll grease her myself, boss." He makes a clicking sound in his throat, and the door closes.

McQueen slides up close behind me, whispers in my ear. "You ready to get it up, boy?"

He puts a hand under Jules' arm, pulls her to her feet. His other hand holds the big knife that nearly gutted me. He twirls it in front of her face, and she cringes. He smiles at me. A filthy, rot-toothed smile.

"You like what I've done, eh? She put up quite a fight, but, in the end . . ." He slaps the broad side of the knife over one eye and laughs like a maniac.

"She's nice and docile-like now though, isn't she?" He reaches inside his leather vest and pulls something long and black from inside.

"You ever heard the joke about the Indian? Goes into the bar, asks all the nice white ladies there, *tickle your cunt with a feather?*" He laughs again and plays the feather around her face, Jules squirming and twisting against his grip. "Aww yeah! Still got a little life in her! Don't worry, girlie. I'm gonna show you one last good time, before your cousin here gets his turn."

Jules struggles against him, trying to escape.

"And after you pop out them puppies, I'm gonna use you up, then gut you like I did your Daddy, and your Mama, and those two little bastard brothers of yours. Then I would have done me the whole pack. Maybe I'll use ya for matching luggage!"

He lets go of her arm and waves the black feather in front of my face. "You like it? Got it off your friend, the Big Chief, when I buried my knife in his chest. Cooed like a baby, he did." His rank breath of mushrooms and dog-shit splashes over my face and soaks through the fog. Inside, my body is shaking, thrashing against the chains, desperate to hold McQueen's throat in my teeth. I try my fingers again and am rewarded with a twitch. Another couple of hours I might be able to move enough to flip him off.

"Big ol' Indian Chief, wasn't much of a . . ."

There's a clamour outside the door, the sound of someone stumbling through a field of empty cans. Raccoons on the prowl. I hear the sound of birds—crows—lighting nearby in the trees. A lot of them.

McQueen's head whips toward the door.

"The fuck is that?" He growls and slides the knife into its sheath, replacing it with a pistol from the holster at his back.

"Don't you two start without me," he whispers, slapping my face with his dirty hand.

The door creaks open behind me, McQueen takes a few steps in the soft earth. There's a high-pitch whistle, followed by another, a shriek, and the report of McQueen's pistol firing into the night. Something crashes from the doorway, and McQueen crawls across the floor in front of me, dragging his own bloody legs behind him, two slender arrows protruding from his knee joints. I can see two inches of wood sticking out the back of his legs. There are two smeared paths of blood trailing from them to the door.

"Fuck!" he screams. "Don't you come in here, you bastard! I'll kill 'em both!"

He has the big knife out and is clawing to get a purchase on any one of Jules' limbs. She crawls into the shadows, as far as the chain will allow. I feel hands at the back of my neck. The tension at my throat loosens, the strap removed, and I fall to my knees with a gasp as all of my senses are returned to me, clear and full. The world rushes in with the air, and the fog comes out in a hacking cough, deep and rough, from the centre of my chest. It burns like fire coming up, then dissolves when it hits the fresh night air.

McQueen lunges and grabs my arm, pulling it out from beneath me and bringing me face first into the concrete floor.

"I'll cut him!" he screams. "I swear, I'll fucking cut him!"

Jules is just out of my reach. I put a hand out toward her. I say her name, coaxing her to come closer. McQueen has my leg, pulled tight against him, screaming at someone behind me. The way he's holding me, I can't turn, and I can't get free. My only chance is to reach Jules.

She edges closer. Closer.

"Please, Jules."

Closer.

"Please."

I stretch my fingers as far they will reach, and I hook them into the collar at her neck, pulling with everything I have left to bring her close enough to reach the clasp on the back. I'm fumbling, twisting at metal, praying to find the mechanism.

McQueen is still screaming. "I'll cut his fucking balls off!"

I feel the point of the knife right at the edge of my thigh, digging in close, a centimetre away from my testicles. He's twisting the tip into me, and I feel an excruciating sting and the hot dribble of fresh blood.

My fingers are trembling. Jules is pulling against me. I don't dare twist or fight any more than I am.

McQueen paws at me with his free hand, trying to pull me back toward him. The collar gives as he sinks the blade an inch deep in the inside of my thigh, and I howl in pain. I lurch back, and he pulls me down in front of him, a human shield.

There's a sound of leaves crackling behind us, a low growl. McQueen's arm goes rigid around my chest. His body stiffens underneath me, and he swings the knife away from my legs, holds it at my throat. We both look into the shadows to see one emerald eye, gleaming from the darkness. He drops the knife, and something warm floats across my back.

Big hands reach out and pull me to my feet as McQueen's screams are muffled by teeth and fur, eclipsed by the sound of bones cracking. She tears his bottom jaw off, his tongue and his throat coming loose with a strong twist of her head, and the screaming stops. Now there's only the sound of blood.

35

I TURN AND bury my face in the wide chest of Bob Dylan's buckskin shirt, throw my arms around him and squeeze.

He wheezes and squeaks like a broken rubber duck, and buckles under my weight.

"Awww, hell," he groans, and I catch him as he falls.

"Bob? Bob!" As I stretch him out on the floor for the shed, I see that he's soaked through with blood in at least four places. One pant leg is black and completely saturated from a wide gash across his thigh.

The sound of Jules tearing into the carcass that used to be McQueen continues behind me. I turn and crouch, crab-walking around the opposite side of him, keeping as much distance between myself and the wolf as possible.

She looks up at me with her one gleaming eye, bares teeth covered in blood and flesh, and returns to her vengeance meal. The feet of a hundred birds batter and claw at the tin roof. The clamour is deafening.

I dig in McQueen's pockets, come up with nothing but a lighter and a tiny, sticky bottle of lube. There's something round, and hard, in his other pocket. I reach carefully underneath gnashing teeth and slip my fingers into his other pocket. I grip it tight in my hand, the cold white jade filling me with resolve. Calming my nerves. Reminding me of who I came here to be.

I pick up the knife and think about cutting McQueen's pants away, cutting them into strips for bandages or tourniquets. One sniff and I know they'd be more likely to kill Bob than the blood loss.

I lift Bob enough to peel away the buckskin shirt and lift the necklaces and charms from his neck. Most of them are on leather straps. I strip the longest necklace of its beads, silently apologizing to whatever Gods or Spirits I might be offending, and quickly run it around Bob's leg, above the gash, cinching it tight until the blood stops oozing from the wound.

I'm so lost in trying to remember my eighth-grade emergency survival class, I don't realize that Jules has changed back until the batter of feet against the roof turns quiet and I hear her weeping behind me.

She's on her knees, in front of what's left of McQueen, her face in her hands, sobbing.

"What have I done? What have I done? What have I done?"

She's rocking slowly as she says it, repeating her mantra of guilt over and over.

She trembles as I put my hand against her shoulder.

"It's okay, Jules. You saved me. You saved us. He got what he deserves."

She turns her face to me, a jagged scar where the open wound had been, but there's still only a hollow pit where her eye should be. The shock of it must show on my face. She drops her gaze and turns away again.

"He deserves much worse. So do I."

"Jules," I say, wadding Bob's shirt up to place under his head. "We're in a load of deep shit here. Magus is going to kill us, he's already . . ." I stop, knowing that me not saying the words won't change it, knowing that she already hears it in my voice.

"I heard what he said. They're all dead. Because of me. My parents. Your dad. Raigan. Now Jamie and Kev . . ." Her voice cracks on the last two names.

"Arthur." I don't know why I say it. She's had enough. I can hear the defeat, the self-loathing, in her voice. I know the sound of it all too well, from years of my own misery. She doesn't need any more tombstones piled on her back. I guess I say it to make it real.

I twist another leather strap under Bob's left arm, where a

ragged slice of flesh is missing, and a deep cut shows white beneath carved muscle. He groans and tries to lift his head.

"Shhhh. It's okay, Bob. You're going to be okay." He swats at me with his other arm. He knows I'm lying. How much blood can a regular person have inside of them? Most of Bob's is on the floor underneath him.

Blood's on the inside, right? Isn't that what he said? Not this time.

"Boys," he croaks at me. "Ain't dead."

Jules throws me out of the way before the words are out of his mouth. She's right on top of Bob. Her one eye trained on his lips. "What did you say? Where?" She shakes him. "Where the fuck are they?"

Bob coughs and sucks a shallow breath that whistles somewhere inside of him. I notice little pink bubbles of foam in the bloody spot around his ribs.

"Get off of him!" I grab her around the waist and lift her off of the floor, off of Bob, as she kicks and thrashes, clawing at my arms. I shove her toward the door.

She turns and growls at me, teeth bared, looking feral and dangerous, wild rage burning in that one green eye like a forest of flame.

I hold her gaze with my own, not flinching. I stare her down. No more games.

"Enough."

Her shoulders hunch around her neck, and she crouches, ever-so-slightly, ready to pounce. Her muscles tighten, and her fists ball at her chest. I remember her doing the same thing in the back room of the Victory. There she looked like an angry mythical goddess. Now she looks like a mad witch, naked, dirty, caked with blood.

"Jules." I try to make the words calm, but strong. If I back down from her, she'll attack. I need her on my side. I can't face Magus alone. I know that. *All three.* That's what Raigan said.

"Bob says that Kev and Jamie are alive. We need to help Bob so he can tell us where they are."

She tenses again, lips curling up over her teeth. I know the face.

Her chest is heaving with anger. I know the feeling.

"I'm not telling you. I'm asking you. Please, Jules. Help me."

Her breathing softens, hardly enough to notice, but I feel her temperature drop. I see the flush fade from her face, and her fists release enough that her fingers take colour again.

BOB IS STILL struggling for breath, a spatter of pink foam forming around the wound in his side. I check the other gashes and cuts, none of them pouring blood the way they had been. I just hope it's from my nursing skills, and not that he's almost out of time.

Jules kneels next to me, fingering the tiny hole where the pink foam is bubbling.

"We need something to seal this. There's some plastic sheet over there." She points to the other side of the shed. "Go cut me a piece big enough to cover this hole. A little bit bigger."

I do as I'm told, and when I return, Jules has a small pail of water and is washing the foam away, pouring water over the wound, and then we watch as the rivulets of water change from clear to red. It shows her where the damage is, and she smooths the plastic over it, pressing my hand against it to hold it in place.

"Keep the pressure on. And give him some water, if you can wake him up."

She moves to the other side of Bob, checking my handiwork, tightening the tourniquet on his leg, then dousing it with water from the bucket.

"This one's the worst, this and the hole in his chest. He might be okay if we can get him down the mountain."

"Thank you." I put my hand on top of hers.

"I'm sorry," she offers, but she pulls her hand away. "All of this. This is my fault. I believed him. I let him use me against you all. I let them destroy my family. Our family."

I pull her close to me, feeling the heat of her skin against mine, and I brush the thick mess of blood-stained hair away from her face. "I thought it was Magus, and McQueen, that tricked me into coming here. It wasn't. I made that decision. It took a long time to realize it, but you're born what you're meant to be. I spent so long pretending to be something I'm not, blaming everyone else, being angry at myself, at them, at the world. I thought I was going crazy."

I pick up the little jade statue from the floor.

"I thought I was a monster."

She takes the bauble from my hand, holds it up to her face.

Examines it. "What is it?"

"It means *hero*. Somebody gave me that for saving someone he loved. I didn't realize that's what I was doing at the time. I've been a goddamn werewolf for about a week now, and I find out it's my birthright, that I'm destined to be with the little pig-tailed girl I only remember from dreams of my distant childhood. I have a town full of cousins, an uncle with a mansion on top of a mountain, and a crazy hobbit-witch aunt who lives in the woods. Most of those people are dead, days after I've just met them. There's a two-hundred-year-old wizard in my ancestral home, threatening my unborn children and the woman who may be my soul-mate, and the only thing close to a father that I've ever known is dying in front of me."

I close her hand around the statue, hold it tight in my own.

"I've spent the better part of thirty years being the monster, and a week being a hero."

I lift her up off of the floor with me, still holding her hands in mine around the little statue.

"I'm not giving up now that I know who I am. Neither should you. You're not Simon Magus' bitch. You're a Strong Wolf."

THE BIRDS CRY out from the trees outside, the thunderous clatter beginning on the roof again. Jules makes the door in two steps. She falls to her knees, laughing. A sweet, infectious laughter. Something I wouldn't have imagined. She's rolling on the ground, half out the door, two little wolves nuzzling at her neck. The jade statue still held tight in one hand.

36

MOMENTS LATER, THE boys are helping us lift Bob from the floor and out into the yard.

"Bob found us," Jamie tells me of their escape.

"We weren't scared," Kev adds. "Simon did something to us. We couldn't move."

"McQueen was going to hurt us, but Simon told him he had to wait. He said we were insurance."

"We knew you'd come back, Finn."

"Bob said you'd save us."

I smile at them, silently thanking Bob for being more of a hero than any of us could hope to be.

I can hear the piano, tinkling some far-off tune, something old and western. The kind of folk-song everybody knows, but can't place. Like "Camptown Races", but slower.

Jules runs silent through the grass, hardly more than a shadow, and one of the SUVs rumbles to life, backing slowly across the gravel, the red lights burning like twin suns in the darkness.

We slide Bob across the back seat, and Kevin gets in beside him.

Jamie climbs in and pulls the driver's seat up as far as it will move. He pushes the button to lower it until the motor grinds and whirrs, with nowhere left to go.

"We can help you fight him," Kevin pleads.

"Yeah," Jamie says. "We'll take Bob down and bring reinforcements."

"People from town."

"The Vargas brothers," they say in unison.

Jules leans into the car, pulls Kevin's head down toward her, and kisses his forehead.

I give him a nod and shut the door, as Jules comes behind me to kiss her other brother.

"Just be careful. Get Bob to the garage so they can get him some help. You don't want to bring anybody else up here. Trust me," I warn them, thinking of Mary-Ellen's demon-face, and the big biker's brains splattering my face.

"Listen to Finn," Jules tells them. "You stay at the garage until I come get you."

"Okay," the boys say together.

"I love you," Jules tells them, and a strange warm look comes over their faces.

"Now *go*!" she whispers, and they roll off toward the little bridge.

"SHOULDN'T WE GET some guns, or something? Go back up to Raigan's? Find some kind of weapons?" Jules says as we step up onto the porch. She looks down at her feet. "I mean, we're naked."

She looks me up and down, a gesture that is exaggerated by her compensating for her lost eye.

"And you're still bleeding."

I nod. "Not for long."

"So that's your whole master plan? We turn into big bad wolves and attack the powerful sorcerer with our teeth?"

I recite the poem. In its entirety, possibly for the first time.

From the South
Three sisters fair
Ran athwart the gloom
Dressed of fur
And fierce of tooth
The maidens of the moon

"Do you know it?" I ask.

"Aunty Raigan used to tell us that when we were little. It's just some old rhyme."

"It's the secret of our power. She was trying to tell me. *Three sisters fair* running *athwart the gloom.*"

"That asshole would have needed to get you a couple inches higher for you to be a *sister*, Finn."

I fix her with a hard glare.

"It's not literally sisters. It means family. Our family. And *fair* means *good*, not just light-coloured. *Athwart the gloom.* Family. Our family, fighting against evil. Against darkness."

"Dark magic. The silver charms, the same as Raigan's, but with his magic in them. That's what the collar was for?"

"To keep us from changing. *Dressed of fur and fierce of tooth.* This whole thing is about him wanting the power behind that transformation. He's afraid of it. He doesn't understand it, so he can't control it. Even like this, in human form, we're more powerful than normal people. As wolves, together, we may be strong enough to kill him."

Jules turns her head slightly, to get a better look at me, doubtless questioning the logic behind my theory.

"I watched him turn the whole of Pitamont into a rampaging horde of mindless killers," I explain. "He didn't have to clamp a collar on any of them. He wasn't playing any games, trying to manipulate them into going along with him. Forty people under his spell with no more than a whisper—*while* he was causing a sandstorm, making himself look twelve feet tall, and pinning me up like a voodoo doll. Why can't he do that here?"

She shrugs, but I see the wheels turning. She's a witch too, after all, she must have some idea how these things are done.

"And why is he so terrified of anyone turning? Why did he need to keep you and Emma under his control? McQueen did all of his dirty work when there were Strong Wolves involved. Simon Magus may be perfectly capable of terrorizing humans and sneaking around in the dark . . ."

It crosses her ravaged face like the coming dawn. Somehow her beauty is even more stark and terrifying in its loss of symmetry.

"He's scared of us."

"You heard the story about his father. Of course, he's scared of us. *We* are the boogeyman, not him, and his magic won't work on us in wolf form—*dressed of fur and fierce of tooth*—especially if all three of us work together."

"*The maidens of the moon.*"

I smile wide and full.

"Exactly. Bob called him *Skinkuk.* He's a coyote. A trickster. A scavenger. A fucking pretender. We're the real thing."

I feel as if I've swallowed the moon and its power and light are seeping out of every pore. I know my power now. It comes from this place, from these people. It comes from me. I am a hero, and it's time to prove it.

"I can still hear the piano. They must be in the parlour. He'll want to keep her close and keep her safe now that she's . . ."

"She's pregnant, Finn. Congratulations," Jules says coldly. "There's only one way up and around that hall. One door in. If we can sneak up on him . . ."

I have the urge to use Bob's Navy SEAL signs, but there's no real plan and no options other than what has already been said. Instead, I take a deep breath through my nose and wait for the fur.

QUIET

Is the thought shared between us, as we step careful across the parquet floor, claws scratching lightly at the glossy finish. A creak in the top of the house freezes us both, mid-stride, and my nose goes to the air, seeking out the scents of sulfur and fish, smells I know as evil and dangerous. All I smell is the house. The lingering hint of burnt bacon from the kitchen, the pine and cedar of the walls, Emma's scent of vanilla and chocolate. The piano continues to play from the parlour. From the edge of the stairs we can see the flickering of candles from inside the room.

Jules is halfway up the staircase when I notice the skip in the tune. The same five notes repeated, the scratch of a record needle bouncing.

His voice comes from the wide room at the front of the house, the room behind me.

"I'm afraid there's no dogs allowed in the house."

He's standing by the window, posed in the shadows, using the darkness to play up his size and power. More theatrics from the Victorian magician. Emma is seated in a chair beside him, neck held high and stiff under the leather collar, Raigan's moon medallion swelling from the centre of it.

With wolf eyes I can see farther into the gloom. Past his magic.

Simon Magus is an old man. Wrinkled and stooped, sparse white hair standing in thickets on his spotty head. He's weak and afraid. I smell his fear. So does Jules.

Kill

Is the one thought I catch as the flash of yellow and grey bounds past me into the dark of the room.

I follow, and we leap toward him, both aiming for the chest, bring him down to the ground then tear him apart.

We find nothing but space. A wisp of grey and he's gone, laughing. Jules crashes down on top of me with a yelp, and I scramble out from beneath her and across the floor, finding room to breathe and turn before I reassess my surroundings. The room is empty, save the two of us, and Magus' laughter bounces from the walls and the ceiling, penning us in with its overwhelming rush of noise.

The music still plays from the parlour underneath it all.

They're not here at all. It's a trap, a distraction.

Smoke rolls across the ceiling above us, a blast of heat and a tsunami wave of sound and air that crashes through everything around us. The furniture flies overhead, splintering against the walls. The windows explode with the crash of a thousand cymbals. A blast of thunder followed by a tinkling rain.

Jules is shaking beside me, back bowed and lips curled, swinging her head in manic circles, one eye wide and panicked. I nip at her hind leg and nod toward the door.

We step carefully around the scattered contents of the room, ignoring the raging heat of the fire now licking at us from every surface. As we come out to the foyer, I can see the black scorch marks where the explosion has disintegrated the kitchen. A gaping hole feeds flame and grey smoke out into the night. The floor shimmers with heat.

There's a huge creaking to our left, and we drop lower, splaying our legs as the stairs come away from the walls, and crumble into tinder. The whole house is ablaze and coming down on top of us. The smoke thick and choking the air. He means for us to burn.

There is another crash and boom above us. The embers begin to fall like hail, spitting down and singeing our backs. The roar is immense, the rocket launch sound of a thousand dragons croaking demon-flame, as our castle burns down around us. The hail becomes chunks of plaster and the clatter of roasting boards hitting the floor, crackling and exploding.

I nudge Jules forward, toward the door, our only chance of escape. One more thunderous crack erupts above us, and I turn my head to the flaming sky just as it falls upon our heads. The beam comes so close to my face that it burns the short hairs on the end of my snout. Jules staggers back, just as the ceiling falls on top of me. Stars burst in my head, and all of my air is replaced by liquid fire.

Darkness creeps in at the edges of my vision, and I fall through the floor into a deep, black void.

37

I FEEL THE weight on top of me shifting. It grinds across my broken ribs, pushing down again. Something sharp inside of me digs deeper into the hole it's made, and I want to scream, but I'm gulping thick air that burns my chest and my throat. The weight shifts again, and there is a cry, a wail like someone giving birth. I open my eyes, and Jules is standing over me, arms smoking, skin sizzling against the red-hot glow of the timber she's lifting off of me. I smell bacon. The weight lifts, and my breath comes, deep and hot, burning hot. I try to crawl, but my paws are just scratching at nothing. I think I'm dying.

The beam crashes to the floor next to me in a cloud of smoke and cinder.

Her arms are sliding under me, lifting me to her chest. I can feel her heart beating, powerful and fast. She swings me backwards as she twists and charges the door, the hinges giving way with a pop, and we crash out into the night air, Jules on top of the door, me on top of Jules. I try to twist away, to move off of her, but I can't. She's up in one more heartbeat, and she lifts me again, her long human legs taking long strides, despite the wolf in her arms who is almost as big, certainly as heavy, as she is.

She doesn't stop until we're at the wooden bridge.

Jules falters, stumbles to her knees, and I slump into the grass, tortuously close to the cool water of the stream. All I want is to put my tongue in that water, lap up the clean, cool feeling into my mouth, into my throat, soothing the swollen, blistered skin, and washing away the pain.

Jules lies beside me, heaving heavy breaths, before she rolls over and vomits into the grass.

After a few seconds, she rolls to her stomach and pushes herself up. Regarding me with concern.

"Change back, stupid."

I can't. I want to tell her. *I can't*.

"Finn. You have to change to heal."

I watch as she twists and spins in ribbons of smoke. Not smoke. Smoke destroys. She becomes air, and moonlight.

She nudges me with her snout.

Change.

As if it's that simple.

Change.

Why doesn't she understand? I'm broken. Killed. Waiting to die.

Change.

She morphs and whirls back into form, long and pale and smooth. The blisters and mottled, ruined skin are healed. Even the scars on her face are thinner, less pronounced. She'll never grow back the eye though.

The things inside of me twitch, knives sinking deeper into places they were never meant to be. A trembling whine escapes my throat. I taste blood.

"You were right, Finn. I like being a hero a whole hell of a lot more than being the bad guy."

She runs a hand through my fur. Scratching behind my ears.

"This is going to hurt," she says, rolling me onto my back and straddling me.

She closes her one green eye and begins to recite strange words, her head bowed in concentration, long blonde hair hanging in waves, tickling at my lips.

I feel heat from between her legs on my belly. I feel her muscles tighten as the incantation becomes louder, faster, more intense. Her heat begins to spread, swarming out from my belly, a thousand ants running under my skin, crawling into every deep part of me, tingling and itching. I yelp and twist beneath her, desperate to scratch them out. I scream inside my head, and it comes from my throat as another whine, begging to be free.

Jules is screaming now, head raised to the heavens, calling out to the moon in some strange, ancient language.

The broken things inside me are melting. The knives are yanked free. I feel like a boiling pot of soup inside, roiling and bubbling. The heat and the itch are inseparable, insufferable. They're going to drive me mad. I squirm beneath her again, but she holds me down, as my insides collapse and liquefy and are reborn and my body screams out in excruciating agony.

The chanting stops. Jules falls away from me, exhausted. I curl up into a ball of bone and blood and fur, wishing she'd just left me to die, pinned under that smouldering beam.

My muscles finally give in to their destruction, and I lose control of what's left of my body. Shaking, twitching. Convulsions take hold and shake me so hard that I bite through my tongue, a fresh spout of hot blood filling my mouth as fireworks explode behind my eyes and fade to black.

Then I hear his voice. Simon Magus. Far off, diffused. The third eye—the dream eye—opens, and I see him, climbing in front of me, scrabbling through the rocks, cursing under his breath. He's shrouded in fog, the corners of the dream filled with dismal grey.

"Damn this infernal place!" He looks back toward me, yanks at something between us—a long metal chain—pulling at my neck. No, not my neck. Emma's neck.

"Move, you stupid bitch!"

I feel the pull of the chain, and softly, ever so softly, I hear her calling me from inside herself.

Finn. Run, Finn.

My chest aches. *Her chest.* She feels empty, hopeless, yet soaked through with sorrow.

"Stop your whining. They're already dead," Magus says as they reach the plateau. He grabs my face—*her face*—roughly, and turns it to look down on the fire, raging in the valley.

"Do you see? All dead." He releases his grip and stomps away. I will her gaze to find two little specks next to the blue line of the stream, just beside the wooden bridge.

The line at her throat tugs again. Her eyes turn to show me Magus moving toward the ruins of Raigan's cottage.

"We wait out the night here, away from the flames. Tomorrow

we leave this miserable place."

Panic. Desperation. I feel Emma inside, thinking about the edge of that cliff, the long drop into the trees.

I SNAP AWAKE in my own body, cold and thin and hairless, but alive. Jules sits beside me, staring at the flames that have swept from the big house to the shed, and are now licking across the treetops, seeking out the rest of the buildings. She's watching her home burn.

"Thank you," I manage to croak through a dry throat full of ashes. I turn on sore muscles and stick my face into the ice of the stream, letting it send a jolt through my body, before I swallow a stomachful and retreat, shaking the wet from my hair.

Even from across the field, the heat is intense, and the flames are bright as day, flickering against her face and dancing across her features, everywhere but the recess of her ruined eye.

"Guess it doesn't matter much," she says quietly. "Maybe this place needed to burn. This fucked up place."

"It's still your home," I say, getting to my feet. "Your brothers' home. Our family's home."

I hold a hand out to her. "Do you want to let him take that from you too?"

"It's already gone, Finn. Look at it. This whole mountain is going to burn."

"And *he* needs to burn with it."

Jules looks at my hand.

"We can't really be heroes unless we stop the bad guy, right?"

Lame, but it works.

WE HAVE TO take the long way around the woods. The flames are already creeping high in the trees surrounding the valley. Our legs carry us fast and sure through the brush, despite the smoke and the heat. I remember stepping out, into the early morning, when the smoke came down over the city. Not even a week ago. I was crazy then. Crazy, drunk, and out-of-control. Running from everything. Hiding from myself. Believing a lie.

The campfire smell pushes us on, past the fire line and up to the trail on the cliff face. The birds that were so absent when the big house took ablaze, swarm in circles overhead as we make the climb, picking our way carefully over the stones. The moon rises beside us, blood orange and huge in the haze. We crest the top of the cliff, and I sniff at the air, high enough to be out of the smoke, but not so far as to have the smell of it out of my nose.

The birds stream above us—ravens, crows, starlings—blackbirds evermore. Magus must hear them. He knows what it means. The candlelight flickering from inside Raigan's cabin suddenly swallowed in shadow.

We edge closer to the cottage, stepping slowly, quietly through the stream, stalking our prey.

Jules moves away from me, further upstream, stealthy and slow, circling into the thick brush and through the woods, flanking the little hut as I walk straight to the front door.

My ankles are still wet when Magus appears, alone. For once he's not dressed in black. It's as if he's naked from the waist down, but the skin is loose and folding with seams along the outside of the legs. Empty pouches, like outward pockets, hang from the crotch, and the ankle cuffs are ragged and tapered.

"Well, well, well," Magus crows, standing in a graveyard of scorched trees and broken totems in front of Raigan's home. "How you have continued to surprise me, James."

He wags a finger at me, holding his strange pants up with one side of a pair of clipped on suspenders.

"I thought you'd be so easy to handle. You were such a disappointing waste. Drunk, slovenly, devoid of hope. Full of misery and resentment. I was sure I'd be able to bring you here, get what I needed, and then send you straight on to hell with the rest of your filthy pack of dogs."

He's walking small circles in the same small area, afraid to face me in the open. Monologuing again. So clever, and so vain.

"Yet, you just keep coming back. You've escaped every trap, every underling, every gambit I've laid in front of you." He pauses. "Maybe I should offer you a position? One seems to have opened up with the untimely death of Mister McQueen."

He laughs, and I inch closer, pulling back black lips to show him my teeth, the teeth I'm going to bury in his chest.

"I suppose I've soured that relationship though. Especially seeing what I've done to poor old Arthur."

The mention of the name stops me in my tracks. He sees the pause, turns his head in mock pity.

"Do you like them?" he asks, hitching the suspenders over his shoulders and adjusting his strange pants. I'm close enough to see what the deflated pouches used to be, and to smell the flayed flesh. "Not as tailored as I usually like. Nor the right colour scheme, but Arthur didn't need them anymore."

A grey and yellow flash behind Magus gives me my cue. I inch forward again, low to the ground, growling with as much anger and ferocity as I can manage.

"They're called *Nábrók* trousers," he says, circling away to meet me in the open grass beside the stream. "There's more than one way to skin a wolf, James. Just like there's more than one way to *become* a wolf."

Magus mutters something and raises his hands as if he's lifting something to the heavens. The sky crackles and jumps with blue light. I set back on my hind legs, hunching my shoulders, ready to fight. Every hair on my body seems to stand on edge as Simon Magus is swallowed up in the same blue flame I've seen flicker to life in the palms of his hands. Sickly grey mist swirls up from the ground, swallowing him whole.

What emerges from the cloud in front of me is not-quite wolf, and not-quite man—a hideous amalgam of creatures, huge and muscular, with long heavy claws, and a terrible wide mouth, gaping from an unhinging jaw, double rows of razor teeth gleaming white inside of it. His eyes are red fire, a nightmare glowing in the night.

The beast roars, throwing its arms back, its wide chest straining with muscle. The sound rattles the trees around us, the birds screaming up into the sky and swirling like a black hole above.

It stomps toward me on cloven demon feet, the ground shaking with each step. That same stench of death and sulfur cutting the air between us. The air sings as its claws slice toward me, and I duck right, then dodge left. I slide under its reach and lunge, sinking my teeth deep into the meat of its leg. A hot, black fluid fills my mouth. It tastes of rot and foul water. I release my grip, shaking the taste from my jaws, and bound forward again, as the thing rears and smashes a fist into the earth, nearly catching my hind leg.

The monster lurches at me, both arms slicing forward, hoping to catch me in a vice grip. I run under its legs, turn and leap, aiming for the back of its neck. One arm swivels with an unnatural pop and crack and catches me by the throat, all four of my legs dangling, useless, in the open air.

The thing turns, gripping my hind legs with its free hand, pulling me close to feel the hellfire of its breath. It hisses into my face, and my body recoils, pulling tenderly at my outstretched limbs, joints twisted at wrong angles. The pressure builds as it tightens its grip, meaning to tear me in half. I feel my spine stretching, ready to pop. The joints of my legs already cracking under the strain. Searing pain fills my legs, my back.

The creature bellows, and I hit the ground, free and still in one piece.

Two wolves—one yellow and grey with one emerald eye; one with olive green eyes and a lustrous black coat—have it by the legs. They tear and pull at its calves, but no meat is coming loose. It cries out, then swings its heavy arms skyward and down in long arcs, swatting them away like errant insects. Jules tumbles into the trees, and Emma splashes into the stream. I leap straight up in the bastard's face, claws out, swiping a black trail across its eyes, a wet cascade of black sewage following me to the ground.

It rises, seemingly larger and stronger with every pain we cause it. The jagged grooves I've carved across its face festering and melting with grey tendrils of smoke and reforming into smooth, unbroken skin.

It roars again, fierce and triumphant, and charges toward me as I shuffle backwards into the treeline.

I duck into the brambles, scoot myself under some thorns, and leap over the roots of an old pine tree that comes crashing down beside me as the beast stomps through the trees as if they were mere cardboard.

I draw it back out into the clearing, Jules and Emma beside me, backing across the stream as it approaches, red eyes glowing from the dark of the forest. There is a rustle behind us. The patter of feet. The two small wolves line up beside us. The straggling remnants of the Strong Wolves standing together at last.

We spread out, Kevin and Jamie moving far outside, circling around beside it, I stay directly in front of the monster, Emma and Jules in between. It turns its skull on a thick neck, measuring each of us, trying to gauge the bigger threat. It comes for me, straight across the stream, but distracted as the other four dive toward its legs. I take the opening and launch myself at its throat, just as it rears up, Kev and Jamie clamping down on its legs, Emma and Jules on its haunches. I catch the throat full and deep, pulling against my cousins in a terrific tug-of-war, until something comes loose, and the creature crumples underneath us. I release my grip, sour filth filling my mouth, and look to my family. Emma has a strip of cloth in her teeth, one of the suspender straps, pulled free. Jules pulls and twists at one of the pouches at its crotch, tears one away with a terrible ripping sound and spits a ragged hunk of skin.

The great beast sputters in blue flame, dissolves in grey smoke, and all that's left is an old man. Magus lies in front of us, frail and white, crawling across the stream.

He struggles to his feet, backing away from us, toward the edge of the cliff. Thick plumes of smoke trail up behind him across the moon.

The Strong Wolves of Binn Connall creep closer around me, the whole family surrounding Magus and pushing him closer to the edge of the precipice, our shoulders hunched, teeth bared, ready to end this, end *him*.

Magus sneers and rolls his hands together. A trick I've seen before. The small sphere of blue lightning rolling over his fingers and across his palms, getting bigger and brighter, more intense. My eyes are drawn to it, the hypnotic sway of it swirling in and out of his hands as he backs away. His hands come together again, the blue flame caught inside, then he draws them out, fingers wide, pulling the flame with them, larger and larger. He's farther and farther away. The birds are screaming overhead. Screaming and swirling. The birds, calling out to each other, to us, waiting for their turn at the table. The ball of flame, so beautiful and full.

Magus throws his arms forward, the blue flame rushing toward us and exploding in a flash, lighting up the night with the sudden blast of a dozen suns.

As the hawk takes wing at the edge of the cliff, I leap. I hear Jules behind me, muttering those ancient words.

My jaws close around him, not the bird, but the man. Old and foul and filled with death and rot and sulfur.

My teeth sink deep, bones cracking, flesh surrendering. His blood fills my mouth, and we fall, the heat and the flames rising up to meet us. It ends, just like it began, *athwart the gloom*.

38

I DREAM OF smoke.

Smoke and blood. Nothing else in this place but the feeling of the earth moving beneath me, the earth spinning, wild and out-of-control, and her green eyes. Dark, olive green eyes, as deep as the sea.

The world is spinning away from me. Above me.

Four wolves standing on the edge of the world

Sisters fair

Running.

Athwart the gloom

Smoke. And blood. *Dressed of fur.*

A monster made of death.

Tearing, ripping, screaming. *Fierce of tooth.*

Blue fire, exploding. Fireworks in the night. Black birds spinning endless circles.

The world turns backwards, white becomes black becomes red.

So much blood. An ocean of blood. Rising and crashing. Pink foam cresting dark waves.

Inching ever closer with the tide.

Hands reaching out.

Plucking me from the abyss.

Carrying me through smoke and heat.

And always my mother's voice calling from a place without time.

Not my mother.

Olive green eyes, as dark and deep as the sea. That voice, dark and velvet.

Sweet vanilla and rich chocolate.

The Maiden of the Moon.

"Finn."

THERE IS A hand in my hand. Delicate fingers, intertwined with mine, an infinite knot.

"Emma?"

She nudges closer and puts her other arm around me, moaning softly in her sleep.

I feel her heat against me, the hard little lump swelling from her belly pushed against the small of my back.

I carefully lift her arm and separate our fingers, slide out of the bed, wince as my bare feet hit the cold hardwood floor.

The house is quiet, and dark. I look out into the yard, three feet high with new snow, the rusted clothesline glossy with ice.

I creep softly into the hallway, gently pushing the door open, Kevin and Jamie on opposite sides of the room, heavy blankets tucked up tight beneath their sleeping faces, Kev's lip shadowed with the darkening peach fuzz of impending puberty.

The fire is crackling in the front room. I find her sitting cross-legged in my father's chair, wrapped in a thick wool blanket, feet poking out to each corner. One hand dangling at her side, a thin trail of smoke rising between her fingers.

"Can't sleep?" I ask her, picking up the mug beside her chair. I can smell the coffee, and the weed, from across the room, but I'm trying to make a point. "You can't stay awake forever, Jules."

"Well, I don't have your wife's fat belly to keep me warm at night." She smirks.

I take a sip from the mug—ice cold—and sit down next to her, stretching my feet out toward the fire.

"Be nice."

She turns her good eye toward me and raises one eyebrow. The patch over her left dancing with reflected firelight. "I'm just jealous. Why should she always get the guy?"

I chuckle and take the joint from between her fingers, taking a deep drag and handing it back.

"Are you sure about this?" I ask, holding the breath and sounding like a bad Darth Vader impression.

"I can't stay here. Who wants to live with their pervo little brothers? Let alone their married cousins about to have inbred mutant babies?"

She catches me mid-exhalation, and I gag on the smoke, laughing and coughing at the same time. Tears fill my eyes, and something hot lodges in my throat. I swig another mouthful of cold coffee and clear my throat.

"Pervos?"

"Bob caught them trying to steal Playboys at the gas station."

She takes a drag and holds it out to me. I just shake my head.

"*In the middle of all things*," I remind her.

"*Always*. Right?" She pulls her knees up tighter, sneaking her feet back under the blanket.

"You can stay here as long as you want, and we're going to rebuild the big house. Bigger, better. Room for everybody."

"Is that what you're gonna call it, *the bigger house*?" She snuffs. "You know I don't belong here. It's not in me. I need . . ."

"More. I know. Just don't get carried away, all right? And if you need anything . . ."

"Yeah, yeah. I can always come home."

I get up and take the cup to the sink, dump out the remnants of cold coffee, and rinse it under the tap.

"Bob's coming up tomorrow to help me clear the road. He can take you to town, catch a bus wherever you want to go." I don't want her to leave, but I know how it feels to be looking for something where you know you can't find it.

She's behind me like a goddamn ninja, wrapping her arms around me. I squeeze her elbows and try to ignore the heat coming from her like a furnace.

"You're naked."

"And you're not. Go get back in bed with your wife, hero."

She slaps me on the ass and saunters away toward the door.

"Tell them I said goodbye," she says, pulling the strap from around her head and hanging it at her neck.

I know what that means.

"Jules."

She stops with her hand on the door.

"You're the hero."

She turns, the tiniest of grins curling up at one corner of her mouth. She gives me a wink and a little salute, then bounds out into the snow. I watch her disappear into the night, a grey ghost against the winter cold, a sudden clamour as a dozen black shadows shake loose from the trees to follow her.

I sit in front of the dying embers of the fire, staring at the hero statue on the mantle.

"Not like she has any pockets," I mumble to the coals.

"WHAT WAS ALL that?" Emma grumbles as I climb in beside her.

"Jules. She's gone."

"Hmmm," seems to be all she has to say about that.

She wraps her arms around me, pulls me close, and presses her soft lips against mine. Electricity jolts through my chest, and the heat of her body seeps into mine. She rolls on top of me, nipping at my neck, then stops and fixes me with those deep olive green eyes. The eyes I've dreamt of every night of my life. The other half of the me I never knew.

"I'm glad you're home," she says.

Home.

Wolf & Devil

DEVIL WOKE UP to the clinking of ice in a glass.

Even half-asleep, he knew the sound. Crystal tumbler. Saturn cut.

He could hear somebody out there, on *his* deck, in *his* yard . . .

Drinking *his* whiskey.

"THAT'S A THREE-hundred dollar bottle of whiskey you're fucking with."

Devil stepped out into the night, pistol first, business-end muzzled with a silencer he'd snuck in from Argentina.

"Better join me then," she said, honey dripping from a dusky voice. Long, slender legs reached out from the shadows hiding her on the far side of the patio table. She hooked nimble feet around the chair closest to Devil and pulled it away from the table, a clear signal for him to sit down and enjoy some of his own booze.

"Nice stems. Where's the rest of you?"

"Come over and have a look, sailor."

Devil clomped out onto the patio, thick-soled boots and boxer shorts the only thing between him and the cool winter night. He took a deep breath through his nose, taking his time before moving toward her.

“I don’t think we’ve met,” Devil said, smiling as he heard the clink of ice in another glass, followed by the screw-top coming off of the bottle. A few short glugs and one of his heavy crystal glasses slid across the table-top toward him.

“Not as of yet.”

The girl leaned in from her dark alcove, winking one brilliant emerald eye. The other eye was covered with a black leather patch. She had a stunning face, framed by a cascade of loose blonde curls.

“You gonna offer a girl a drink?”

“Seems like you already helped yourself, kid.”

She leaned back, face disappearing into the dark, replaced by a slender hand and an empty glass full of half-melted ice.

“I could use a refill, Pops.”

Devil grinned, reached across for the bottle and poured her another.

“So what’s with the eyepatch, señorita?”

“Wizard battle gone wrong. What’s a girl to do? You don’t like it?”

Devil strained to see the rest of her through the darkness.

“No, from what I can tell, it suits you, Jules. It is Jules, right?”

Her Cheshire cat smile gleamed there in the black.

“Hmm. Finn said you were smart.”

“So what are you doing in my backyard at two A.M. on a Wednesday?”

“Finn said I should look you up. He thought we might have a little fun together.”

“But how did you get in? That fence is seven feet high, reinforced, and alarmed.”

“I just hopped on over. I could smell this Yamazaki single malt from a block away.”

The ice in her glass clinked as she took a sip. Devil found himself staring at her full red lips on the glass, parting just slightly to let the amber liquid slide past those perfect white teeth, and along her tongue, swirling once through the warm insides of her mouth before being carried down her throat.

Jules leaned forward again, licking those luscious lips, and nodded her head toward the concrete slab off to one side of the yard, where a tall shrouded figure loomed.

“Sex swing?” She grinned, popping her shapely eyebrows at

him.

Devil laughed out loud, almost spitting Japanese scotch out his nose. “Heavy bag.”

She regarded him quietly for a moment.

“You keep that stuff outside?”

“I don’t want to stink up the house.”

“What do you do when it snows?”

“I put on pants.”

Devil watched her with a wary eye, silently battling his own raging libido in his mind. How old was this girl? Jimmy’s cousin. Old enough to be a stripper. Old enough to lose an eye fighting some crazy fucking magician. Jimmy’d told him the whole wild story. In any case, she was old enough to be a fucking werewolf, right?

“You want to take this conversation inside, like civilized adults?”

“Is that what we are?” Jules looked Devil up and down, taking in this man in his four-leaf clover print boxers and motorcycle boots, covered with strange tattoos, not seeming to mind the cold any more than she did. Finn was right. They’d get along just fine.

She stretched her legs under the table, working out the last knots from the change that brought her here, running through the streets of this strange neighbourhood, leaping his fortress walls. She might not even bother bewitching this one. Let Simon Magus take his tricks with him to his grave. This guy knew all about what she was, and didn’t seem to care. She was just a woman, seducing a man. The old-fashioned way. Naked in the moonlight.

Jules folded her legs up, slid out from the chair, and stepped up the patio stairs into the light, letting him drink her in, like a three-hundred dollar bottle of whiskey. This was a man who appreciated the finest.

And she was the finest.

Devil watched her as she slinked out from the shadows, every bit of her smooth, honey-gold, and perfect.

“What’s with the ink?” she asked as he slid up behind her at the door.

“Wizard battle. A little protection can’t hurt.”

“Seven foot-high fence, alarms, tattoos of magical protection . . . You are a careful boy.”

"House of bricks."

She spun to face him, slid her arms around, and clamped her hands on his ass, pulling him in hard and smashing his lips with hers.

"Little pig, little pig," she said, that Cheshire cat grin beaming wide, showing Devil the long canines as she pushed her hard nipples and soft curves against him, grinding against the barely contained erection about to burst out of the thin layer of cotton between them.

"You ever make it with a big bad wolf, Devil?" she purred.

"Not as of yet."

Wolf & Devil:
Demon Days

Coming Summer 2017

Acknowledgements

Many thanks to the family and friends that always see me through; to the amazing crew at Tyche books who made this thing happen; and to all the madmen who put all of these monsters in my head - thanks for a lifetime of reading and watching and daydreaming

About the Author

Axel Howerton (or #AxelHow, if you're into that whole hashtags & brevity thing) is the genre-hopping, punch-drunk author of the Arthur Ellis Award nominated Hot Sinatra, the gothic urban fantasy Furr and the forthcoming Wolf & Devil series. His short fiction and essays have appeared the world over, in no fewer than five languages, and more than 30 (but less than 1000?) publications. Axel is the Prairies director of the Crime Writers of Canada and a member of the Canadian Science Fiction and Fantasy Association, the Calgary Crime Writers, and the Kintsugi Poets. He is also the editor of the books AB Negative and Tall Tales of the Weird West, and the organizer behind one of Canada's first recurring "Noir At The Bar" events, #NoirBarYYC.

Visit Axel online at axelhow.com to sign up for the GotHow? email list and receive free exclusive ebook collections, sneak peeks, and more!

Axel@axelhow.com

CPSIA information can be obtained at www.ICGtesting.com
Printed in the USA
LVOW08s1411121016

508108LV00002B/1/P